PUFFIN BOOKS

GRANDMA AND THE GHOWLIES

Just when old Mrs O'Pheeley decides to sell her old house and buy a bungalow instead, five little ghosts turn up and make things difficult. Not that they are scary, or even badly intentioned (at least, four of them aren't) but they do need a home – and a loving one at that!

Mrs O'Pheeley is determined to live her life alone and in peace, but somehow the ghowlies always seem to turn things upside down . . .

This is a charming and funny story which will make any children who are afraid of ghosts wish they had some after all!

URSULA MORAY WILLIAMS

GRANDMA
— AND THE —
GHOWLIES

Illustrated by Susan Varley

PUFFIN BOOKS

PUFFIN BOOKS

Published by the Penguin Group
27 Wrights Lane, London W8 5TZ, England
Viking Penguin Inc., 40 West 23rd Street, New York, New York 10010, USA
Penguin Books Australia Ltd, Ringwood, Victoria, Australia
Penguin Books Canada Ltd, 2801 John Street, Markham, Ontario, Canada L3R 1B4
Penguin Books (NZ) Ltd, 182–190 Wairau Road, Auckland 10, New Zealand

Penguin Books Ltd, Registered Offices: Harmondsworth, Middlesex, England

First published by Andersen Press Limited 1986
Published in Puffin Books 1989
3 5 7 9 10 8 6 4 2

Printed and bound in Great Britain by
Cox & Wyman Ltd, Reading
Filmset in Plantin

Contents

1 The Old House   7

2 The New House   13

3 Winty   18

4 Selling the House   22

5 Buying the House   27

6 The Willarbees at The Beeches   34

7 A New Home for the Willarbees   43

8 Return of Winty   53

9 The Doll   56

10 The Stolen Doll   61

11 Television   70

12 The Health Visitor   76

13 Going Abroad   82

14 Adieu to the Willarbees   91

15 Return from Holiday   97

16 Winty Behaves   106

17 The Flower Show   114

18 In Search of Timfy   121

19 All One Big Happy Family   131

To Anthea Morton-Saner

1

The Old House

Knock-knock-knock-knock . . . .

'Who's there?' said Mrs O'Pheeley.

Nobody answered.

She went to the door and there was nobody there.

Tap-tap-tap-tap-tap . . . .

'Who is it?' cried Mrs O'Pheeley.

There was no reply. She opened the door, but the doorstep was empty, and the garden path had nobody on it. No footsteps. Nothing.

Rat-tat-tat-tat-tat . . . .

It sounded like a crowd of children stamping their feet and chattering just outside the door. Mrs O'Pheeley thought it was her grandchildren, and ran to let them in. But there was nobody to be seen at all.

'What a pity!' said Mrs O'Pheeley. 'I did want to sell my house and get something smaller, but nobody will ever buy it if they keep having to go to the door and find no callers after all . . . .'

She sat toasting her toes by the fire for quite a few minutes, during which time she could hear more scrapings and tappings outside, and some voices like children playing in the garden. There came one or two more taps at the door.

'Whoever you are . . . ' Mrs O'Pheeley said very loudly, 'will you please state your business and go away? Thank you!'

There was silence for a while, and then a chorus of thin voices all sprang to life outside, singing in unison and quite softly:

7

'We are the Willarbees!
We never were
We'll never be!
The bad old days we'll never see!
Oh happy, happy, happy we!'

As the song came to an end a thread of pale nothingness began to stream through the keyhole like fluff,
with tufts in it from time to time, as if four or five little
creatures were holding hands and each pulling another
one after it.

Their thin voices repeated the song until the thread
turned itself into four or five small, soft, shining
phantoms, who made a half-ring round Mrs O'Pheeley's chair, clutching each other's thin hands and
smiling. They never stayed still for one instant, but
hopped from foot to foot and melted into one another

and came apart again like froth on a pool of water.

Mrs O'Pheeley knew that they were phantoms or ghostlings or ghowlies or something of that kind.

For a long time she had suspected that her house was haunted. Her grandchildren had assured her that this was so. It hadn't mattered when she lived there alone, but now that she wanted to sell it and leave, the whole situation was different.

The phantoms began to introduce themselves:

'This is Miss Willarbee, Mrs O'Pheeley. She's the oldest of us all. She was born a hundred years before yesterday! But she never grew up—so sad!'

The shadows seemed to cluster round Miss Willarbee as if giving her support. Their small empty arms wound round her knees. For a moment they were just a mass of weaving fluff.

'I'm sorry to hear that,' said Mrs O'Pheeley practically.

Miss Willarbee emerged looking brave.

'I don't mind very much,' she said, 'except that I never knew what name I was given. But here is little Victoria Willarbee! *She's* got her name on a gravestone!'

'*What?*' cried Mrs O'Pheeley. 'Is that true?'

'Oh yes! It's in the graveyard,' they chanted in chorus. 'Mary Victoria Willarbee, aged six years. Isn't that a beautiful name, Mrs O'Pheeley?'

'I never saw that name on any stone in the graveyard,' said Mrs O'Pheeley, nonplussed. She made a point of knowing the names on all the gravestones round the church.

'No?' cried the ghostlings in surprise. 'But how sad!

9

How sad!'

Mrs O'Pheeley felt crushed, as if it were all her fault that little Victoria had no place in the graveyard to call her own. She decided to ask the Rector to allow her to search again in the Register of Burials.

'Here is little Timfy,' the ghostlings went on. 'He's a tomorrow Willarbee! One minute he's here and the next he never was! Show her how you cannot be, Timfy!'

The small shadow that was Timfy Willarbee went in and out like a light.

'He will never be born,' the Willarbees sighed. 'It is very sad!'

'And this is Beth,' they continued, pushing forward a pale, willowy mite who very nearly had a faint sweet smile. 'She is a long-long ago, like Miss Willarbee. She'll never be born either. It is very sad!'

'I suppose you are—ghosts—ghosties—ghostlings . . . ?' Mrs O'Pheeley asked them.

'We're ghowlies!' said one of the wraiths.

'Ghoulies!' said another.

'Ghowlies!'

'Ghoulies!'

'Ghowlies!'

'*Ghoulies!*' corrected Mrs O'Pheeley, pronouncing it with the 'oo'.

'Yes, just like we said!' agreed all the Willarbees.

Mrs O'Pheeley found herself at a loss to know what to say about the long-ago Willarbees. Finally she pulled herself together.

'Why have you come to see me?' she demanded.

'We need a home to live in,' said the Willarbees. 'We

were happy till we heard you were going away. But if the house is to be sold and the new people don't like ghosts, what will become of us?'

'Can't you go on living in odd corners as you have with me?' said Mrs O'Pheeley severely. She did not enjoy being taken to task by a posse of nostalgic ghostlings.

'Oh no!' they sighed. '*You* didn't mind us, so it didn't matter, but people who hate ghowlies can do dreadful things to us. They can destroy us—utterly! Would you like to be utterly destroyed, Mrs O'Pheeley?'

'It is my house, after all!' snapped Mrs O'Pheeley, not answering the question. 'I suppose I can do as I please with it!'

The ghostlings clustered closer to her. The very smallest suddenly wrapped itself round her hand, feeling like a soft shawl or a spider's web.

'Please take me to live with you, Mrs O'Pheeley,' it said.

The softness of the little creature melted Mrs O'Pheeley's heart. But when she closed her fingers on it, it melted away.

'I don't want to desert you,' Mrs O'Pheeley said in a gentler tone, 'but I'm getting old, you know! I shan't be able to run this house much longer. It is a very cold house.'

'Oh it is! It is!' they chorused.

'And there is so much work to do!' said Mrs O'Pheeley.

'There is! There is!' they agreed.

'I don't want to be a burden on my children,' she

told them. 'I thought I would sell the house and go to live in a small bungalow which is warm and easy to look after. I can buy it with the money I get for selling this house.'

'Selling *us*!' said the phantoms reproachfully.

'I shall soon be a ghost myself!' Mrs O'Pheeley reminded them.

'But you have *been*,' they chorused. 'We have never been—not quite! And we never will be now! Not ever—ever—ever! It's so sad!'

'You said you were happy,' Mrs O'Pheeley objected.

'Only while you are here,' said the chorus. 'How can we be happy when you go away?'

One by one they began to stream back through the keyhole. Soon it was as if they had never been in the room at all.

'I don't believe in dreams,' Mrs O'Pheeley told herself, 'but if I did, I would say I must have dreamt it.'

2

The New House

Mrs O'Pheeley lay awake for most of the night, listening for the ghowlies and wondering what to do. She didn't hear anything, which was a comfort. It helped her to make up her mind to sell the place and go ahead with her plans. She thought she would buy a new bungalow with no ghosts in it. If she went straight to the estate agent in the morning, she told herself, it could all be arranged and finished with very quickly. She could move house and be settled in before the ghowlies knew what had happened. After all, if it did seem a little mean, they were not unpleasant ghostlings, they didn't frighten or harm people, and quite possibly the new owners would come to tolerate them, just as she had done.

Of course she did not mention their presence to the estate agent, but she told him quite frankly that she was tired of living in an old house, and she wanted a brand-new bungalow nearer to the shops.

She was leaving the estate agent's office when she ran into her two grandchildren, George and Emily, who were shopping for their mother.

'Are you buying a new house, Grandma?' they asked her.

'I am by way of doing just that!' said Mrs O'Pheeley, and even as she spoke the estate agent came to the top of his steps and called her back into his office.

Mrs O'Pheeley climbed the steps again, followed by George and Emily.

'I think I have got just the bungalow you want,' the

estate agent said. 'It really sounds just the one you are looking for! Would you like to come straight away and have a look at it?'

'But I haven't sold my own house yet,' said Mrs O'Pheeley, but the estate agent brushed that aside. 'Just come and have a look at it,' he suggested, 'and by all means bring your grandchildren with you!'

George and Emily squashed themselves into the back of the estate agent's car, and within minutes they were all walking up the path of a charming new bungalow with apple trees in the garden. Mrs O'Pheeley knew by the look and feel of it that this was exactly where she would choose to live for the rest of her days. But she let the agent show her all over it and open every cupboard and door before she admitted that yes, this was the kind of house she had pictured, and if she could sell her own house quickly she would like to buy it and move in as soon as possible.

'Shall you bring the little ghosties with you, Grandma?' asked George and Emily.

The agent turned on them as if he had been shot.

'There are no ghosts in *this* house, my dear,' he assured them, but Emily would not be quieted.

'Grandma's got them in hers,' she said, and the estate agent reacted as if she had mentioned dry rot and woodworm and unexploded bombs all rolled into one.

'I trust there is no such thing, madam?' he said stiffly. 'You hardly mean to tell me that your house is supposed to be haunted?'

'Well, not really,' said Mrs O'Pheeley, frowning at George and Emily. 'We hardly ever hear them, and I don't know what my grandchildren are talking about!'

'*We* see them!' Emily said importantly. 'When we stay with Grandma they come and talk to us. There is Miss Willarbee, who is hundreds of years old, and Victoria, who is buried in our graveyard . . . .'

'She *says* she is,' Mrs O'Pheeley contradicted her before she could stop herself, and the agent gave her a sharp look.

' . . . And Timfy,' the grandchildren went on. 'He has never been born, poor little thing! And neither has little Beth. They have nothing to remember, isn't it sad? They love Grandma, and I'm sure they won't want to go on living in her house without her. They would *love* this bungalow!'

'Now, now, now!' protested the estate agent. 'My new houses have no ghosts in them! I should never sell them if they had! But old houses are a bit different, of course. And we do have some Americans on our books . . . .'

'And Americans *love* ghosts!' said Emily in delight.

'Not all of them do! Not nearly all of them!' said the agent, looking nervous. 'In fact, very, very few want to *buy* a house with a ghost in it. How *many* ghosts did you say there were?'

'Four or five,' said George evasively. 'And they aren't naughty. At least, four of them are not, are they, Grandma?'

'No, no!' said Mrs O'Pheeley nervously. 'Certainly four are not. But I didn't know there were five . . . .'

'The last one is very small,' said Emily, 'and he isn't often naughty. His name is Winty, and I really like him best!'

'Then why don't you and George take them home?'

15

Mrs O'Pheeley suggested tartly. 'They all want a really good home to be happy in. They told me so themselves. Why don't *you* have them?'

The grandchildren looked shocked and solemn.

'Oh no, Grandma! Mum and Dad would never allow it!' they said together.

'Very well then,' said Mrs O'Pheeley brightly. 'We will find another home for them! And in the meantime if you will send me the necessary contracts, Mr Agent, I will buy this bungalow and arrange to move into it at once. And you can get busy finding a rich American who would like to buy my beautiful old house and who would enjoy my little ghostlings. They really are a charming little crowd. Aren't they, George? Aren't they, Emily? They are such dears!'

'Oh *yes*, Grandma!' said George and Emily fervently.

The estate agent did not speak all the way back to his office.

'I know your house well, madam,' he told Mrs O'Pheeley, opening the door for her. 'It is a very charming house, and in the ordinary way I am sure I should find a purchaser ready to pay a very high price for it. But with ghosts in it I am not nearly so certain. I think it would be best to advertise it and delay proceedings until that purchaser can be found.'

'But meanwhile somebody else may come and buy my beautiful bungalow!' said Mrs O'Pheeley.

'Well,' said the estate agent, 'there is that possibility. But I think we'll have to take the chance. At any rate I will call on you tomorrow morning and make a thorough itinerary of the house and garden to put in my advertisement. You won't object to a board at the gate of course, madam?'

'Oh no, not at all! Lots of boards!' said Mrs O'Pheeley happily. 'And put TO BE SOLD IMMEDIATELY on it! It will make people keener.'

She took George and Emily to have coffee and ices before going home. She found they had become very depressed.

'Don't you like the new bungalow I have bought?' she asked them.

'Oh yes, Grandma, it is beautiful, and we liked it while you were buying it. But now it's all over we are thinking how we loved your old house, and the ghosties in it. It makes us very unhappy!' said George and Emily.

'Well it isn't mine yet!' snapped Mrs O'Pheeley, paying the bill.

3

Winty

That evening Mrs O'Pheeley sat by her fire making plans.

Oddly enough George and Emily's protests made her all the more determined to move as soon as possible. She decided to give them a party in the new bungalow, and Emily should help her to furnish the guest room. She realised she had almost said 'the ghost room' and she laughed silently into the glowing embers of her fire.

When she looked up the four little ghowlies were there again. They had come through the keyhole without being noticed, or perhaps they had come down the stairs, or any other way that ghostlings travel. They were standing beside her and looking very sad and pitiful. The smallest was slowly creeping on to her knee.

'Good evening,' said Mrs O'Pheeley, putting on a bright and hospitable voice.

'Good evening, Grandma O'Pheeley!' said the ghostlings quite flatly.

Mrs O'Pheeley did not know whether to be flattered or offended at being called Grandma.

'Have you really bought a new house, Grandma?' asked the phantom called Timfy.

'Yes I have,' she said brightly. 'A very nice new house! A bungalow, at No. 7 Caldicott Road. Quite close to the Post Office and the shops,' she added, since there was no reaction from the ghosts. The smallest had stopped climbing on her knee. The place, halfway up her leg, where it had stopped climbing felt cold and damp, as if someone had put a wet cloth on it and then removed it. And a moment ago it had felt so warm and friendly.

'We think it is very unkind of you!' said the tallest ghost. 'We are very surprised that you can be such an unkind old lady!'

'I don't see that it is any business of yours!' said Mrs O'Pheeley crossly. 'It is my own house, I suppose, and my own money, and you haven't any claim on it, or on me. I can surely do as I please!'

'We belong to the house,' the phantoms reproached her. 'We have been here for years and years and years . . . .'

'Well then,' said Mrs O'Pheeley, 'you can just go on being here, can't you? And take your luck! I've only been here for ten years myself. You must have had lots of other owners before I came.'

'We liked you best,' the ghostlings said. 'You never bothered us, and your grandchildren used to play with us. Some of the other people used to scream when they saw us. Wasn't it silly?'

'Perhaps they were frightened,' said Mrs O'Pheeley, 'perhaps *you* frightened them.'

'We never did!' came their soft little voices. 'We always behaved nicely to them. All four of us did.'

'All four of you?' Mrs O'Pheeley repeated. 'I thought there were five of you?'

'Well, not really,' said the ghosts. 'There was one more, but we turned him out. He was just a nuisance, and he got us a bad name in the neighbourhood. We

19

don't have him with us any more.'

'Well, what do you want me to do about it?' Mrs O'Pheeley asked after a pause.

'We want you to find us happy homes,' chorused the little ghosts. 'When you sell this house the next people are sure to take this place all to pieces and put it together again. They will clean out all our lovely corners and paint them nasty colours, and open up the cupboards. They will *discover* the place. We will be so terribly frightened and unhappy! Can you find us a really nice family who would be glad to have us— something like your grandchildren without their parents?'

'There are not many families who want to adopt four ghosts or ghowlies!' said Mrs O'Pheeley, smiling. 'Either the parents like them and the children don't, or else the children love them as my grandchildren do, and the grown-ups detest them. You are asking me to do something very difficult.'

'Please, please try,' said the sad chorus.

The smallest phantom climbed into her lap once more. It was just as if a large soft moth had settled on Mrs O'Pheeley's folded hands. It was warm and weightless, but she could see and feel its large pleading eyes looking up into her face.

'Please don't sell the house until you have found us somewhere else to live,' begged Miss Willarbee at her side. 'If you knew what it is like to have your home sold about your ears!'

'It may not be as bad as you think,' said Mrs O'Pheeley. 'You ought to give it a chance!'

'Very well, Mrs O'Pheeley,' they said meekly.

At that moment Mrs O'Pheeley felt a sharp pain in her left ankle, as if a wasp had stung her, or a small dog had bitten her very hard.

The ghostlings jumped backwards, and little Beth slithered off her lap.

'Oh my goodness!' she heard them mutter as they vanished into thin air. 'Wherever has he come from? What is he doing here? It's Winty!'

4

Selling the House

Mrs O'Pheeley sat for a long time expecting to see the fifth ghostling that had been named by the Willarbees, but the room remained quiet and empty. The flames flickered in the hearth and all was perfectly silent. There might never have been a phantom in the house. The only remaining sign of their presence was the echo of a sharp, stinging bite on her ankle. The kind of bite that might have been made by an angry mouse. Even that pain was fading away.

Just to satisfy herself Mrs O'Pheeley rolled down her stocking and looked at the very small red spots that had almost drawn blood but not quite. And she still had the warm feeling in her lap of the weightless little creature who had cuddled down among her fingers.

She did not understand what the Willarbees had meant in talking about Winty. There was no sign nor sound nor feel of any fifth ghostling. The whole room felt perfectly unhaunted.

She got up and began to make herself some supper.

Mrs O'Pheeley spent a quiet night, except that she felt just a little bit guilty about the Willarbees.

They were quite right, in a way, she really ought to try to find them a suitable new home before she moved into her bungalow. On the other hand, whoever bought the house might be glad to have such pleasant little ghosts to go with it. Mrs O'Pheeley decided to wait until some prospective buyers were sent along by the agent to view the place.

Nobody came for three or four days, and her only visitors were George and Emily.

'Have you seen the Willarbees again, Grandma?'

'Not since last Friday. Not a sign of them. I think they must have gone,' said Mrs O'Pheeley.

George and Emily searched the house from top to bottom in vain.

'They aren't here now, but I don't think they have exactly *gone*,' said Emily. 'They wouldn't leave you just like that, would they, Grandma?'

'I have no idea,' said Mrs O'Pheeley. 'Would you like tinned apricots or a banana for your puddings?'

George and Emily were bored without the Willarbees, and they left early. Mrs O'Pheeley went to the estate agent's office to follow up the purchase of her new bungalow.

She noticed to her satisfaction that a board had been erected beside her garden gate, announcing that her house was For Immediate Sale and Please Apply To The Agents.

When she returned from town the board was lying on its back in the road.

'There's shoddy workmanship for you!' said Mrs O'Pheeley. She rang up the agent, who assured her that the board had been fixed, by their most reliable man, with nails, and was not in the least likely to fall over.

Mrs O'Pheeley scrutinised the board, and sure enough, the nails had been removed, and were lying in a neat little pile on top of the gatepost.

'Vandals!' said Mrs O'Pheeley very crossly.

The agent's man arrived in a car to put the board up again.

He had not been gone five minutes before the board was flat on its back once more, and again the nails were piled neatly on the gatepost.

Mrs O'Pheeley kept an eye on the man all the time he was hammering and fixing the notice board. She only turned away when he had driven off in his car.

And when she looked back, the board was lying on its back and the nails were piled on the post. There just wasn't any natural explanation for it.

While she was still staring George and Emily came by on bicycles.

'We are sorry we left you so early, Grandma,' they apologised. 'We didn't help wash up. Have the Willarbees come back?'

'I haven't seen them,' said Mrs O'Pheeley, 'but I wish you would put that board up again, George, and then just watch it from behind the holly bush.'

'Why?' George asked. Mrs O'Pheeley explained her reasons.

'Oh, *that's Winty*!' they exclaimed in great disgust. 'We knew he'd come back, and he has!'

'And who exactly is Winty?' asked their grandmother.

'He's just Winty! And he's horrid. He spoils everything!' said George. 'His father was a poltergeist — you know, Grandma! One of those things that throws everything about the place and rings bells and plays pianos that are not there. Poltergeists are not like the Willarbees! Winty isn't like them either. They don't like him, and we don't either. He's just a nuisance!'

'He won't do any harm, I suppose?' said Mrs O'Pheeley, nervously thinking of the people coming to view the house.

'Well, not if you call *this* not doing harm!' said George, gloomily picking up the board and nails. 'Have you got a hammer, Grandma? I'll put it up again.'

'Then Winty will pull it *down*!' said Emily.

'Oh no he won't!' said George. 'Because I'll make a sign of the cross in the ground first, with the stick. Winty doesn't like the sign of the cross because he is naughty. The Willarbees don't mind it at all, because they are good.'

'Oh really?' said Mrs O'Pheeley, surprised.

'You ask the Rector!' said George, busy with hammer and nails.

It was quite true that this time the board stayed in its place and nobody removed it again, but when Mrs O'Pheeley mentioned it to the Rector she didn't get much satisfaction.

'Are there really some old Willarbee graves in the churchyard?' she asked him.

'Not to my knowledge,' the Rector said, 'but of course some of the stones are so old you can hardly see the names written on them any longer. It is perfectly possible that the name WILLARBEE is somewhere on one of those gravestones. Though it is much more likely to have come down to us as WILLOUGHBY. There were Willoughbys in the village before I came here, but they have all died out now.'

'So sad!' murmured Mrs O'Pheeley.

She took her little kitchen knife and went rootling round the churchyard looking at the tombstones. The Rector had told her that the Burial Registers were locked up at Dorchester.

She found a few Willoughby graves, but they were all old men or old ladies . . . and then, all of a sudden, she came upon a small and ancient gravestone beside a wall. It was almost hidden in ivy and grass.

Mrs O'Pheeley scraped the surface clear, and scratched at the letters with her little knife.

Before long the letters could plainly be seen:

'MARY VICTORIA WILLARBEE. Aged six years.'

It gave her quite a shock. She decided not to tell the Rector. It was the kind of secret she preferred to keep to herself. But she told George and Emily about it.

'There you are!' said George. 'They were bound to be right! You may even find Timfy Willarbee there, though probably not. I don't think you'll find Miss Willarbee either. I guess she's too far back. And of course Beth won't be there . . . .'

'What about Winty?' said Mrs O'Pheeley.

'Oh not *Winty*!' they said in shocked surprise.

5

Buying the House

That evening the Willarbees were back, all four of them, looking a great deal more real and more solid than they had done before.

'Good evening, Grandma Feeley,' they said politely.

Mrs O'Pheeley did a rapid count to see if there were a fifth Willarbee among them. She was not at all anxious to meet Winty. But there were only four—Miss Willabree, Timfy, Victoria Willarbee, and little Beth.

'Good evening, my dears,' said Mrs O'Pheeley kindly.

'Have you found us a home yet, Grandma Feeley?' the Willarbees wanted to know.

'Well, not quite yet,' said Mrs O'Pheeley. 'You see, I haven't sold this one yet. To tell you the truth, I have a prospective buyer coming to see it tomorrow morning.'

'We will be there,' said the Willarbees in one voice. Mrs O'Pheeley could not tell whether it was menacing or friendly. But she did not want them to be there.

'You will stay—invisible, my dears, won't you?' she coaxed them, thinking to herself that any purchaser coming face to face with four phantoms might well ask for a reduction in the price of the house.

'Oh yes, Grandma Feeley,' they promised earnestly, but Mrs O'Pheeley had to acknowledge that it would be very much in their own interests to spoil a sale and keep the place for themselves.

'In the meantime I will do my best to find you a good

home of your own,' she promised them. Pleasure glowed on their strange little faces.

'Oh *thank you*, Grandma Feeley,' they said gratefully, and although she did not know where to begin to look Mrs O'Pheeley knew she would have to try.

The opportunity came in quite an unexpected manner.

That evening she went to a concert in the town, taking with her Emily, who was musical.

On her other side sat a woman whom she might have ignored, but during the interval Emily ran off to greet her music teacher, and Mrs O'Pheeley and her neighbour fell into conversation.

The neighbour, whose name was Mrs Morrison, ran a children's home outside the town. 'No, not a state home, it is all my very own,' she told Mrs O'Pheeley. 'The state helps with the money side, of course, but I choose the children. I love children, and children love me. Such tragic cases, many of them—unwanted, unloved—some of them haven't had a word of love said to them since before they were born!'

'Are they—difficult?' Mrs O'Pheeley asked, interested, and thinking of loving four little ghostlings . . . well, five . . . .

'Of course!' said Mrs Morrison simply. 'Wouldn't you be difficult if for years and years nobody had loved you? That's why I try to get away now and again to listen to music and forget how difficult they are.'

Emily had come back and was listening.

'Would you have room for four more?' Mrs O'Pheeley enquired.

'Five!' said Emily.

Mrs Morrison blinked and stared at Emily.

'Of course!' she said simply. 'We can always double up if necessary. Is this one of them?'

'No, I'm not!' said Emily. 'But they'd be easier to have than me. You wouldn't have to wash their clothes, and they don't eat much and . . . .'

'Emily, be quiet!' said her grandmother. She began to explain to Mrs Morrison, who listened with the greatest interest until Beethoven's Third Symphony interrupted the conversation.

'I think she'll take them,' said Emily as they went home. 'She sounded so sympathetic, and she'd just love little Beth.'

But all Mrs Morrison actually said was that here was her telephone number.

In the morning a gentleman arrived with his wife to view the house.

As they had predicted, the Willarbees were present, hovering invisibly in the background of Mrs O'Pheeley's sitting room. She had been telling them her hopes about the children's home where Mrs Morrison loved children so dearly, and would welcome them all and give them a happy home.

The Willarbees were overjoyed at the prospect.

'They have pets there, and little gardens,' Mrs O'Pheeley told them, 'and they do lessons and have holidays and go to pantomimes and to the Tower of London!'

'My great-great-great grandfather *lived* in the Tower of London!' said Victoria Willarbee in awe.

'Then you can go and see his grave,' said Mrs O'Pheeley practically.

'On Traitors' Hill!' murmured Victoria. 'He was hanged and drawn and quartered in the Tower. It was so sad.'

'So you see it is most important that I should sell this house as soon as I can,' said Mrs O'Pheeley, shuddering a little. 'I want to go to my nice new bungalow, and get rid of this one, and whether you go with it or find a new home is up to you. I'll do my best to help you, but you must do your own bests as well. And particularly this morning I want you not to interfere in any way with the purchaser who is coming to look at the place. Could you possibly just *disappear*?'

'Oh but Grandma Feeley, we want to see who might be buying us!' the ghostlings objected. 'If they're nice we'll stay with them, and if they aren't we'll go to the children's home. We just want to be happy! We don't mind so much about the Tower of London.'

They promised to be quiet, and soon after that Major Bodkin and Mrs Bodkin came in, and Mrs O'Pheeley showed them round the house.

It was while they were sitting drinking coffee in the sitting room that Major Bodkin's hat fell off his knees and before he could pick it up it started walking round the room. Major Bodkin made a grab at it, but the hat merely lifted a few centimetres off the floor, jumped across his hand, and landed on the table beside him. Then, quite suddenly and calmly, it was on his knees again.

Major Bodkin looked very embarrassed, and clutched it as if he hoped Mrs O'Pheeley had not noticed what was happening. She was busy explaining the central heating to Mrs Bodkin, and neither of them had noticed the hat at all.

'You might like to see the boiler and the deep freeze and the washing-machine,' said Mrs O'Pheeley, leading the way from the room.

Major Bodkin clapped his hat firmly on the back of his chair and stumped after them.

When they returned the hat was still there, but a bright red rose was stuck into the ribbon on the side of it.

'Do you have grandchildren, Mrs O'Pheeley?' Major Bodkin asked, treating the matter as a great big joke.

'I do indeed, Major,' said Mrs O'Pheeley. 'I have George, who is ten, and Emily who is nine. They live close by and they are always running in to see me.' She too had noticed the rose, and something told her it was not George or Emily who had put it there.

'It is a lovely house,' said Mrs Bodkin. 'I love it all! I love the *feel* of it . . . !'

'Yes, my dear,' Major Bodkin agreed. 'It has a very pleasant feel indeed!'

As he spoke the light bulb exploded suddenly above his head. The glass flew about but nobody was hurt.

Mrs O'Pheeley apologised deeply.

'My dear madam, it wasn't your fault,' said Major Bodkin, busy sweeping up the fragments with the hearthbrush. 'These things just happen, don't they?' He sucked at his thumb where a splinter of glass had made a nasty little cut.

Refusing any plaster he and Mrs Bodkin went away, still saying how much they liked the house, and promising to go straight to the agent to talk things over.

When they were gone Mrs O'Pheeley rounded on the Willarbees who had been lurking invisibly in the background while the visitors were present.

'You promised not to interfere!' she said angrily.

'You had no business to play tricks on those nice, kind people! You could see for yourselves how pleasant they would be to live with! What do you *mean* by it?'

'Oh, Grandma Feeley, it wasn't us! We didn't! We didn't!' the Willarbees cried. 'We never did a thing! You must believe us—you must!'

'Then who put the rose in Major Bodkin's hat?'

'Winty did!'

'And who bust the electric light?'

'Winty did!'

'And he made the hat walk round and round,' added Timfy Willarbee.

'Fetch him for me!' ordered Mrs O'Pheeley, but Winty was not to be found.

'He doesn't live here now, you see,' explained the Willarbees.

'Then where *does* he live?'

The ghosts all shrugged their flimsy little shoulders.

'We don't know!' they said.

The Willarbees at The Beeches

Mrs O'Pheeley sold her house to the Bodkins and moved to her pretty new bungalow.

Mrs Morrison agreed to have the Willarbees, and Mrs O'Pheeley took them along one evening in a taxicab.

Although they were excited at the idea of their new home the Willarbees clung to Mrs O'Pheeley. Little Beth had a shadowy hold of her hand. 'I wanted to stay with you,' she said.

'No, no, no, my dear! No ghowlies, no animals, no birds in cages, no anything!' said Mrs O'Pheeley firmly. 'I mean to live a perfectly untrammelled life!'

She introduced all four of them to Mrs Morrison at The Beeches, and tried to explain about Winty, who had not been seen for some days.

'Oh, we have far worse than that here!' said Mrs Morrison cheerfully. 'We'll give him a little garden of his own, and perhaps we'll let him look after the chickens.'

'If he turns up,' said Mrs O'Pheeley doubtfully.

'*If* he turns up!' Mrs Morrison agreed.

The children at The Beeches took the Willarbees entirely for granted. They paid very little attention to them at first, but then gradually they all became good friends, and Mrs Morrison, meeting Mrs O'Pheeley in the town, said that everyone was settling down very nicely.

'And *no* Winty!' she smiled.

'And no Winty!' said Mrs O'Pheeley in relief.

Emily, shopping with her grandmother, was still sore from a row with her mother.

'I'd like to go to The Beeches too!' she said. 'And so would George. We have a rotten home. Nobody has loved us since the day we were born! It's much nicer to be a ghowlie!'

'Oh, Emily, how *can* you?' said Mrs O'Pheeley, deeply shocked, and stopping short in the street.

'All right—I can't!' said Emily hastily. 'I didn't mean it! Only I do think Mummy might let me have my hair styled like the girls on telly!'

'I shall never take you out again if you speak of your mother like that!' said her scandalised grandmother. 'And I certainly shan't let you help to decorate my new house.'

'Sorry, Grandma, I didn't really mean it!' said Emily. 'Only it would be a kind of *change* to be a ghost!'

It took days and weeks to settle into the new bungalow. When the carpets were laid and the curtains were up and the lighting was fixed and the heating was adjusted and the drains were altered and the chimneys were swept and the draughts were excluded and the garden was dug Mrs O'Pheeley actually found herself looking around for something to do.

She didn't look for long.

The very next morning all four Willarbees were waiting on her doorstep.

'We've come back,' they told her. 'We couldn't bear it any longer! Winty came, and everything he did was blamed on us. The other children told tales, and the nurses hated us. Mrs Morrison was kind, but she was always busy, and she hadn't time to love us. Nobody had. Beth nearly faded away, didn't you, Bethy?'

'I think so,' said the shadowy little phantom that was Beth. 'It was so sad!'

'It was Winty's fault,' Timfy said. 'It would all have been happy-and-all-right if it hadn't been for Winty . . . .'

'But where is Winty now?' asked Mrs O'Pheeley.

'He's *there!*' they whispered. 'And Mrs Morrison thinks he's lovely! She doesn't know how bad he is! He's awful!'

Mrs Morrison was hard on their heels.

She was dreadfully upset, she said, that the ghostlings had not been happy. But she was bound to admit that they had upset all the other children at The Beeches.

'They wail at night,' she explained, 'and the night staff don't like it. It wakes up the children, and they don't like it either.'

'What about Winty?' Mrs O'Pheeley asked.

'Oh he's a dear little fellow,' Mrs Morrison said. 'Full of mischief, but he's so affectionate! The other children love him!'

'He steals their sweets and they think it's us,' said Victoria when she had gone.

Mrs Morrison had not refused to take back the Willarbees, but it was quite plain that she did not want them.

'Would you rather go back to your old home?' Mrs O'Pheeley suggested. She did not want to have them all in the bungalow, and it was quite evident that they would not be really happy there. It was all too light and

36

airy for them. Surrounded by other children they had survived, even if they cried a little at night, but on the new, bright housing estate they were entirely out of place. Little Beth pined, and became as damp and grey as the rag with which Mrs O'Pheeley wiped the kitchen floor.

The Willarbees said they *would* like to go back to the old house.

Mrs O'Pheeley took them after dark.

'You must promise . . . *promise* not to annoy Major and Mrs Bodkin!' she told them. 'After all, it was years before you made yourselves known to me, so you can just as easily hide away from the Bodkins.'

'Yes, Grandma Feeley,' they promised her.

Two days later they were back again on the doorstep.

'The Bodkins have a dog!' they chorused. 'And a cat! And a terrible parrot! The dog growled at us, and walked backwards whenever it saw us. The cat spat and fluffed at us. And the parrot called out: "Ghostie! Ghowlie! Whoo-oo-oo-oo!" till Mrs Bodkin put a pillowcase over its cage. We never went near them, but they seemed to know we were there. We thought it was only Winty who made people miserable!'

Mrs O'Pheeley took them all in her arms and comforted them. It seemed quite strange to be cuddling ghostlings.

'You can stay with me until we find something more suitable,' she promised them. But she still told herself firmly that she did not want to live with any cats, dogs, birds or ghowlies. She wanted peace and quiet in her old age, and as for the Willarbees, they must—er—well they must fend for themselves . . . .

But they did not want to fend. During the daytime they hung themselves like sheets on the clothes-drier in the garden.

And at night the Willarbees wailed.

It sounded like cats, or foxes, or somebody's radio left on too loud, but it disturbed everybody, and Mrs O'Pheeley became very unpopular. When she turned out the Willarbees and shut the door upon them, they all came back and sat along the garden fence in a row, looking so dejected that she was forced to let them in.

Nobody else could see them as she did, but it was very disconcerting to have a row of phantoms staring at the windows and dumbly imploring to be allowed into the house.

Not that they liked the bungalow. They spent their

time prowling from room to room, whimpering and wailing.

Mrs O'Pheeley thought she might ask the Rector what to do about her ghosts, but Emily assured her that it would not be any good.

'They aren't *bad* ghosties, they're only miserable,' Emily explained. 'Once they are happy you will never see them again.'

Victoria Willarbee brought home a cat.

At first Mrs O'Pheeley thought it was a ghost cat, it was so thin and fierce and had such bright yellow eyes, and such thick black fur that crackled when you rubbed it. But it accepted food when she offered it, while the Willarbees never did, and it slept quite solidly on her lap in front of the fire. Sometimes little Beth climbed up and slept beside it.

Mrs O'Pheeley tried to shoo it away as she had tried to shoo the Willarbees, but it would not be shooed, and it seemed to love the Willarbees.

The Willarbees loved it too, and were much more contented and less miserable when they had a cat to play with.

They were just beginning to settle down and fade nicely into the background of Mrs O'Pheeley's life, when George arrived with the news that he had heard of another haunted house, only twenty miles away, which was perfectly empty, and the Willarbees could all go and live there.

'I thought you would be glad to hear about it, Gran!' he said.

This time Mrs O'Pheeley did not ask the Willarbees if they wanted to move.

She invited them to go for a bus ride with her, took the cat in a basket, and set out to catch the bus at the end of the road.

The house that George had described was nearly two miles from the bus stop at the other end of the journey. By now the Willarbees knew they were being removed to some strange neighbourhood, and once off the bus they lagged behind, looking suspicious and unhappy. But they did not want to be completely deserted by Mrs O'Pheeley, so they drifted along not too far behind her, anxiously peering round each corner as they came to it.

When they arrived at the drive gates of a very old property, Mrs O'Pheeley guessed this must be the place they were looking for. The Willarbees, who had been very uneasy while they walked through housing estates, now began to perk up and look interested, for they loved old houses.

'You see?' Mrs O'Pheeley told them. 'This is just the kind of place you have been looking for! It must be as old as old. Look at those chimneys sticking up over the trees! And look at these woods! Nobody ever goes near them by the look of it. Don't you think you would like to live in a place like this?'

'Oh yes, Grandma Feeley! Yes we would!' clamoured the Willarbees.

They rounded a corner and there was the old house in front of them—as derelict a mansion as one could wish to see. So old, it might have grown out of the earth from the seeds of time—the windows broken, the walls in ruins, the doors falling in.

Such a rush of gratitude filled Mrs O'Pheeley's heart

that for the moment she could not speak. She just stood still holding the cat basket, while the Willarbees with a shout of joy, rushed forward hand-in-hand to take possession of their new home.

'Go on! You go too!' said Mrs O'Pheeley, emptying out the cat. It followed the phantoms, mewing.

As the Willarbees entered the door of the derelict old mansion they turned round for one brief moment and seemed to wave to her. It was the nearest they came to saying goodbye.

No thanks, no apologies, no appreciation, Mrs O'Pheeley thought, turning away with an odd emptiness inside her. Funny things, ghowlies, they didn't seem to have any—any *hearts*, somehow.

She turned round and hurried back to catch the bus.

A New Home for the Willarbees

Mrs O'Pheeley went home to her new bungalow to live at last a life of peace and quiet.

She bought some hens and some seeds for her garden. She laid out flower-beds and put wire round a run for the chickens, who quite soon began to lay eggs.

Mrs O'Pheeley joined the Women's Institute and the Mothers' Union. She began to be very contented and she soon forgot to worry about the Willarbees.

You just had to be very firm with ghosties and ghowlies, she told herself. They looked after themselves all right, and it was up to you to do the same.

Just now and again a pang of loneliness and regret smote her. It wasn't that she *wanted* ghowlies in the house, she admitted. It wasn't that she minded their going away to be happy without her, but when she came home from women's meetings in the late afternoons, or when she was alone after supper, the bungalow did feel most extraordinarily empty. It was strange, thought Mrs O'Pheeley, that a brand-new house could feel quite so empty and unloved.

She met Major and Mrs Bodkin at the library, and asked how they were getting on in her old home.

'Oh very well indeed!' they told her. 'It seemed rather peculiar at first, and the animals took a little time to settle down, but now they are quite all right, and we are all so happy there! It is such a friendly house!'

Mrs O'Pheeley smiled faintly and wondered why she had ever come away.

George and Emily did not come to visit her nearly so often in her new bungalow. There wasn't much for them to do there without the Willarbees.

George said he was going to visit them at their new address. He said he would cycle there and back.

'You can't!' said Emily. 'It's much too far to cycle!'

'No it isn't!' said George. 'Not on my new racing bike. I'll be home by supper time!'

'You ought to leave them alone,' said Emily reprovingly. 'You'll only unsettle them. They must be perfectly all right or they would have come back to Grandma. Wouldn't they, Gran?'

'I suppose so,' said Mrs O'Pheeley with a little shiver. But like George she was longing to know what had happened to the Willarbees.

George set off, carrying sandwiches, early the next morning.

He had not cycled fifteen miles before he met the cat limping home, its eyes wide with horror, its fur standing on end, and its paws blistered and sore. It was thinner and more starved-looking than when Victoria had brought it home.

I suppose it *is* the same cat? thought George, getting off his bicycle.

But the cat, after a look of recognition and a half-mew, laid its ears flat and bolted out of sight. It was as if in future it would trust no one ever again.

George pedalled on feeling thoughtful.

It was a long ride, even on a fine day, and he was glad enough to come within sight of the old park gates that his grandmother had described to him.

Nobody was around, and he did not feel bold enough

44

to cycle up to the house, so he leaned his bicycle against the side of the gate and walked rather slowly up the drive.

Not that he was afraid of ghosts, George told himself, but it was quite different meeting the Willarbees on his own ground, so to speak, which was in his grandmother's house, from coming to look for them in entirely strange and new surroundings.

Grandma O'Pheeley had told him the house was tumble-down and empty, but suppose it wasn't? Suppose it was inhabited by people who resented his coming to call and look for phantoms that perhaps they had no idea were there? How was he going to explain himself? He began to wish he had brought Emily, although her bicycle was old and slow, and quite likely to break down even before they had come halfway. But Emily was good at taking situations in hand and saying the right thing at the right moment.

George was almost certain she would have caught and made friends with the cat. The memory of the cat still worried him. Why was it running away as if for its life?

Then the thought arrived—probably there was a dog in the old house? And if there was a dog it meant there must be people, and if there were people how should he explain himself?

I could be selling insurance, or checking drains, thought George, but he knew that someone of his age would hardly be likely to be employed doing either of these things.

I could be asking my way somewhere, thought George. But why come all the way up a mile-long drive

45

to do it? Any cottage in the village would have told me. I could be doing some research for a project for an exam, he decided, only I don't know the name of the house or the people who used to live here . . . .

And then he decided to make a project of the Willarbees, and to ask the people who lived in the house if they knew anything about the Willarbee family, and what they could tell him about their descendants.

At this moment he rounded the last corner of the drive and came within sight of the strange old ruin Grandma O'Pheeley had described to him.

There was only one difference. Mrs O'Pheeley had described it as a perfect ruin, whereas part of the old house was still standing. Many of the windows were broken, but not all of them, and the doors, while some hung from their hinges, still guarded the entrance to empty halls and emptier corridors.

However it did not look like the kind of house anybody lived in, and this was a great relief to George.

He walked more confidently across the ancient carriage sweep in front of the house, climbed the steps, and looked in at the door.

Everything inside was very quiet, yet it did not feel quiet. There was the faintest stirring of some kind if life within. Was somebody really living there?

George put his head inside the door and listened. Nothing to see. Nothing to hear. Yet he almost felt he was listening to somebody who was listening to *him*.

'Willarbees!' he called in a loud whisper. 'Miss Willarbee! Timfy! Victoria! Beth! It's me! It's George! Are you there?'

Something did move at last. Far away at the back of the house he heard slow, deliberate footsteps.

All George's courage evaporated and left him terrified. He looked back the way he had come, but the carriage sweep was wide and the drive so distant he would be seen long before he crossed it. Oh why had he left his bicycle at the gates?

Because the approaching steps were not *nice*, they were not friendly and benevolent, they were strange and ominous. The Willarbees did not walk like that, they glided, or glid, or whatever ghostlings do. These were *frightening* steps, and George wasn't surprised that he had met the cat running for its life. He felt like running too.

But if he ran he felt that the steps would come faster and faster after him, and he wouldn't have a chance of escaping before he was caught and seized—by *what*?

George's knees began to tremble, and he clung to the side of the broken doorway, waiting for whatever was going to happen to make up its mind to do it.

The footsteps came closer, and they were accompanied by a kind of clinking or clanging, as if someone were carrying a tray full of metal objects.

Now George *knew* that he was terrified, but his legs would not move, and he was just about to sink down on his knees on the broken tiles of the entrance hall, when a familiar whisper at his elbow breathed up into his face, and the voice of Timfy Willarbee reassured him:

'Don't worry, George! You needn't be afraid! I can manage him! It's only my Great-great-great Uncle Willoughby! He might even be pleased to see you!'

There was Timfy, calm and concerned, holding out a

transparent hand to George and stroking his knee.

'I th-think I'd rather g-go home!' said George, still seized by a horror which he could not explain.

'Oh no! Not before you have met my uncle!' said Timfy, as the footsteps came closer and closer. 'You mustn't be frightened. Yes, of course he's a ghost, whyever not? But he won't hurt you, at least, not if you are polite and friendly and mean him no harm. But there's just one thing I must warn you, George. Don't be surprised at anything you may see. You might find he looks a little—peculiar!'

For Timfy spoke only just in time to prevent George from giving a yelp of sheer horror.

For the man plodding up the hall towards him was not only a great deal more solid in his suit of armour than any of the Willarbees, but he had his head tucked underneath his arm.

'Bring him in, Timfy!' said the man in armour.

Most unwillingly George let himself be led into the old hall by Timfy Willarbee, down a very long dark corridor into a room where there was a bright fire burning, but so many dark and shadowy corners that one could not see much else.

'Timfy and I are making toast,' said the great-great-great uncle, subsiding into a deep and shabby armchair. 'Would you like to join us?'

It was so disconcerting to have an invitation issuing from underneath an armpit that George could not find words to answer, but Timfy did it for him.

'Yes please, Great-Uncle Will,' he said simply, and some toast was put into George's hands.

The old man seemed to drop off to sleep, if one could

judge by the head, which he now placed carefully upon his knees with its eyes closed.

'Where are the others?' George whispered, when faint snores came from between the parted lips.

'In the cellar,' replied Timfy. 'They don't like it here, and neither did the cat. I like it very much myself. I'm going to stay here for ever and ever. It is just my kind of place. If you want to take them home with you I would advise you to do it now. They are very unhappy indeed, and my great-great-great uncle hates them. Go into the hall, and down those stairs to the right. Close the door when you go out. Goodbye!'

George fled from the room, but for a moment he looked back at the sleeping ghost.

'But what would happen,' he whispered, 'if you took his head away from him—*now*?'

'Something horrible!' said Timfy. 'Do go quickly! I don't expect I shall ever see you again! Goodbye!'

George closed the door and fumbled his way down the stairs. It was terribly dark, but presently he could see and hear the faint shapes of the three Willarbees, crouching in a corner of the cellar and sobbing.

When they realised it was George they began first to whimper and then to shriek with joy, enfolding him in their cobwebby embrace as if they would never let him go.

'Have you really come to fetch us home, Georgie!' they asked him. 'We tried and tried to be happy, but we couldn't. The cat escaped, but we didn't know how to. It was so sad!'

'Hush, hush! HUSH!' George pleaded. 'We'll none of us get out if you make such a noise! Timfy wants to stay here, but he thinks you had better come home with me. I don't know what his Great-Uncle Willoughby wants, but if you don't come quietly he may try to stop you from leaving.'

'Oh he will! He will!' moaned the Willarbees.

'He's horrible!' shuddered Victoria. 'I wish Timfy luck with him! Let's go! You lead us, George, and we'll be as quiet as mice! We don't want to be ghowlies in a house like this!'

It was no problem for the Willarbees to be quiet, but George had to take his shoes off and tiptoe down the passage and across the hall. He could hear Timfy making his great-great-great uncle some more toast.

At one moment George tripped over a hole in the carpet, but at the next they were out of the front door and across the drive. Nobody came after them.

The twenty-mile bicycle ride home seemed a mere jogtrot once they had left the drive gates behind them. One Willarbee perched on George's shoulders and the others perched just anywhere. They overtook the cat within two miles of Mrs O'Pheeley's bungalow, looking exhausted, but it put on a spurt of speed and followed them in.

Mrs O'Pheeley tried to look pleased to see them, and listened sympathetically to George's story.

'Timfy is there for good, Gran. You won't have to bother about *him* any longer,' George consoled her.

'But don't you mind leaving your brother behind?' Mrs O'Pheeley said, turning to the other little phantoms. 'You may never see him again!'

'Timfy isn't our brother. He's a sort of cousin about nine times removed!' said Miss Willarbee. 'No, we don't mind not seeing him again if he is happy. He's nothing to us!'

They haven't any hearts, thought Mrs O'Pheeley, looking at the strange little creatures. But then with nobody to love them, where could they find any love to give away? She was just thankful she had been lucky enough to arrive home herself without meeting Great-great-great Uncle Willoughby, who from George's description sounded a most unattractive old gentleman.

Well, there was her peace and quiet shattered again, and this time she could not see a solution to her problems.

Timfy, it was true, was accounted for, but there were still three Willarbees needing homes, and a very starved and frightened-looking cat. It was easy enough

51

to feed the cat, but the little ghostlings accepted nothing in the way of food, even if George ate enough for the lot of them.

'Try them on buttered toast,' he suggested with his mouth full, for he was positive he had seen Timfy sharing slices with his Uncle Willoughby. But the ghowlies shook their heads and refused the toast. It was obvious that whatever was eaten in the haunted house had quite another flavour.

They were tired, however, and all three were settling down comfortably beside the fire, when there came a banging on the front door, the letterbox flap opened and closed, and Winty came crashing into their midst.

8

Return of Winty

He was less than a metre tall, and the most turbulent little creature Mrs O'Pheeley had ever seen. A small pair of fierce and hollow eyes shone out of a billowing sheath of cloudy drapery that at one moment was a shirt, and at the next became a kind of plaid. First he had feet and hands, and then he had nothing, except a kind of shirt tail to balance on as he twisted and twirled and faced the company. One even caught sight of a wicked grin and sharp flashing teeth, and then one just saw a blank.

Mrs O'Pheeley was immediately reminded of the vivid nip on her ankle, the second time she had met the Willarbees face to face, and instinctively she tucked her feet underneath her chair.

The three Willarbees jumped from their seats and joined themselves together in a transparent but ominous wall of defence.

'Go away, Winty!' they chanted in chorus. 'We don't want you here! Go away! Go! Go! Go!'

For answer, Winty rushed at them.

There was a flurry of shadows and clouds, some shrieks and some bitter sobbing. Out of the flurry emerged the crushed shape of little Beth. She fled to Mrs O'Pheeley's lap, but the next moment another shape was after her. Sharp nails, even claws tore at Mrs O'Pheeley's hands; wails and growls filled the air, and a dreadful choking silence in the disturbance on her knees told her that one or other of the combatants was being suffocated.

'No, no, no!' Mrs O'Pheeley cried, trying to get a grasp of the churning mass of softness that was struggling there. 'Winty! Winty! How *dare* you?'

Something leapt from her knees and bounced on to the ground, so soundlessly that she saw only a kind of veil coming between her and the fire. Then the hollow eyes glared at her again.

'Winty! How dare you?' Mrs O'Pheeley repeated more bravely than she felt. 'And how dare you come into my house like that without asking or knocking? Go back to The Beeches at once!'

The fierce little phantom seemed to wilt. The fiery eyes drooped, and instead of a turbulent ghostling a mere shadow stood before her in the firelight. It looked wretched.

'I didn't like it there,' the shadow muttered. 'I want to go to a nice old house like we had before! But there's dogs now where we was, and a parrot and a cross old man. And they all got cross at The Beeches. It wasn't *my* fault!'

'Are you sure it wasn't your fault, Winty?' came the calm, thin voice of Miss Willarbee, the oldest of the ghostlings.

'Oh it's sure I am!' said Winty, suddenly cocky. 'I didn't howl at night, I didn't frighten the staff, I didn't pinch the babies, I didn't . . . .'

'All right, Winty, all right!' said Mrs O'Pheeley, suddenly very tired and exhausted. 'I will go and see Mrs Morrison in the morning and you can come with me.'

'*I* will take him back to The Beeches,' said Miss Willarbee majestically. There was no reply from Win-

54

ty—only a rather unpleasant growl.

'Now please all of you go and sleep in the spare room!' Mrs O'Pheeley implored them. 'You have all slept there before—except Winty, of course.'

'I don't want to sleep with Winty!' sobbed little Beth.

'Very well, dear! You can sleep on the sofa in my room,' said Mrs O'Pheeley generously.

One by one during the night the other Willarbees drifted through the keyhole into Mrs O'Pheeley's bedroom. She could hear them whispering and singing, in and out of her sleep. Next door she could hear Winty stamping and slamming about, and throwing things on the floor.

'One has to remember his father was a poltergeist,' she told herself, as a pot of flowers was hurled from the window-sill. 'And his mother can only have been a banshee. In the morning I shall tell Mrs Morrison that he really is her responsibility now. I cannot possibly take him back again.'

The wail of terror that arose from the spare room as the cat came through the window woke neighbours in several houses round the estate.

The cat, scared out of its wits by the noise, shot back out of the window again, and everything was quiet for the rest of the night.

9

The Doll

After breakfast the next morning Mrs O'Pheeley prepared to set out for The Beeches with a very subdued phantom beside her. Winty might almost be said to be sulking.

She found Miss Willarbee drifting at her elbow.

'Leave it to me, Mrs O'Pheeley,' Miss Willarbee said. 'I will take Winty back! You, sir!' she said to Winty, quite sternly for a ghost. 'You will come with me and say you are sorry to Mrs Morrison!'

The two ghostlings left the bungalow side by side.

With only two phantoms left Mrs O'Pheeley felt quite light-hearted. She asked Beth to pick roses for the house and set Victoria to clearing up the mess that Winty had made of the spare room. It seemed very strange to be giving orders to little ghowlies, and stranger still to see them obeying her.

'Poor, poor Granny Feeley!' said Victoria, sweeping away.

'I *love* getting flowers!' said little Beth.

Mrs O'Pheeley forgot about them in doing her accounts and bottling fruit. When she looked up they were gone. Beth's flowers, two pale roses, were drooping without water in a jam jar, and the dust, earth, and broken crocks Winty had scattered were swept into a neat pile inside the door, but on examining them Mrs O'Pheeley found there was nothing broken after all.

The ghostlings had climbed over the wall into the churchyard at the edge of the new estate. Wide-eyed and happy they were drifting among the graves, to the astonishment and horror of the sexton, who caught glimpses of them as he dug the scanty flower-beds, and was considerably shaken by what he saw.

He was more shaken still when his trowel, an old and trusted friend, was gently removed from beside him on the grass. One minute it was there, and the next it was not. He *knew* he had had it only five minutes before, and now it was nowhere to be seen. Very unhappy, he began searching for it. He searched and searched, and after a whole twenty minutes he found it, just exactly where he thought he had put it down, beside a tomb-stone.

'Place looks to be haunted!' said the sexton, bewildered and perplexed.

Victoria, who had borrowed the trowel, had meanwhile been burrowing in the leafmould under the wall, close to her own tiny grave. 'I know it's there! I know it is!' she repeated, digging with the sexton's trowel.

Little Beth was wholly engaged in reading Victoria's name on the stone. 'If only I had one like that,' she said wistfully. 'It's so—so sad!'

But Victoria paid little attention to her or to the inscription.

'I know it's here!' she kept saying. 'I know it's here from long, long ago. It *is* here! IT IS! It is! Oh Bethy, look! Look!'

The sexton's trowel had unearthed something hard and white, shaped like a doll. And it *was* a doll! The china arms came into view, then two legs and feet, all jointed and carved in the fashion of long ago. The remains of a cotton dress fell away from the china body, and some of the hair was lost from the head, but the face was there, smiling, and as Victoria wiped the leafmould off its cheeks, the face she used to know was as familiar as it had ever been.

'Put back the trowel, Beth,' she told the other Willarbee.

Beth drifted across the graves with the trowel.

The sexton, finding it, looked up and saw in the distance, and for the briefest moment, a little ghostling girl kissing the face of a doll. Then both phantoms were gone.

When he examined the soil underneath the wall it looked as if a dog had been burying a bone there. Quite recently too.

He went back to his planting, shaking his head. Graveyards were strange places, he thought, but he liked them all the same.

Victoria and Beth fluttered back to Mrs O'Pheeley's bungalow, Victoria clutching her doll.

'Is it nice?' Beth kept asking curiously. 'It looks like a baby. Is it one of us?'

'It's a doll,' Victoria told her. 'It was my baby doll. Have you never seen a doll before?'

'Never, never, never!' chanted little Beth. 'Isn't that sad?'

'I want to show it to Miss Willarbee and Granny Feeley,' Victoria said, but when she went into the bungalow two visitors were just arriving to bring plants for the garden and have coffee. Victoria only had time to lay the doll on the table, before rushing away to hide herself, with Beth, in the hall cupboard.

The visitors came into the sitting room and began to make themselves at home. They exclaimed in astonishment at the doll on the table.

'But Mrs O'Pheeley! My dear Mrs O'Pheeley. Where on earth did you find this most fantastic doll?' they cried.

Mrs O'Pheeley, coming in with the coffee tray nearly dropped it in her astonishment.

'Why? Well . . . ! I—I—didn't really know it was there!' she said in great embarrassment.

'Of course you didn't!' the visitors said. 'There must be a number of interesting things hidden under the soil in your garden! The earth hasn't been turned over for years! It used to be part of the old Manor House when the Willoughby family lived there, many many years ago.'

'The Willarbees, did you say?' asked Mrs O'Pheeley.

'The Willoughbys. Sir Geoffrey and Lady Willoughby,' repeated the guests. 'Long before our time. It has all died out now. Such a pity!'

One of the ladies was examining the doll.

'It just needs a good wash under the tap,' she said. 'Very carefully, of course! Just look at these joints! They don't make them like that today! I believe my grandmother had a jointed doll. But look at those eyes, and the nose, and the dear little mouth! Oh I know they make lovely babies in the shops now, and they walk and talk and all the rest of it, but where would you find one made like this? The workmanship, my dear! It must be worth a lot of money!'

There was the slightest movement in the hall cupboard and a wave of resentment seemed to cross the room. One of the visitors shivered a little as if she had

59

felt a draught.

Mrs O'Pheeley, still perfectly bewildered, began to pour out coffee for her guests, and when they looked for it again, the doll was gone.

'Do let me look at it just once more before I go,' begged one of the visitors. 'I want to tell my husband about it. He's quite an authority on antiques.'

Mrs O'Pheeley looked round the room. There was no doll to be seen. She went into the kitchen. No doll there either. It was very embarrassing.

'Never mind! Never mind!' said the ladies, getting up to go. They thought Mrs O'Pheeley had hidden it on purpose, and their friendly manner became a little cool.

'You must come and have coffee with us when—er—when—er—when you have quite settled in!' they said, shaking hands rather stiffly.

They were hardly out of sight before Victoria and little Beth drifted out of the hall cupboard clutching the doll.

'It was mine, Granny Feeley, long, long ago!' said Victoria. 'I buried it in the churchyard when I was a little girl. I wanted it to have a grave like the other people. Only then I got ill and nobody could find it for me. You can carry it, Bethy,' she told the smaller ghostling. 'Just fancy, Granny Feeley, she's never had a doll before!'

Little Beth became even more transparent as she reverently nursed the solid china body of the doll.

She was still looking down at it when the door burst open with the force of a windstorm, and Winty came charging into the hall.

10

The Stolen Doll

Before Mrs O'Pheeley could find a word to say to him Winty had rushed at Beth and snatched the doll out of her arms.

'That's mine now!' he exclaimed, and was out of the door again in a flash. Little Beth was left with her mouth wide open, but Victoria was crying—a faint, ghostly sobbing that tore at Mrs O'Pheeley's heart.

She would have run after Winty, only Beth came creeping into her arms, while at the same time a paper envelope, far more solid than a phantom, lay on the ground where Winty had been.

Mrs O'Pheeley picked it up and read the letter inside:

'Dear Mrs O'Pheeley,

If your little friends had not called upon me this morning I was coming to see *you*! I am afraid I cannot keep Winty with me any longer. He is a very naughty and upsetting little creature. He disrupts all the children and the staff are tired of being knocked about and bitten. Also he does the most dreadful things. We gave him the hens to look after, but all the eggs that the children had for breakfast went off bang. I am sorry that I cannot ease you of your little ghostlings, for I can quite see the problem it must be. I think I picked the wrong one, for dear Miss Willarbee tells me she would like to stay and help me to look after the children. This will suit me very well as all the children love her, and she will see to it that naughty little Winty does not come back.

Trusting that it will suit you as well,
I am, dear Mrs O'Pheeley,
Yours very sincerely,
Madeline Morrison.'

Mrs O'Pheeley dropped the letter, by one corner, gently into the wastepaper basket, looking thoughtful. Then she turned her attention to the sobbing Victoria.

'I'm sure he will bring your doll back,' she comforted her.

'He won't! He never will! He'll smash her up and throw her in the pond!' wailed Victoria. 'I shall never see my doll again!'

'So sad!' echoed little Beth, laying her cobwebby hand on Mrs O'Pheeley's arm.

'Well, you did without it for years,' Mrs O'Pheeley said more sternly. She thought to herself: I can't stand that sobbing going on day and night, day and night, for ever.

'Yes I did!' sobbed Victoria. 'But I knew it was there!'

'I didn't know,' whispered Beth. 'I didn't know what it was or what it wasn't, or whether it was something I wanted or not. It was a great surprise when Victoria found it in the graveyard. I had never seen anything like it! It had no clothes on, poor thing!'

Mrs O'Pheeley found that the ghowlies were becoming more articulate these days, and talking more than they used to do. And little Beth in her arms had just a trifle more substance. But it also meant that Victoria's ghostly sobbing was more penetrating, and like a season of rain it showed no signs of stopping.

'Suppose we think of something better to do than cry,' Mrs O'Pheeley said.

'What?' asked the little ghosts.

'We could make a milk pudding,' said Mrs O'Pheeley, but the idea of sitting down later to eat a pudding that had been made with a sobbing little phantom at her elbow made her feel very depressed.

'When your doll comes back I might make it some clothes to wear,' she said, just as she might comfort Emily.

'What for?' asked Victoria. '*We* don't wear clothes! We just wear *us*.' She sobbed more bitterly than ever.

Mrs O'Pheeley was about to telephone Emily and George's mother to ask her to send Emily along immediately after school, when the windowpane shattered with a terrible *bang*! and Victoria's doll came flying through the air, landing with a thump on the floor at Victoria's feet, amid a shower of broken glass.

The glass fragments, as Mrs O'Pheeley saw them, fell all over Victoria, while a great, jagged splinter landed on top of Beth, but neither of the ghostlings was hurt. Nobody shrieked or bled—come to think of it, had they any phantom blood to bleed with?

The doll, scratched and battered, was snatched up by Victoria, Beth left Mrs O'Pheeley's side, and the two vanished with their prize into the shadowy depths of the hall cupboard. It was the only hiding-place in the bungalow.

Mrs O'Pheeley went to the door, but there was no sign of Winty.

The broken pane looked worse than ever from outside. Before telephoning the glazier Mrs O'Pheeley swept up the pieces inside the living room for fear that the grandchildren might cut themselves. And she realised she was including the Willarbees with George and Emily.

Now there was no more sobbing and wailing, and just for the moment, no Winty! Perhaps after all there might be a period of peace and quiet. As she swept, Mrs O'Pheeley cleared away the clutter of the day before, and had pangs over the remains of a china dove and a coloured flowerpot full of freesias. It worried her to think that the little demon who was Winty should be free and roaming on the housing estate, even if he was afraid to go back to the old house. But when she looked at the shelf again her treasures were whole once more.

If only she could persuade Winty to come with her to Great-great-great Uncle Willoughby's home she felt sure the old gentleman would keep him in order. Though it did seem rather hard on Timfy who had never worried anybody.

Timfy was gone. Miss Willarbee was gone. After all, there were only three ghowlies left. It wasn't as bad as it had been. Mrs O'Pheeley tried to count her blessings.

But they had never been a nuisance before she left the old house. In spite of her dear little bungalow Mrs O'Pheeley wished from the bottom of her heart that she had put up with all the inconveniences and stayed where she was.

That night she was particularly careful to lock all the doors, though the window had repaired itself and there was no sign of Winty. And there was something absurd about trying to lock out a ghost! Mrs O'Pheeley remembered the way they had come sifting through the keyhole the first time she had met them. But it was the best way to show Winty that he would not be welcome in the bungalow.

She wondered if Mrs Morrison would be plagued with him at The Beeches, but something told her not. Now that Miss Willarbee was there Winty might well stay out of sight. He seemed to have just a little respect for Miss Willarbee.

Mrs O'Pheeley decided to call on the Rector in the morning to see if he could help her.

It being Saturday Emily was round quite early, perfectly delighted to find Victoria in residence, with Beth and the doll.

Mrs O'Pheeley left them happily playing Mothers in the living room. She did wish Victoria would allow her to make some clothes for the poor, jointed thing, but perhaps Emily could persuade her.

The Rector welcomed her very kindly, and brought in coffee.

Mrs O'Pheeley tried to explain her troubles.

'I do understand about there being ghosts or some kind of visitations in your *old* house,' the Rector said, 'though Major and Mrs Bodkin seem very happy there and have not complained . . . .'

'Major and Mrs Bodkin have no ghosts,' Mrs O'Pheeley said flatly. 'They all moved out with me!'

The Rector looked at her quite sharply.

'You don't mean to tell me, Mrs O'Pheeley, that you have ghosts in your *new bungalow*?'

Mrs O'Pheeley went rather red as she realised how foolish she must sound.

'I'm afraid that is just what I do mean,' she said bravely.

The Rector sipped his coffee, saying nothing, but by the way he said nothing it showed just how little he believed in Mrs O'Pheeley's story. She sipped her coffee too.

The Rector broke the silence first.

'Have you had a word with your doctor?' he enquired gently.

Mrs O'Pheeley realised at once that he thought she was having hallucinations. She was very mortified and offended.

'I don't think that is necessary,' she said firmly. 'What I want to know is—can you tell me any way of getting rid of ghosts in a house?'

'Well,' said the Rector, 'in an extreme case they can be exorcised, of course . . . .'

'And what does that mean?' asked Mrs O'Pheeley, who knew pretty well that it meant saying prayers in the house, and sprinkling the rooms with holy water. But she did not know what effect it would have on *her* ghosts.

'It means they would go away and never come back again,' said the Rector, still treating it all quite lightly. 'But it doesn't always work on poltergeists . . . .'

'And what *happens* to the ghosts that are not poltergeists?' Mrs O'Pheeley asked anxiously.

'Why! I wish I could tell you, but I can't!' said the Rector. 'We don't know a lot about these manifestations, I only wish we did. I've always thought they just go out spiritually like a light, and vanish . . . .'

'Do you mean it *kills* them?' said Mrs O'Pheeley.

'If you put it that way,' said the Rector. 'I prefer to think that it gives them rest from their troubles. But poltergeists are rather harder to get rid of.'

Mrs O'Pheeley thought of Victoria and little Beth, and their happiness when everything was going right. They didn't want to be got rid of.

'The bad old days we'll never see . . . Oh happy, happy, happy we!'

She realised she couldn't bear to have the Willarbees put out like a light.

'I don't really want to *lose* the phantoms,' she said unhappily. 'It's just the poltergeist that is so difficult. He's impossible!'

'Perhaps, if you were to come to get fond of him?' the Rector murmured. 'These things react so violently to people's feelings. So far as I know they are seldom dangerous . . . !'

Mrs O'Pheeley thought of the broken window. True, nobody had been hurt, but they might have been.

'Let me know if I can be of any further help to you,' the Rector said kindly.

'There is just—the Parish Register,' Mrs O'Pheeley said. 'If one knew a little bit more about the Willarbee—the Willoughby family, I thought it might possibly help me to get on better terms with the—the . . . .'

'Why of course!' said the Rector. 'I'll look up the names and let you know. Once I have the registers back from Dorchester you can see them for yourself.'

He telephoned her the next day, when he and Mrs

O'Pheeley spent a considerable time looking up the ancestry of the Willoughby family.

Victoria's was the only name actually mentioned, and Mrs O'Pheeley was a little shaken to find out how very old her tombstone was. Miss Willarbee must have been one of half-a-dozen very ancient unmarried Willarbee daughters, and there was nothing faintly resembling Timfy, or Winty, or Beth.

'Winchester Alexander Willoughby, died aged 35,' was the very nearest to his name. It seemed terribly likely that Winty too, never was.

'I think I know little Victoria,' Mrs O'Pheeley said.

'Oh really?' said the Rector, but he did not sound very convinced, and she was too embarrassed to speak of Timfy or Beth. As for Great-great-great Uncle Willoughby she really did not want to know much about him. He would have to have a good many more 'greats' anyway to have his head cut off in a righteous cause.

'Thank you very much, Rector,' Mrs O'Pheeley said, taking her leave.

11

Television

Watching television that evening Mrs O'Pheeley felt the now familiar warm feeling of something climbing into her arms.

Sure enough, little Beth was there, while at her feet Victoria sat, nursing her doll. The doll now wore a filmy, wispy sort of garment, rather like Beth's covering, and its joints did not look so aggressively naked. Victoria was rocking it to and fro, and Mrs O'Pheeley found herself rocking the ghostling on her knee, as she had once rocked Emily and George. Neither of the phantoms was looking at the television screen. Their attention seemed to be far, far away. One might almost say they were looking into the past.

The black cat that had been missing for a while now crept in by some way of its own and sat down by the fireside at her feet.

It was such a quiet and cosy scene that Mrs O'Pheeley was quite upset when George came whistling up the path and let himself in by the front door.

'*Well*!' George said. 'You do look comfortable! What's that thing Victoria has got hold of? And Gran, can we watch "The Bloodbreakers"? Dad says he won't have it in the house!'

'Oh then I think not!' said Mrs O'Pheeley hastily, but even as she spoke the pleasant gardening scene on the screen began to fade out, while its place was taken by a violent and noisy battle going on between one set of demonic characters and another.

'Oh thank you, Gran! You are a sport!' cried George, delighted.

'No!' cried Mrs O'Pheeley, but no sooner did she change the station than the dreaded film crept back again.

'No, George! It's so bad for the little girls,' said Mrs O'Pheeley, but the phantoms were taking no notice. It was as if they could not see the screen.

'It doesn't matter to *them*! They don't see it!' said George impatiently. 'Oh do leave it, Gran! It's fantastic! Don't keep turning it off!'

Mrs O'Pheeley was baffled. If only she and George were looking at it perhaps she could put up with it for just a little while. She knew it was spoiling George if his father had said no, but he didn't often come to see her, and even if it were a bad reason it was rather nice to have him.

While she hesitated the colour became more and

more violent, the action more animated, and the sound louder and louder.

'It's great, Gran!' said George excitedly. 'I didn't know you had such a super set!'

'Turn it down, dear,' said his grandmother, and George did, but to no avail. The sound, the colour and the action grew more and more violent until it filled every corner of the room. Mrs O'Pheeley rushed to the connection and pulled the plug out. The quiet that followed was almost menacing.

'Oh, *Gran*!' said George.

'It was much too loud!' said Mrs O'Pheeley crossly. But the silence only lasted a few minutes.

Slowly but surely and all by itself the screen came back to life. The noise began again, the violent colour, the action, till it was as deafening as before, and the plug which Mrs O'Pheeley had pulled out was back in the socket where it had been originally.

'Did you do that, George?' asked his grandmother.

'No, Gran, I didn't!' said George, looking startled.

'Well, pull it out again at once!' ordered Mrs O'Pheeley.

George obeyed, and felt a mighty push that toppled him head over heels backwards on to the sofa. The plug was snatched out of his hand and snapped back into the socket.

'It's Winty!' George shouted. 'Quick! Get him, Gran! He's there!'

Mrs O'Pheeley was just in time to see the little poltergeist vanishing through the kitchen door before George regained his feet and raced after him. The little ghost girls shrieked, and the doll nearly fell into the fire. The cat vanished, spitting.

George chased Winty out of the kitchen by way of the open window, which he shut with a bang! but not before a piece of cheese and the breadboard had clattered to the floor.

'Don't you *dare* come in again!' George shouted across the garden. Mrs O'Pheeley could not help noticing that no one ever spoke to Winty kindly. They always yelled angrily at him.

She took to comforting Beth, who was shivering and appeared badly shaken. If all ghostlings were like Beth, she thought, she would not mind at all if they came into her home, but Winty was not like Beth.

'I want to stay with you for ever!' said the little phantom, and for the first time Mrs O'Pheeley felt a surge of love towards her.

'Perhaps you shall, dear, perhaps you shall!' she said to her, but she knew it was a question of getting rid of Winty first.

'*Ruining* the film!' said George crossly. He switched on the picture, but now whatever he did it would only show the gardening programme.

'Rotten set! Goodnight, Gran!' said George, going home.

Darkness fell outside, and the ghostlings melted into it. Mrs O'Pheeley thought she felt a kiss brush her cheeks, and then next moment they were gone.

'Goodnight, Beth! Goodnight, Victoria!' she called, but there was no answer. The little black cat got up, yawned, and disappeared after them.

Mrs O'Pheeley felt curiously lonely. The house felt not so much lonely as deserted. She was quite glad when the telephone rang, and it was Emily.

'I've got a good idea, Granny!' she said. 'George says you are having an awful time with those ghowlies again, especially Winty. Why don't you advertise them?'

'*Advertise* them?' exclaimed Mrs O'Pheeley. 'What on earth do you mean, dear?'

'Well, you've seen those kinds of advertisements ...' Emily said, 'like "Who will give a happy home to..."' and then there's a picture of the children. They get heaps of replies!'

'But I haven't got a picture of the Willarbees!' Mrs O'Pheeley said helplessly, thinking of Winty and Beth and Victoria sitting under an artificial palm tree at the photographers.

'No, of course you haven't,' Emily agreed. 'But you can *talk* about them, I mean *write* about them. You can write so people just long to give a home to the Willarbees. I know you can!'

'Would your mother be persuaded to give them a home?' Mrs O'Pheeley challenged her.

'Um—no, Gran,' Emily admitted honestly. 'I don't believe she would.'

'Well, I'll have to think about it,' said Mrs O'Pheeley.

After much thought she wrote:

'HAVE YOU EVER TRIED TO FOSTER A PHANTOM?

Three little children of long ago need fond and happy homes, together or apart. Only child-lovers

with infinite patience need apply.
Very rewarding.'

She put her telephone number but not her name, and went to bed feeling perfectly convinced that nobody would answer the advertisement. Before locking the doors she put her head out in the garden to smell the velvet dark, and the tang of the rising dew.

'Goodnight, Winty!' she called, but the only reply was a mew from the little cat, which rubbed itself round her legs but remained outside.

12

The Health Visitor

In the morning when Mrs O'Pheeley was leaving the house to post her advertisement to the newspaper, she found Winty waiting for her on the doorstep.

'Good morning, Winty,' she said kindly.

'Good morning, Granny Feeley, and goodnight too for last night,' Winty said sweetly. She had never had a polite word from him before.

'Are you going to sell us to the newspapers?' he asked her.

'Oh Winty, no! Not like that!' said Mrs O'Pheeley, aghast. 'I just want to find a nice, kind home where you would all be happy. You can see for yourself that a bungalow is not a very suitable place for you to live in. There must be some nice kind people living in *older* houses who would be glad to give you a home. But you would have to be very good, of course!'

'I don't want to go and live with other people. I want to live with you,' Winty said sulkily. 'I won't be good if you make me go away! I'll begin all right, like I did at The Beeches, but after that I'll be awful! I'll throw all their things about and smash their pictures and pinch their babies and . . . .'

'Oh, *Winty*!' exclaimed Mrs O'Pheeley, horrified.

'Well then, not their babies, but just their grandmas and their grandpas and make them jump! And I'll let their budgies out of their cages and put the cat in the larder and salt in the jam pudding!'

'Winty! Winty! WINTY!' cried Mrs O'Pheeley

frantically. 'How can you be so dreadful? Don't you *want* people to love you?'

'Yes of course I do!' shrieked Winty, jumping up and down. 'But they never do! They don't! They don't!' And suddenly the odd little creature collapsed into heartfelt sobs and flung himself at Mrs O'Pheeley's feet.

'I want to stay with you and have a grandma like George and Emily!' he wailed. 'I want to have someone to say "Goodnight, Winty!" and "Be a good boy, Winty!" But they never, never do!'

'Didn't Mrs Morrison say that?' Mrs O'Pheeley asked, surprised.

'She just said "Night-night, children! Sleep well!"' said Winty. 'I'm not children, I'm a ghowlic and nobody loves me! Nobody ever really loves ghowlies! So I'll just go on throwing everything about and it serves them right! I will! I will!' cried Winty, jumping to his full height, which was not very tall.

'Now, Winty!' Mrs O'Pheeley reproved him. 'You are really not being very sensible. You are trying to start the wrong way round. First you have to be good, and *then* people will love you!'

'They didn't at The Beeches,' said Winty, 'and I was ever so good and happy till Mrs Morrison spoilt it all.'

'Did you never tease the other children?' asked Mrs O'Pheeley.

'No, never. Well, only sometimes,' said Winty.

'Or steal their sweets and say it was Victoria, Beth and Timfy who took them?'

'Well, just now and again!'

'And did you never tell fibs or break things up or

77

shriek at night to frighten all the neighbourhood?' pursued Mrs O'Pheeley, wondering meanwhile who on earth would be likely to offer a foster home to Winty.

'Um!' said Winty. He turned his back on her.

'Now I must post my letter,' said Mrs O'Pheeley. 'Please let me come by.'

Winty did not exactly step aside, but she was able to walk right through him.

As she reached the gate she heard him say plaintively: 'I want to stay here with you.'

Mrs O'Pheeley was touched, but she knew Winty was not to be trusted.

'I'm afraid I don't want you in my house,' she told him coldly. 'But I don't mind if you stay in the garden. Just for a little while,' she added, 'and only if you behave yourself.'

'Why do you have Victoria and Beth in the house when you won't have me?' said Winty. 'Don't you like polterghowlies?'

'I like *good* ghowlies,' said Mrs O'Pheeley firmly. 'Beth and Victoria never give me any trouble. But I don't really want *any* ghowlies in my new home. I am doing my best to find new families for them.'

'And for me?' asked Winty suspiciously.

'*Yes*!' said Mrs O'Pheeley walking out of the gate.

When she came back Winty was still sitting on the doorstep, sulking, but he made a great parade of getting up and vanishing in a cloud of contempt.

Mrs O'Pheeley did not expect to have any replies to her advertisement, but to her great surprise, she did.

A woman telephoned who said she had second sight, and would like to help send the phantoms back to where they came from. But the Willarbees would not hear of that.

'We want to go on, not backwards,' Victoria explained. 'That's just another way of getting rid of us for ever. We like being us! We like today and tomorrow! We don't want yesterday! We want next week and the year after! Please don't send us to that lady, Granny Feeley!'

Mrs O'Pheeley had not liked the idea very much herself. She decided not to go any further with it.

The next phone call was from a lady who had been a hospital nurse, and now lived in an old farm.

'I should love to have the little darlings,' she said. 'But I already have two ghost hounds and the skeleton of an owl that flies about on Halloween. Do you think they would live happily together?'

'No!' said Victoria, listening.

'I don't like owls,' said Beth.

The third call was from a little girl.

'Please can your ghosties come and live with me? They can live underneath my bed,' she said.

'I'm not going to live underneath a bed!' said Victoria.

'Nor me!' said Beth. 'And you wouldn't make us go anywhere that Winty went, would you, Granny Feeley?'

Mrs O'Pheeley had been going to do just that, although she felt very guilty about it. It would have been so much more convenient to send Victoria and Winty away and to keep Beth. Perhaps she might even adopt her, but an added problem had arisen.

Some while ago she had promised to take Emily for a holiday to see the châteaux of France, and the date was fast approaching for them to leave.

But she could hardly let little Beth stay in the house by herself, neither was she anxious to leave all three ghostlings there without her. She could not imagine what the neighbours might find out, nor what might happen in her absence.

While she was explaining to the Willarbees that she simply had to make some arrangements for them by the end of the month, a stranger came up the garden path and rang the doorbell.

It was a lady from the Social Services department, who dealt with adoptions and foster children. She was anxious to know why she had not been told about the little ghowlies, and what Mrs O'Pheeley thought she was doing by advertising them all on her own.

'You see,' Mrs O'Pheeley explained, 'I really didn't think it concerned the Social Services. They aren't real children at all—they're—um—well . . . .'

The health visitor stared at her very oddly.

'Of course I'd *love* you to find them homes,' said Mrs O'Pheeley. 'It would take an enormous weight off my shoulders. They are really very sweet, at least two of them are. One is rather naughty, but I think if a nice grandmotherly person were to have him he might be good. Have you got anybody like that on your books?'

'Let me see the children first,' said the lady practically. Mrs O'Pheeley looked round the bungalow but they weren't there, and then she looked in the hall cupboard but they weren't there either.

It was while the health visitor was looking under the stairs that she received such a pinch that she yelped aloud. Getting to her feet she looked round sharply, but there was only Mrs O'Pheeley, who was the last person to do anything like that to a guest.

'Something pinched me—hard!' said the lady.

'I'm so very sorry. That must have been Winty, the naughty one!' apologised Mrs O'Pheeley. 'He bit my ankle the first time I met him. But he is usually very polite to me now.'

The health visitor looked up and down the hall, but there was not the smallest sign of Winty.

'I'll make a report to our department, and see if we are able to help you,' she said doubtfully. 'Quite frankly, I don't see how we can, but I'll try!'

She would not stay for a cup of coffee but departed as quickly as she had come.

'What did she want, Granny Feeley?' the Willarbees asked, following Mrs O'Pheeley into the kitchen.

'She may be able to find homes for you all!' she snapped at them, rolling pastry so hard that the board rattled. 'And if she can find one you'll *all* go, all three of you, do you understand me?'

The little ghosts melted away.

For three days Victoria's doll lay unclaimed underneath a chair. Of Winty there was not a sign.

13

Going Abroad

Emily, as usual, was sensible.

'I wouldn't worry about the Willarbees, Granny!' she said. 'They can look after themselves while you are away. George can come and feed the cat. It's not a ghostie-moggins anyway, it eats too much.'

'It's Winty I worry about,' said Mrs O'Pheeley. 'It's difficult enough packing up one's valuables and taking them to the Bank and telling the neighbours and the police and warning one's insurance company, but what will happen if Winty goes in and smashes everything up just for spite?'

Her fears were put at rest by Mrs Morrison of all people, whom she met at the superstore. Mrs Morrison all but embraced her.

'I've been going to ring you up, my dear,' she exclaimed. 'I'm so grateful to you! You can't *think*! Come and have a coffee and I'll tell you just what I owe you for sending me that sweet Miss Willarbee to help me. She is so wonderful with the children!'

They sat at a little round table in a café called The Big Brown Owl. Mrs Morrison went over Miss Willarbee's virtues one by one.

'And she's such a *lady*!' finished Mrs Morrison. 'All the children have better manners since watching her eat.'

'Eat?' exclaimed Mrs O'Pheeley, surprised.

'Well she does rather pick at her food, but she does it so gracefully! And she gets all the children round her and tells them stories by the hour together! I shall always be in your debt, dear Mrs O'Pheeley!'

'In that case,' said Mrs O'Pheeley bravely, 'would you consider having—er—three of them back for a few days while I am on holiday in France?'

Mrs Morrison's face fell. Then she pulled herself together and said:

'Victoria and Beth, yes! Timfy, as you told me, has a good home elsewhere. But Winty—*never!*'

The table began to rock very violently. The coffee cups tipped over and the coffee flowed. The people at the next table looked shocked.

Mrs Morrison clutched at the tablecloth and then at her dripping skirt, while a waitress with a tight face hurried over to mop up the coffee. Both ladies declined a second cup, and while Mrs Morrison was getting up to leave she received such a bite on her ankle that she rushed out of the café, leaving Mrs O'Pheeley to pay the bill.

In the morning she sent a note of apology and enclosed a pound note.

'I really am sorry I had to leave you so suddenly,' wrote Mrs Morrison, 'but I hurt my ankle quite sharply on the corner of the table. The people next to us should have been more careful in causing such an upset! I hope you got no coffee on your dress? By the way, I told Miss Willarbee of your concern at leaving your house empty, and she assures me that Winty would never harm the house without you being in it. She said *he would not be able to,* and you would be quite safe to leave it empty. I do hope this will reassure you. And I will gladly have Victoria and Beth to stay while

you are abroad, so just send them along to me . . . .'

At last Mrs O'Pheeley was able to look forward to her holiday.

'I told you it would be all right!' said Emily.

At the moment she could not inform the Willarbees because they kept well out of sight, and life was much more peaceful without them.

Winty stayed so invisible that it was difficult to believe he had been responsible for the scene in the café, but Mrs O'Pheeley had few doubts on that score.

She and Emily had their passport photographs taken, and packed their bags, bought their tickets, and arranged to be driven to the station by Emily's father.

At the last possible minute, that is to say on the evening before they left home, the Willarbees turned up suddenly in the hall. Mrs O'Pheeley had hoped they might not turn up at all, but she was strangely glad to see Beth.

She welcomed them warmly, and told them of her plans for them while she was away.

'We know,' the Willarbees said sadly. 'We've known all about it for a long while. But we don't want to go and stay at The Beeches.'

'They are expecting you,' Mrs O'Pheeley said, her heart sinking into her boots. 'Mrs Morrison knows you are coming, and Miss Willarbee is so *much* looking forward to seeing you again! It's only for a fortnight . . . ' she added.

'How long is a fortnight?' asked the Willarbees.

'Well, it's just a fortnight since you came back from staying with Timfy and his Great-great-great Uncle Willoughby,' said Mrs O'Pheeley. 'Do you remember?'

'We don't want to remember backwards, only forwards,' said the Willarbees plaintively. 'Please may we stay here and not go to The Beeches?'

'If you don't mind being alone with Winty!' said Emily cunningly. She had come over to help her grandmother write the final labels and finish packing the suitcases.

The Willarbees gave in immediately. They said nothing while Mrs O'Pheeley telephoned for a taxi, led them into it, and drove them to The Beeches.

Up to the very last minute she was afraid that Winty might appear and make trouble, but he did not.

She slept quite badly, listening for him, but heard nothing, and when Emily and her father arrived in the morning she turned the key in the lock of her bungalow, thinking with deep gratitude that this was almost too good to be true.

Only as she came down the garden path did she hear the front door, that she had thought locked, close with slam that shook the windows. She and Emily looked at each other, but Emily's father had started the car engine and thought it was Mrs O'Pheeley herself who had slammed the door. They got into the car and drove away to the station.

I do hope—I do *hope* that Miss Willarbee was right about Winty not going into the house while I am away! Mrs O'Pheeley thought to herself, enjoying Emily's calm and quiet commonsense. But then after all it wasn't Emily's house.

She could not help thinking about it in the train, all the way to London, but after that the past faded rapidly into the present in the hurly-burly of catching the boat train to Dover, and keeping an eye on their cases, and buying fruit and biscuits for their lunch, and answering all Emily's excited questions about the châteaux in France.

One thing was perfectly certain. Winty was *not* with them today! They passed through the passport section, and only she and Emily were there together. By now she had a kind of premonition when Winty was around, and Winty wasn't. He had been left behind like a bad dream, and Mrs O'Pheeley began to enjoy her holiday very much indeed.

They boarded the cross-Channel ferry, and Emily squeezed her grandmother's arm as the boat drew away from the dock, nosing its way quietly into the open sea.

Gulls flew over their heads, lying on the wind like children's kites, only their beady eyes moving as they followed the boat. The English coast fell away behind them, and the fresh, cool sea breeze patted their cheeks as they leaned on the ship's rail.

For a long time Mrs O'Pheeley thought Emily was still at her side, but when at last she looked down she found Emily had gone to buy chocolate, and the Willarbees stood beside her, gazing out to sea, just as if they had always been there.

Emily came back with Mars bars.

'Oh no!' she exclaimed in disgust. 'Not *them*! Did you have to come?' she scolded the Willarbees.

'We didn't like it at The Beeches,' said the Willarbees plaintively. 'We wanted to come with you to France. We have never been to France.'

'Winty is not with you, is he?' said Mrs O'Pheeley in alarm.

'Oh no, Grandma Feeley! Winty doesn't know how
to talk French . . . ' said the Willarbees. 'He has stayed
at home to annoy the neighbours!'

Mrs O'Pheeley's spirits, so high a moment ago,
dropped to zero. Then she remembered that whatever
Winty did could not be traced to her while she was out
of the country, and she revived again. Let him do his
worst! She was determined that she and Emily should
have a good time. It was irritating that the Willarbees
had insisted on coming too, but after all, they were
invisible to everybody else, and they did not play
mischievous tricks like Winty.

And once on the other side of the Channel there was
so much bustle and confusion that the Willarbees got
lost, and Mrs O'Pheeley hardly had time to think about
them until the passport officer opened her passport
and gazed with puzzled suspicion at the page where,
under the section: DEPENDANTS, somebody in a
thin and ghostly hand had written: 'The Willarbees.'

'Vill—ar—bees?' questioned the officer. 'And which is that?'

Emily, feeling superior and secure in having her own passport, now came to her grandmother's aid.

'They're just our dolls,' she said flatly.

'Dolls?' said the officer, looking at her with a frown that was almost fatherly. 'It is forbid to write dolls in a passport! It is forbid to write *anything* in a passport! You must not touch the passport of your grandmother!'

'I'm sorry!' said Emily.

'Did you really write it, Emily?' asked Mrs O'Pheeley when at last they were on the train, 'because we ought to rub it out!'

'No, don't do that, Granny,' said Emily, 'because, if they are still with us when we get home, we can *put them in quarantine!*'

'Into quarantine?' exclaimed Mrs O'Pheeley.

'You have to do that when you bring things into the country,' said Emily, 'dogs, cats, budgies, snakes— because of rabies.'

'But Willarbees don't bite!' said Mrs O'Pheeley helplessly.

'Winty does!' Emily rejoined, and Mrs O'Pheeley remembered with a jolt that Winty *did*.

Emily was so sensible. If she thought it best to leave the Willarbees' names on the passport then leave them she would. But where were the Willarbees?

'If they take the next ferry back to England without us, will they still have to go into quarantine?' she asked her grand-daughter.

'What does it matter,' said Emily airily, 'so long as

they don't bother us?'

Mrs O'Pheeley felt quite ashamed of her own heart-less feelings when she saw Victoria and Beth sitting on empty seats opposite to them and looking sad. When two more travellers came into the compartment and sat down on top of them the ghostlings merely removed themselves to the luggage rack, and folded themselves into the spaces between the travelling bags.

14

Adieu to the Willarbees

It would have been a perfect holiday, Emily thought, if her grandmother had not been so cross. And Mrs O'Pheeley thought it would have been a perfect holiday if they had been able to travel without the Willarbees.

But they were there all the time, or rather they were half there, which was worse—in the hotels, in the trains and buses, and endlessly, in the châteaux.

Mrs O'Pheeley liked to believe she was not plagued with nerves, like some people, but if she had any nerves at all the Willarbees surely got on them. It was bad enough getting herself and Emily safely across the crowded streets, but she could not prevent herself from looking round all the time to see if Victoria and little Beth were coming safely behind them, and while she was doing this some frantic automobile surged up on the wrong side of the road and threatened to knock her flat, while the driver yelled and gesticulated.

'Leave them *alone*!' Emily kept telling her. 'They can look after themselves! Even if they do get under a taxi it doesn't matter!'

'Oh, Emily, how cruel!' panted Mrs O'Pheeley.

'You know I don't mean it *that* way!' Emily said patiently. She was rapidly becoming the guide to the tour, and held her grandmother very firmly by the arm as they stepped into the crowded streets. 'I just mean they can't get *hurt*! But *you* can, Granny! And if you aren't frightfully careful and much more sensible you'll end up being a Willarbee yourself!'

'It might be much more convenient,' panted Mrs O'Pheeley, skidding down the side of a taxi. 'At least I couldn't be hurt any more either!'

'Ha!' exclaimed Emily in scorn. 'Not when you got that far, but think of all that comes first! Bang! Crash! Everybody screaming! Police whistles blowing—ambulance—hospital—me all alone in Paris! Lots and lots of blood! Nobody to look after me! You unconscious! Me crying and sobbing! Nobody speaking English! Me not speaking French! Dad sent for! Hours and hours before he comes! YOU DEAD!! And then who's to say you'd ever be a Willarbee after all? Most people aren't. Most people have all those yesterdays behind them, and so have you. I don't expect we'd ever meet again . . . .'

'Oh, Emily, we *would*!' expostulated Mrs O'Pheeley. 'You know what the Bible says!'

'Well, maybe in years and years and years we might!' Emily conceded. 'But by that time I'll be as old as you and I'll have children and grandchildren and I'll have forgotten what you look like . . . .'

'Oh Emily!' Mrs O'Pheeley said again, hurt.

'I'll have photographs, of course,' Emily went on thoughtfully, 'but you will look so old-fashioned . . . .'

'Oh *Emily*!' said Mrs O'Pheeley piteously. 'But if I did become a Willarbee,' she added, cheering up, 'I need never leave you! I would be able to be with you all the time, like Victoria and Beth!'

'Ugh! How awful!' said Emily. 'I don't mean to be horrid, Granny, darling, but—oh *no*! What would my husband say?'

'Oh of course I see what you mean!' said Mrs O'Pheeley hastily. 'I was only joking. But now then, let's see which is our first château, and where are those Willarbees?'

She took charge again, and the tour went on, with lovely château after lovely château, and as little notice taken as possible of the Willarbees.

The phantoms changed in character as they travelled. Sometimes they were missing for hours on end in the shadowy arcades of the buildings they visited. Sometimes Mrs O'Pheeley and Emily quite forgot about them. And sometimes they seemed to meet and communicate with other spirits and other forces that it was hard to identify. At these times Emily and her grandmother felt lighthearted, sometimes for as much as two days at a time. They knew that the little ghosts were happy, and Mrs O'Pheeley became less crabby, and Emily less concerned. Slowly the holiday developed into the kind of tour they had planned and hoped for.

Mrs O'Pheeley spoke French very fluently. She and Emily were taken by the guardians into the secret depths of old castles and introduced to the most ancient rooms and valuable possessions. Always the Willarbees followed, but sometimes they lagged behind and disappeared.

After a while it was easier to forget about them and to take it for granted that they would come back again.

And reappear they did, one morning very early, standing hand-in-hand at the foot of Emily's bed in the big hotel bedroom which she shared with her grandmother.

'There is a lady wants us,' they announced together, repeating it over and over again till Emily sat bolt upright on her pillows, thinking she was dreaming.

She said nothing, but the ghostlings came a little closer and repeated urgently: 'We have come to say goodbye! There is a lady wants us in the château!'

The previous day they had visited and explored one of the oldest and most beautiful châteaux in the north of France. The Willarbees had been delighted with it, and true to their habit, had disappeared into its shadows and failed to return.

This had not worried Mrs O'Pheeley and Emily, because they always came back in the end, but here they were, at seven o'clock in the morning, formally saying their goodbyes as if it were the most natural thing in the world to part for ever at this stage of the holiday.

Suddenly Emily did not want them to go.

'Wait! Wait!' she urged them. 'Don't go off just like that! Think it over! Think about it before you leave Granny and me! And ask her first! Don't just *go*!'

Mrs O'Pheeley turned over in bed and sat up like Emily.

'Granny, they want to leave us—for good!' said Emily urgently. 'Tell them not to! Tell them they can't! Tell them to wait a little while! Do *forbid* them to go!'

'Granny Feeley doesn't want to keep us,' said the ghostlings sadly. 'You don't want to take us back to the bungalow! We know you don't! And if you do take us back you will put us into quarantine, we heard you say so. But there's a lady in the château who wants us! She's kind and lovely! She lost her little daughter long, long ago, and she goes round looking for her. It's so sad. But if she had us she wouldn't be lonely. The guardians are sorry for her—they hear her crying at night. It is *very* sad. But if she had us she wouldn't cry any more and we'd all be happy.'

Suddenly Emily felt so guilty she could hardly bear herself. Mrs O'Pheeley felt just the same.

They hadn't wanted the Willarbees. And the Willarbees whom they had thought so cold and heartless had known it, and had minded. And because now they had found a home for themselves and somebody to love them, Mrs O'Pheeley and Emily saw them in quite a different light. The dear Willarbees, the faithful, kindly Willarbees—not like Winty, but just like themselves. And the Willarbees were now casting them off, not *being cast off*, but drifting away quite firmly and for ever and ever.

'Don't go! Oh please don't go!' pleaded Emily. 'We're going home tomorrow! You can come too, can't they, Granny? And if Gran doesn't want you at the bungalow I'm sure I can persuade my parents to let you come and live with us!'

The Willarbees stood expressionlessly saying nothing.

'We've got a nice house,' Emily rattled on. 'There are attics and a big garden and . . . .'

'Is it an old house?' Victoria asked politely.

'I believe it is Victorian,' said Emily.

The ghostlings did not sniff, but they looked as if they did.

'Of course, they are talking about a *château*!' Mrs O'Pheeley reminded Emily, but she too longed to keep the Willarbees. After all these weeks life would seem curiously empty without them.

'We would love to give you a happy home . . . ' she ventured. 'Of course, there is Winty . . . .'

The ghostlings shuddered.

'There is no Winty here!' they said impassively, 'The lady will have only us. And she already loves us dearly.'

'It is so sad!' burst out Emily.

'Yes,' agreed the Willarbees. 'It is very sad.'

But even while they were speaking they faded out. One minute they were there and the next they were gone.

Emily and her grandmother looked at one another in disbelief. They felt perfectly stunned as the truth slowly sank into them that the Willarbees, and of their own choice, were gone at last.

15

Return from Holiday

Mrs O'Pheeley and Emily returned from their holiday a great deal more depressed than when they set out.

On the last morning they bought presents to take home, also long French loaves and chocolate, and a best hat for Emily.

On the ferryboat they sat quietly in chairs watching the water, surrounded by their parcels. From time to time both hoped to catch a glimpse of a Willarbee coming after them, but no Willarbees came.

'The main thing is that they are happy,' Mrs O'Pheeley kept saying to cheer themselves up, but in their inmost hearts both she and Emily were feeling very miserable and guilty and rejected.

Emily's father met them at Dover when they had been through Customs. No officials had taken any notice of 'The Willarbees' written in Mrs O'Pheeley's passport. In fact, when she came to look for it, the writing was now so faint it was very nearly not there any more.

Emily's father took Mrs O'Pheeley back to her bungalow after tea.

By now she was feeling so depressed she did not mind if the house were upside down or the garden uprooted. Whatever it was like she knew it would feel as empty as a tomb, and if Winty was around it would feel worse.

But the house was warm and welcoming. The flowers in the window-boxes were blooming whole-heartedly.

The garden was in perfect order. All the grass edges were cut, and the dead roses snipped off.

'Who did all this?' Mrs O'Pheeley exclaimed, as Emily's father carried in the cases.

'Don't know! Must have been George!' said Emily's father, which surprised Mrs O'Pheeley because George never did any gardening if he could help it. She was glad she had brought him back a nice present from France.

Emily's father drove away, and Mrs O'Pheeley unpacked her cases and sat down on a chair, wondering if it really felt as if she had come home.

Emily did. The moment she set foot on her own doorstep she became a new person, full of life and spirits and bursting to tell her parents about the places they had seen and visited. It was as if the Willarbees had never been.

It had made it all the harder for Mrs O'Pheeley to leave their cheerful household and to return to the empty bungalow, which seemed so much barer and less cosy than her old home, which she had always been glad to see.

'A cup of tea will do me good,' said Mrs O'Pheeley, 'One thing the French don't know how to make is a nice cup of tea!'

She went into the kitchen, and when she returned with a tray and a teapot Winty was sitting in her chair, much more solid than she remembered him, and much more polite.

He sprang up as she came in, and carefully closed the door behind her into the kitchen.

'Good afternoon, ma'am,' said Winty, standing

aside to give her back her chair. 'I was only keeping
your place warm! I trust you have had a good holiday?'

'Why yes—no—yes . . . I don't exactly know!' said
Mrs O'Pheeley, overcome with the shock of seeing
him, and to her horror and humiliation she put down
the tray, sat down in her chair, put her head in her
hands and burst into tears.

'Dear, dear! Poor Granny! Poor Granny!' said
Winty, and the strangest little bony hand passed over
her hair. 'What happened to you then?'

It was so wonderful, so comforting, to hear a note of
sympathy, Mrs O'Pheeley cried more than ever. But
having cried and blown her nose and sipped at the cup
of hot tea Winty had poured out for her, she found
herself telling the story of the tour, up to the minute
when the Willarbees had, quite suddenly it seemed,
decided they had had enough, and walked out on her.

'You don't want to cry for *them*!' said Winty in
contempt. 'Wishy-washy-wambly little Willarbees!
They only think about themselves! You've got *me*!'

Mrs O'Pheeley gave a little shiver that she could not
quite suppress.

'It was little Beth,' she whispered. 'I loved little
Beth. I though she loved me too. I wanted to adopt
her.'

Winty kicked the table, but not violently.

'The silly little muppet!' he muttered. 'Who could
possibly want a whimsy little ghowlie like that when
they've got *me*!'

'But, Winty, you can be so awful!' Mrs O'Pheeley
pleaded.

'I'm not awful!' said Winty. 'How ungrateful you

are! Haven't you seen your house and garden? Well then!'

'Oh, Winty! Did you really do all that?' Mrs O'Pheeley said gratefully. 'I thought it was George!'

'*George*!' spat Winty. 'The only time he tried to prune the roses I jabbed such a splinter into his hand that he never came back!'

'Well, it's all looking lovely,' said Mrs O'Pheeley, feeling better already. 'Did you water the seedlings and trim the edges and snip the roses and . . . ?'

'All—all of it!' said Winty with a self-satisfied smile. 'Every bit of it I did. Just me.'

'And I never brought you anything from France!' said Mrs O'Pheeley regretfully.

'Yes you did, Gran,' said Winty. He pounced on the long French loaf. In a minute his sharp little teeth had nibbled up the whole length of it, and in another minute they had raced all the way down again as if the bread was a flute. By the time he had turned it round and run up it for the second time there was not much of the bread left.

'Like a bite?' Winty offered, breaking off a piece of crust.

Mrs O'Pheeley accepted it, and this was all she saw of her souvenir loaf. Winty had already eaten all the rest. No jam, no butter, no anything. But then French loaves are very delicious.

'But I haven't eaten any of your other food, Granny Feeley,' Winty said. 'I didn't think I ought to take it without asking you.'

'Really? That was nice of you, Winty,' said Mrs O'Pheeley. 'Did you get very hungry without anything to eat?'

'No! Oh no! No! No, not at all,' said Winty. 'I don't *have* to eat! I just like eating!'

'The Willarbees don't eat at all,' said Mrs O'Pheeley.

'Oh *them*!' said Winty with the utmost disgust. 'Of course they don't! They've got no insides to eat into. And no teeth either! I'm quite different!'

'I know you've got teeth, Winty,' said Mrs O'Pheeley, wrily smiling as she remembered her bitten ankle.

'Shall I wash the tea things for you?' Winty offered, and without waiting for a reply he bundled the cup and saucer on to a tray and whisked it into the kitchen.

There was a crash as a saucer broke, and then a cup bounced on to the floor and rolled under a chair. Mrs O'Pheeley shuddered.

'Careful, Winty! Please be careful!' she called, but Winty appeared in the doorway polishing the crockery with a teacloth.

'No harm done! Not to worry!' he announced, and certainly the cup and saucer looked quite undamaged.

'Then—what was it that broke?' Mrs O'Pheeley asked, bewildered. 'Didn't you drop the china? I heard something go smash!'

'That's right! Just this!' said Winty, carelessly. To her horror he dropped the saucer on the floor and hurled the cup against the wall. There was a resounding crash but when he picked them up both objects were as perfect as ever.

'Aren't they *cracked*?' Mrs O'Pheeley asked, astonished.

'No, Granny ma'am! Not even cracked!' said Winty, tossing the cup to the ceiling before he caught it and put it into Mrs O'Pheeley's hands. He jumped on the saucer and then offered that too.

'It sounded so terrible,' said Mrs O'Pheeley help-lessly.

Winty giggled.

'You should have heard my dad hurling china!' he said. 'You would have thought it was a whole porcelain factory being smashed up! My mam used to shriek and yell at him! Oh they did kick up a noise between them!'

'How dreadful!' shuddered Mrs O'Pheeley.

'Shall I show you?' offered Winty.

Suddenly he rushed at the dresser and swept every plate, cup, saucer and dish to the ground. Then he jumped on them, bouncing like a ball and smashing the lovely pieces into smithereens. The noise was intolerable. Mrs O'Pheeley put her hands over her ears and closed her eyes.

When she opened them again someone was knocking at the door.

Mrs O'Pheeley ran to open it, thinking it might be George, but it was the neighbour from next door.

'Have you had an accident?' he asked kindly. 'We heard a most terrible noise, and my wife made me come round to see what had happened.'

'I only just—broke a saucer!' said Mrs O'Pheeley, trying to block out the sight of the devastated kitchen, though why she should protect Winty she could not imagine.

'Is that all?' said the neighbour, looking disappointed.

He peered across her shoulder, and Mrs O'Pheeley was bound to look too.

The kitchen was perfectly tidy. Nothing lay broken on the floor except a single odd saucer that she knew had been cracked for years. The blue and white plates stood in their usual places along the dresser. The blue and white cups hung on their hooks. On the top shelf the three meat dishes followed one another like ships at sea, and lower down a geranium in a painted pot stood undisturbed on its saucer, blooming happily.

'So kind of you!' Mrs O'Pheeley said faintly. 'Would you like a cup of tea now you are here?'

The neighbour accepted. He peered all round the room while she was refilling the kettle, and Mrs O'Pheeley could not blame him. It was all so very peculiar.

She felt easier now the neighbour was there, but there was no sign of Winty, and he did not come back during the whole evening. She wondered if he were sleeping in the house, and rather hoped not, though she knew he could get in through a keyhole.

Although she felt extremely cross with him, she could not let him go to bed without a word, and opening the door a little she put out her head into the cool night air.

'Goodnight, Winty,' she called into the darkness.

16

Winty Behaves

Mrs O'Pheeley would not admit, even to her self, how much she missed the Willarbees.

George and Emily were busy with school. Winty lurked, or sulked, she was not sure which, and peered at her out of corners. When she called him he did not reply, but when she went to look at the chickens she found they had been fed, and the seedlings had been watered and the toolshed tidied. Of course, it could have been George, but she had a strong suspicion it was Winty.

However George did come to see her on his way home from school and he offered to feed her hens.

'The neighbours have been doing them,' he told her, 'but you can't expect them to go on doing it now you have come home.'

'Of course not, dear,' said Mrs O'Pheeley, and George went off down the garden. He was back in a moment, nursing his hand.

'There's a mouse in the chicken food,' he complained, showing small teeth marks.

'Oh dear! Oh dear! Come quickly and put it under the tap while I get the disinfectant,' said his grandmother.

She washed and plastered George and gave him some tea.

'You don't think it was Winty who fed the hens, do you?' she asked him over toast.

'*Winty*? Good gracious no! He never does anything

useful like that!' said George scornfully. When he left
the bungalow his back tyre had a puncture and he was
forced to walk home.

Winty came in to finish up the buttered toast.

'You shouldn't *do* these things, Winty!' Mrs
O'Pheeley scolded him, quite glad to see him again.

'What? Feed the hens? Bite George? Give his silly
old bicycle a flat?' said Winty. 'Whyever not?'

'Well, it isn't kind,' said Mrs O'Pheeley. 'And it isn't
at all necessary. George has never done anything to
harm *you*.'

'Oh well!' said Winty.

'You certainly shouldn't bite anybody,' went on Mrs
O'Pheeley. 'It is perfectly disgraceful, and there is no
excuse for it at all. I never heard of a boy your age *biting*
people.'

'Well, you have now!' said Winty rudely.

Mrs O'Pheeley simply picked up her knitting and
turned her back on him.

'Shall I wash up for you?' Winty offered.

'No thank you. I don't want another scene like
yesterday,' said Mrs O'Pheeley.

'I never do the same thing twice! Not ever I don't!'
said Winty, bouncing up and down. 'I don't want to
bring that silly old carrot in from next door again!
You'd much better let me wash up for you!'

'No thank you, Winty!' said Mrs O'Pheeley firmly.

'Well then, can we play a game? What kind of game
can we play?' asked Winty, burrowing in a drawer.

Mrs O'Pheeley had a darts board, and a box of
snakes and ladders, which was Winty's choice.

She tried to teach him the rules, but Winty would

not learn. He raced up the ladders, but screamed with rage when he had to come down the snakes, and finally he ran away with the counters and refused to say where he had put them.

'I shall not play *any* games with you again, Winty!' said Mrs O'Pheeley. She went away to wash up the tea things, and when she came back again Winty was knitting. She watched him for a little while, his face screwed up in a fierce frown, his sharp little hands pulling and tugging at the wool till it broke, and then knotting it up again.

He knew she was watching him, but he did not look up.

'I am knitting for you,' he muttered, and the stitches slipped off the needle one after another and avalanched down to the bottom of her work. 'It is like snakes and ladders!' said Winty. 'Only there aren't any ladders to climb up—only these silly old snakes!'

Mrs O'Pheeley took the knitting quite firmly out of his hands.

'You are spoiling it,' she said. 'I could teach you how to knit, only you are so impatient I don't believe anybody could teach you anything!'

Winty went out like a light and Mrs O'Pheeley was alone all the evening.

She found herself thinking of Beth—little clinging Beth who wanted to stay with her and be adopted.

How infinitely comforting to live with a ghostling like that instead of a wild, noisy little poltergeist like Winty! She hadn't the energy to cope with Winty. George hadn't been as bad as that, even at his worst. But Emily hadn't been *quite* so loving as Bethy, not after she went to school. George and Emily's father had been a dear little boy, but that was so long ago, and if he had been tiresome and naughty she had forgotten it. Besides, she had been young then and she was too old to cope with naughty boys now.

Emily had taken the little ghost cat to live in her home while they were away, and it did not seem inclined to come back. Probably it found Winty rather disturbing to live with. But it did rather leave her with nothing. Except Winty. And he only came in when he wanted to.

Mrs O'Pheeley put her knitting to rights and began to feel sorry for herself. Once she had begun she felt very sorry for herself. And then very, very sorry for herself. The tears began to roll down her cheeks, and she went into her bedroom to find a hanky.

While she was there another knock came on the door, and this time it was not the same neighbour, but his wife.

'Ah, Mrs O'Pheeley!' she exclaimed. 'We thought you might be feeling a bit lonesome after your holiday, and my husband and I wondered if you would like to come in and have a cup of tea and a sandwich and watch the telly a bit . . . .'

Mrs O'Pheeley was most grateful to go. She couldn't tell the neighbours about Winty, but she told them all about the châteaux—well, not quite all, and about the journey—not quite all about that either, and the joys of Paris, and what Emily had said and done.

She went home feeling infinitely cheered and comforted, to find her bed turned down with her hotwater bottle in it, and a hot drink standing on the bed table with a saucer on top of it to keep it hot.

She thought for a moment that Emily or her mother had dropped in, but then she remembered that all the family had been going to a concert that evening, so Emily would not have had time to come.

'Thank you, Winty! Oh thank you, *dear* Winty!' she exclaimed, sipping her cocoa, and in case he had not heard she repeated it into the darkness outside, wondering where Winty had gone to sleep.

'Do you want to come and sleep in the house?' she asked him, but there came no reply. Only the night stayed very quiet, and she slept better than she had for weeks.

The next morning she thanked him in person, for Winty was in the kitchen eating sugar.

'It's a pleasure, Granny Feeley!' said Winty amiably.

'Wouldn't you like to have a bedroom of your own in the house?' Mrs O'Pheeley offered him, feeling more warmly towards him than she could ever remember in the past.

'No thank you,' Winty replied. 'I might get on your nerves. I'll go on sleeping in the garden shed. It's not very comfortable, but it will do. I'm going to be good, Granny Feeley, I'm going to look after your garden and your chickens and see that no harm comes to you, and you will be ever so proud of me! I won't break your china any more! I'll just be *good*!'

'Oh Winty, how wonderful!' said Mrs O'Pheeley, looking at him with something like affection.

She could not help noticing that he was becoming a great deal more solid looking than he had before. Much

110

more, in fact, like a little human child. She longed to brush his hair and cut his nails, but she dared not suggest it. It was gratifying to have him even suggesting better behaviour, and she left it at that.

It was terribly difficult to believe he meant what he said, but perhaps he did mean it—just for the minute.

And really, for the next few days he was a model of perfect behaviour. It was not only that the garden jobs got done, and could be seen to be done, but astonishing to relate, *Winty could be seen doing them!*

'I see your grandson is working hard,' Mrs O'Pheeley's next-door neighbour remarked, when to her knowledge George had not been near the house all the week. 'Good little chap, that one! Feeds the hens, weeds the paths, and never looks up while he's doing it! *My* grandson is all for motorbikes, and won't ever give me a hand, not ever!'

'He *is* a good boy!' Mrs O'Pheeley agreed, not liking to add that her grandson wouldn't help in the garden either. She wondered how many other people had noticed Winty.

She soon found out. The health visitor came to call and asked why Winty wasn't at school like all the other children on the estate.

Mrs O'Pheeley didn't know what to say. She felt very guilty, as if she ought to have seen to it that Winty went to school like the others. But the only explanation she could think of was: 'Well, you see—he isn't that kind of a boy . . . .'

The health visitor looked at her keenly. 'Do you mind if I go and have a word with him?' she asked. 'I think my colleagues in the Education Department

111

would be interested in him. There might be a place found for him in a special boarding school and . . . .'

As Mrs O'Pheeley watched she saw Winty go out, just as plainly as a picture changing on a television screen.

But a little further down the garden, through a pergola which divided it from the vegetable patch, a new scarecrow spread and waved its arms. Malice gleamed through the hollow eyes of its turnip head, and it swayed a little, turning with the wind.

While the health visitor walked down the garden to find Winty Mrs O'Pheeley shook her finger at the scarecrow, imploring it to behave, and indeed it stood quite still and showed no sign of life as the health visitor strode to the end of the garden, glanced inside the shed and came back again.

'It was just my little garden boy,' Mrs O'Pheeley explained. 'Perhaps he's really over school age.'

'Well, I can't see him around,' said the health visitor. 'But it looks as if somebody has been sleeping in your garden shed.'

'Well yes! It is a kind of summerhouse,' said Mrs O'Pheeley.

'Very beautifully set out,' remarked the health visitor. 'Basin! Running water! Shower! And the furniture is most attractive! Do you sleep out there yourself?'

Mrs O'Pheeley had to admit that she never did.

'Your grandchildren do, then?'

Mrs O'Pheeley admitted that they often came to see her.

'And er—sanitation?' asked the health visitor.

Mrs O'Pheeley blinked. It had never struck her that sanitation was lacking. Phantoms, after all, don't have any use for loos.

'There is one inside the back door,' she said. The health visitor seemed satisfied. When she left the scarecrow slowly let down its arms and went on weeding the path.

Mrs O'Pheeley watched the health visitor's car out of sight. To her great relief the tyres were not flat, and there did not seem to be anything wrong with it.

'*Good* boy, Winty!' she called down the garden, blowing him a kiss.

Winty took no notice at all, but the next time she went to the door she found a small posy of flowers on the doorstep.

The shed was just as bare as it had always been. It was very peculiar . . . .

17

The Flower Show

George and Emily went less often to see their grandmother.

Mrs O'Pheeley did not feel lonely because she had
Winty, and slowly her mistrust of him faded away.

'I'm so glad you have an odd job boy, dear Gran!'
said Emily's mother, dropping in with a leaflet about
the village Flower Show. 'I know it's not a big garden,
but we did feel it was a bit much for you to tackle all
alone. I hoped Georgie would come and help you, but
you know what Georgie is! He'd rather take his bicycle
to pieces than chop a bit of wood! And Emily is always
babysitting. I think it's rather sad when one's children
grow up!'

Emily's mother was a very busy person, occupied in
so many different directions that she hardly ever came
to call. Mrs O'Pheeley had lunch with the family on
Sundays.

She promised to enter flowers for the Flower Show,
and in the bungalow garden she discussed with Winty
what classes she should choose.

'Six matched eggs,' she decided, for Winty had done
wonders with the hens. They were fat and healthy
looking, and laid a tremendous quantity of fat brown
eggs. Mrs O'Pheeley sold them to the neighbours.

The flowers were splendid too. Nobody on the estate
had such roses or such delphiniums, or such big white
daisies.

'We must enter all of these,' said Mrs O'Pheeley,

getting quite excited.

Winty was just as enthusiastic. In the evening he came into the house and they sat together watching gardening programmes or looking at gardening books.

Winty collected a large quantity of slugs and snails from the flower-beds and tipped them all over the fence after dark into the neighbours' gardens.

When she found him doing it Mrs O'Pheeley became very angry and scolded him severely.

'But *why*?' insisted Winty. 'We don't want them winning all our prizes, do we?'

'But Winty, it's a *competition*!' said Mrs O'Pheeley. 'We must all play fair!'

'Then they can tip them all back again!' said Winty sulkily. He did not speak to Mrs O'Pheeley for two days.

The morning of the Flower Show dawned bright and clear. A huge marquee had been erected in the field behind the school and everybody was told to bring in their entries before twelve o'clock.

Winty was in the chicken run quite early in the day, feeding the hens, and putting a drop of Mrs O'Pheeley's brandy in their water to encourage them to lay big eggs.

Not that they needed much encouragement. Mrs O'Pheeley found it quite hard to select six large brown smooth eggs, they were all so big and splendid.

'Come and help me choose the roses,' she told Winty, but he made excuses, and while she was cutting delphiniums and daisies he went back to his ordinary garden jobs as if he had lost all interest in the Show.

Emily and George came to lunch. Emily was wearing her new French hat. George cycled over, because he was entering for the Cycling Marathon, which was twenty times round the school field, and he was determined to win.

They both tolerated Winty but they did not like him. Winty had a habit of disappearing when he saw them arrive.

He played a silly little game with Emily's French hat. One moment it was on the top of the steps and the next hanging on the house door. Emily was furious at first, but when she saw it walking, head high, across the garden, she burst out laughing, and she and Winty chased each other silly, till her grandmother called her in to dinner. Winty never ate with them, nor did he eat very often with Mrs O'Pheeley. Now and again he snatched a bite, but on the whole he only ate about once a day, and as often as not it was a raw egg or some vegetables out of the garden.

He did not go with them to the Flower Show, and this was a relief, because Winty was much more visible these days, and an in-and-out kind of character was difficult to explain away.

Miss Willarbee was at the Show, though nobody noticed her, also Mrs Morrison and The Beeches children.

Quiet, refined and elegant, it was difficult to distinguish Miss Willarbee from anybody else, and The Beeches children clung to her and quarrelled to hold her by the hand.

She greeted Mrs O'Pheeley with a wan smile, but did not enter into conversation.

They all made their way to the marquee, where the

judging had taken place during the dinner hour, and Emily dragged them at once to the Children's Posy section, where she found she had won a third prize.

Filled with ecstasy Emily stood gazing at the green card on the table, till roused from her reverie by George, who came rushing across the tent to announce: 'Gran's roses have won First Prize!'

It was perfectly true. A large red card propped up in front of the vase announced that Mrs O'Pheeley was the winner of the First Prize in the Rose section of the Flower Show.

'And the daisies!' shouted George.

'And the delphiniums!' cried Emily.

'And the eggs!' cried George and Emily together.

Mrs O'Pheeley was overcome with embarrassment. Her friends came hurrying to congratulate her. Neighbours and acquaintances crowded round the stall. She had never been so famous in all her life before. And she did not really enjoy the sensation. She had not expected for one moment that she would win, and she could not help remembering the slugs and snails and caterpillars, and all the work Winty had put into raising her roses and her daisies and feeding her hens.

'Why Gran, aren't you *proud*?' asked her grandchildren, seizing her hands.

'Oh yes, dears! Very, very!' replied Mrs O'Pheeley, but something inside her was hammering away that everything was not quite as it should be.

She gave her prize money to the cause, which was the Save the Children Fund, but when, at the end of the day, she came to collect her flowers, with Emily to help carry them home, her worst fears were realised.

The roses, stiff, glowing scarlet as they were, were like no roses she had seen growing in her garden. She could have sworn they were made of paper. And the daisies—they looked and felt so artificial Mrs O'Pheeley could not believe they could ever have deceived a judge. The delphiniums were made of silk.

As for the eggs, when she picked them up one after the other they collapsed between her fingers like little puff balls and all that was left was the broken shiny shells.

Emily shared in her grandmother's horror and humiliation.

They rushed to find the judges, but it was too late. Nobody would listen to them. Two of the judges had gone home, and the two that were left would not believe a word of what Mrs O'Pheeley said to them.

'I assure you, dear madam, we had *experts* judging the flowers,' they insisted. 'And in every single entry yours was judged the very best in its class. And as for the eggs, we had a farmer's wife judging those, and she said she had *never seen eggs of such a size and quality*!'

There was nothing more they could do about it.

Mrs O'Pheeley and Emily were forced to take the flowers home with the remains of the eggs, and they put them straight on the bonfire that Winty had lit at the end of the garden.

'I thought you might be needing it,' he remarked with a sidelong grin.

George, to their surprise, was helping him. He had won his marathon, and was so pleased with himself he had ridden straight back from the prizegiving to show off to somebody, and there was nobody to show off to

but Winty.

'Oh Winty, how *could* you be so dreadful?' Mrs O'Pheeley and Emily burst out together, unwrapping the flowers and the eggshells and hurling them on to the fire.

'It wasn't fair!' said Winty peevishly. '*You* won all the prizes, but you never did anything for the pretty flowers like I did! They put *your* name on all the nice red cards, but it ought to have been: GROWED BY WINTY!'

18

In Search of Timfy

Winty got over it, and Mrs O'Pheeley nearly forgot the Flower Show. She couldn't alter things now, anyway, and she had not kept the prize money. But it was difficult to have any real peace of mind.

Winty gave little trouble, but she could not help thinking of the other ghostlings, some near, some far — Timfy, Miss Willarbee, Victoria and little Beth in the vast French château — were they really well and happy? Did they long for England and the old house they used to live in, and the doll they had left in the hall cupboard, and the little black cat, and sitting by the fire at night telling stories? And if they were sad and homesick, how would they ever find their way home again? And what would become of them if they did?

Then Timfy Willarbee, living with his terrible uncle, not twenty miles off — he was in and out of her mind all the time. What if he was lonely and frightened? What if his uncle ill-treated him? Would Timfy know how to run off and get on a bus? In the old days she had taken the view that what became of the Willarbees was their own affair, but lately her sense of responsibility towards them had grown and grown, and she found she was thinking about them most of the time.

Even Winty noticed her restlessness.

'Why are you so miserable, Granny Feeley?' he asked her. 'Are you thinking about *us*?'

Mrs O'Pheeley was startled to hear him speak of

himself and his fellow ghostlings as 'us'. Up till now he had always kept himself apart.

'Well, yes in a way I am,' she admitted. 'I'm thinking of Timfy all alone there with his great-great-great uncle in that dreadful big house. I'm thinking that he may not be happy. And I'm wondering if his uncle is cruel to him, as he was to Miss Willarbee, and Victoria and little Beth. And if he is cruel, what is Timfy to do?'

'Shall I go and find out?' offered Winty.

Mrs O'Pheeley was so overjoyed by the suggestion that she threw her arms round Winty, and for a moment clasped the thin bones of a cold and spiky little ghost. He wriggled away, but she felt he was not displeased, and he added: 'But I don't know how to get to the place.'

They were both silent, thinking.

If I go, Mrs O'Pheeley thought, the old man will see me, and we'll never know how things really are.

'You could go by bus,' she told Winty lamely.

He did not reply. He did not think the suggestion worthy of an answer. But a long while afterwards he said: 'How stupid!' very loudly, and kicked a saucer into the grandfather clock. The saucer broke into a hundred pieces, and Mrs O'Pheeley jumped up with a scream, but when Winty picked it up the saucer was quite whole again, and there was not a mark on the grandfather clock.

'Oh Winty, how *can* you?' she said crossly.

George came in to watch a programme he was forbidden to see at home. He too noticed that his grandmother was worried because she let him turn it on without an argument.

'What's wrong?' he asked above the clamour of the entertainment. 'What are you worrying about, Gran?'

'I'm thinking about Timfy!' she confessed. 'I'm wondering how he is getting on. I can't help worrying about him and that awful old great-uncle he has gone to live with. I'm afraid he may be so unhappy!'

'You don't want him *back*, do you?' said George, aghast. 'Surely it's better not to know!'

'Oh George!' said Mrs O'Pheeley. 'But he may be very, very unhappy, and it could be so cruel to leave him there!'

'Do you want me to go and find out?' asked George lightly.

'*Ha!*' exclaimed Winty fiercely.

'Shut up! Nobody wants your opinion!' said George, and a certain amount of scuffling went on under their chairs.

'*Don't!*' cried Mrs O'Pheeley. 'All right, Winty! You did offer first, but you hadn't any idea how to get there! Now George *does* know how to get there, don't you, George? And wouldn't it be a good idea for you both to go together?'

Both George and Winty were silent. They stared into the television screen as though absorbed by what they saw there.

'How would we go?' asked Winty at last.

'I shall cycle!' said George firmly. Having won the marathon there was no question with him of travelling any other way.

Winty put out all the lights and the television screen. They knew it was him, because the light outside was shining brightly and at the same time his banshee wail

123

filled all the corners of the room.

'Oh don't do that! We'll have the neighbours in!' cried Mrs O'Pheeley. 'Georgie, can't you take him too?'

'If he likes. It's all the same to me!' said George coldly.

There came a tattoo of delight on his shoulder blades, and a crow of pleasure from Winty. The lights came on again.

'I always wanted to ride a racing bike!' Winty said.

'You won't be riding it, but I don't mind if you sit behind me,' George said graciously.

They started early in the morning.

Mrs O'Pheeley watched them go with a mixture of anxiety and relief, together with the happy realisation that at last she would have a day to herself. She accepted an invitation from Emily's mother to go and make jam.

George pedalled furiously, pretending he was on another marathon, this time forty miles long. He supposed Winty was clinging on behind him, but it was hard to tell. The little poltergeist had no weight, and the hands with which he gripped George round the waist could hardly be felt.

Only when they came to a hill and George got off at the steepest part to push the bicycle, the pedals continued to go round and round, and the machine pulled itself out of George's hands.

'*Ride*!' hissed a command in George's ear. 'You don't have to do any work!'

George rode, and the pedals raced away under his feet even on the steepest of slopes. This encouraged him to ride faster and faster, till before he expected it they were within sight of the gates of the old house where Timfy had gone to live with his great-uncle, the Cavalier Willoughby.

George jumped off his racing machine rather suddenly. Now they had come to this part of the enterprise it all felt different, and something told him very urgently not to go on.

He leaned his machine against one of the crumbling pillars of the gate.

'Y' don't want to go in they—ar!' said an old man walking past with his dog. 'It's na—asty in they—ar!' The dog too raised its head and howled as it passed the gateway, but whether it howled at its master's tone or because it saw Winty George could not be sure.

Winty did something so quickly that George did not see it, but the dog began to whiz round suddenly in frantic circles, snapping at its tail.

'Drat that—dang ye!' said its master, hauling it along by the collar. They passed from sight.

George was shivering a little.

'Come on! Let's go!' said Winty, in imitation of George's favourite television thrillers. But George hung back.

'Er—um! Well—er—er—um!' he murmured. 'I'm kind of out of breath after all that riding! I guess I'll just rest a little . . . !'

A sound came from Winty that was as like a raspberry as a poltergeist can blow. He strutted forward through the gates, flashing in and out of invisibility like

125

a sheet of summer lightning.

'You wanted to come!' he jeered at George. 'And now you're frightened! Ha, ha, ha!'

'I'm not frightened, just getting my breath!' said George, but even he could hear how foolish this sounded.

'Wait one minute!' he shouted after Winty. 'I'm just coming!' All his old terrors, nearly forgotten, had returned.

There came a cackle of hollow laughter as Winty vanished round the corner of the drive. George rode after him, but he was nowhere to be seen. Then he rode back and tucked his bicycle behind the entrance gates. He thought he could conceal himself better without it. After which he took a deep breath, thrust his hands into his pockets, and strode forward.

The old house came into view, but Winty had vanished. Still, the mere fact that he was—he must be—somewhere in the building gave George the courage to go on.

The last few steps across the gravel sweep and up the steps were the worst. The stillness of the old bricks and stones was rather like the stillness of a monster waiting to pounce upon him.

George watched the broken windows, hoping in vain to see Winty, or Timfy Willarbee or even Great-great-great Uncle Willoughby peeping out, but nothing peered at him except cobwebs.

He listened, but there was no sound to be heard against the sinister silence. Nothing moved, nothing spoke, nothing laughed. Nothing did anything at all.

Very bravely George pushed open the broken hall

door and looked into nothingness. It was as if the building had been empty and deserted since the beginning of time. There were no footsteps in the dust on the floor, although certainly within the last few weeks to George's knowledge people had been crossing it. Last time he had visited the place he remembered there had been a feeling, a *knowledge*, of a far away hidden movement that had spoken of life within, but today there was nothing at all.

Where was Winty? Where was Timfy? Where was the ghost-uncle he remembered, and which some terrible fascination made him long to see again? He ventured a little further inside the old house and listened.

Nothing. A most dreadful and sinister nothing. The nothing of something frightful hidden in a corner and waiting to burst out. Or was that just his imagination after all, and was the nothing just *nothing* after all?

But if so, where was Winty? Now that he had disappeared he seemed the only link with real life that George could cling to. He dared not even turn his head to walk back the way he had come. He just stood still, while his knees shook and trembled and knocked against each other like drums in a jazz band. Then he began to walk slowly backwards towards the door.

The fresh, sweet air from outdoors blew into the hall round the backs of his legs, and made him feel braver. Besides, he was nearly outside now. And suddenly he realised that he could leave the house now, this very minute, and leave Winty behind too. Never mind that he hadn't seen Timfy or his uncle, this hardly seemed to matter any more. It was much more important to escape while he could, because once he had made contact with whatever was going on inside this horrible house he might never be able to leave again. He might be mopped up and become part of the haunting like Timfy and Winty, prisoners of the ghastly old man without a head.

He took one more step backwards and came into contact with the frame of the old front door, which, already hanging on one hinge, fell in with a fearful crash. George could hear the echoes reverberating down the corridors and on and on throughout the house.

He was about to leap over the broken door and flee, when something passed him like the wind. He had a fleeting glimpse of Winty pulling Timfy by the ear, and then they were both past him and across the gravel.

'Come quick, before it's too late!' shrieked Winty, and even as they ran, the clanking footsteps of the phantom cavalier sounded behind them deep within the house. Faster and faster the steps approached, but as George took the last of the stone steps at a bound the building slowly and solidly collapsed upon itself behind him. The pillars crumbled, the windows splintered and disintegrated, the walls fell into piles of rubble, all with a terrible dying roar.

Dust rose in clouds from the ruins. When George looked back it was just settling, but of Great-great-great Uncle Willoughby there was not a sign.

Winty and Timfy were at the gate, drifting round George's bicycle.

'Will he come after us?' shuddered George.

'No, never!' said Winty.

'It's rather sad!' said Timfy. 'I was just teaching him to put his head on to eat his toast with. But he wasn't very nice. I didn't want to stay there really. I was so lonely.'

George knew that his grandmother would not be all that pleased to see three of them coming home together, but there was nothing to be done except pedal back as fast as possible.

'I suppose you can both sleep in the toolshed?' he asked them.

'No he can't, it's mine!' said Winty. 'And if he comes too I'll smash it all up! I'll smash the flower-pots and pull up all the plants and throw the potatoes over the fence and put things in the mowing-machine and bring in all the slugs I can find and . . . .'

'Oh Winty!' cried George, horrified and pedalling hard. 'How can you do all that to Grandma when she has been so kind to you?'

'I know,' came Winty's voice, quite softly behind his ear. 'I can't! It's a great pity, but I can't because I love her! I want her to be my grandma too!'

All One Big Happy Family

Mrs O'Pheeley and Emily were watering the flowers when George rode in at the gate with Winty and Timfy perched somehow behind him.

'They've come back,' said Emily gloomily, 'and they've got Timfy with them!'

'Not his uncle too?' quavered Mrs O'Pheeley.

'Oh no, no, no! Of course not! He's not that kind of ghost!' said Emily, thinking it was impossible to imagine a cavalier with his head tucked underneath his arm tramping the small rooms of her grandmother's bungalow.

'I don't know what I'm going to do with them, or where I'm going to put them!' cried Mrs O'Pheeley in despair.

'Well, Winty has got the toolshed, why not let Timfy have the coalhouse?' suggested Emily. 'It must be much more comfortable than that dreadful place you told me about!'

'There isn't a house any more!' panted George, putting down his bicycle in the middle of the lawn. 'It fell down while we looked at it. It's just a pile of dust and stones now.'

'But what about Timfy's uncle?' asked Mrs O'Pheeley, very concerned.

'He is no more!' said Winty piously.

'So sad!' said Timfy cheerfully.

Mrs O'Pheeley looked at them. One-and-a-half little ghostlings—for Winty almost looked like a boy these days—and nowhere for them to go except her clean little modern house which was not in the least suitable for ghosts or poltergeists. She looked at Emily, and Emily shrugged her shoulders and shook her head. Like her grandmother she did not know what was to be done about the ghowlies.

And at that moment Miss Willarbee walked in through the gate.

Mrs O'Pheeley thought at first that she had come to tea, before she remembered that ghowlies don't eat tea. Then she just thought she had come to call, and was rather touched that Miss Willarbee should have troubled to come and see her all the way from The Beeches.

'Come in and sit down, dear,' she invited her.

'I've left!' said Miss Willarbee. 'I'm not going back to The Beeches ever again!'

'Oh Miss Willarbee! Whyever not?' cried Mrs O'Pheeley.

'There was too much work to do,' said Miss Willarbee in a flat but discontented voice. 'Work, work, work, from morning till night. Mrs Morrison expected everything of me! Just everything! I've never been used to working like that. It isn't fair to expect it. I told her I had had enough, and here I am!'

Mrs O'Pheeley was wondering where on earth she could put Miss Willarbee to sleep.

'The larder!' Emily urged her in a whisper. 'She doesn't eat, so she can sleep in the larder!'

'But I haven't got a larder,' whispered Mrs O'Pheeley. 'She might have the airing cupboard . . . .'

'Yes, that would do!' agreed Miss Willarbee.

She half smiled at Timfy and frowned at Winty, who

put out a nearly transparent tongue at her, and drifted towards the toolshed.

'I'm off!' said George, retrieving his bicycle. 'Do you want a lift, Em? You can ride on the carrier.'

The grandchildren left. The ghostlings proceeded to their allotted quarters, Timfy to the coalshed, Winty to the toolshed, and Miss Willarbee to the airing cupboard.

'But what will happen when they get tired of being there?' Mrs O'Pheeley tormented herself. 'Or Winty quarrels with Timfy? Or Miss Willarbee gets sick of them both? And what about the neighbours? We are almost back to where we were before! Am I never going to have any peace and quiet?'

To her surprise she found she was not as frustrated as she would have been a few weeks ago. There was almost a comfort in having the little phantoms rustling about the place, even if it was rather inconvenient.

'We can manage!' said Mrs O'Pheeley.

She petted Timfy, until Winty bit him, and then she petted Winty, and Miss Willarbee called him that horrid little banshee. The next morning the whole contents of the airing cupboard were strewn on the carpet, and Mrs O'Pheeley did not know what to do.

Miss Willarbee helped her to put everything back again. Winty worked in the garden, Timfy stacked coal, and the day passed quite peacefully.

George and Emily came to tea and to watch the last instalment of a serial they wanted to view. 'But really we've come to see how you are getting on with the dreadful ghowlies!' said George, putting her arm about his shoulders. 'It's a great shame you should be landed with them like this! Em and I are thinking what we can do about it . . . .'

They were sitting peacefully in front of the television set with slices of cake on their knees when there came a double knocking at the door.

'Oh *no*!' groaned George, but he did not offer to open it.

'Who's there?' called Mrs O'Pheeley.

Nobody answered.

Tap-tap-tap-tap-tap!

'Who is it?' called Mrs O'Pheeley.

There was no reply.

Rat-tat-tat-tat-tat! Then there were very faint, high voices like the wind blowing in the leaves.

Mrs O'Pheeley got up and went to open the door.

There on the doorstep were Victoria and little Beth.

Mrs O'Pheeley opened her arms and enfolded their frail, gossamer-like bodies with their frail twig-like limbs.

'My darlings! Oh my darlings!' she heard herself saying.

'We got tired of being French ghowlies!' said Victoria. 'The lady didn't want us both—only one. So we left her. It was very sad, but we couldn't be parted. We came back on the ferryboat the same way we went. I expect she will find herself another ghostie, poor thing.'

Mrs O'Pheeley was already worrying about where on earth she was going to put them to sleep, and pleased as she was to see them she could not help thinking of the little ghosts hanging on the washing lines in the garden, and the crowded house, and how the neighbours were bound to notice something peculiar. True, they had managed before, but now there was Winty as well, and Winty was bound to be awkward.

He crept away now to lurk in the toolshed, so Mrs O'Pheeley was able to take Beth in her arms and cuddle her to her heart's content.

'We will sleep in the hall cupboard,' said Victoria, so that was a problem solved, though not the problem of Winty, and not the neighbours.

Mrs O'Pheeley hardly slept a wink all night, and when the dawn was creeping through the window Winty climbed in too, and sat on the end of her bed.

'Good morning, Grandma Feeley,' said Winty when he saw she was awake.

'Good morning, Winty dear,' said Mrs O'Pheeley.

'I think I am going away for ever,' said Winty solemnly.

'Oh no, no, no!' cried Mrs O'Pheeley, sitting bolt upright on her pillows. 'Why? Why? Why?'

'I can't be here with Miss Willarbee and Timfy and Victoria and Beth!' said the little poltergeist. 'I'm not the same as them and you don't like me!'

'Oh I do, Winty! I do!' pleaded Mrs O'Pheeley.

'You like Beth better than you like me!' accused the ghowlie, pointing a skinny finger at her. 'You would like to keep her for ever!'

'I like you *and* Beth!' protested Mrs O'Pheeley. 'I love you both! I don't want either of you to leave me! Please stay! Please stay!'

'Miss Willarbee hates me, and so do the others!' Winty said gloomily. 'There really isn't room for all of us here. I think I shall go back to The Beeches and

135

make poor Mrs Morrison's life a misery!'

'Oh Winty, how *dare* you?' cried Mrs O'Pheeley. 'If you ever leave me or do any such thing, I shall never, never love you any more!'

'*Do* you love me, Granny Feeley?' asked Winty plaintively.

'Yes, I do!' she said simply.

A kind of glow spread all over the phantom that she could see even in the half light.

'Better than Beth?' he pursued.

'Oh you are terrible!' cried Mrs O'Pheeley half laughing and half crying. 'As if it mattered which of you I love best! I love *both* of you best! But Beth loves me too. That's what makes all the difference.'

'I love you too!' said Winty quite slowly. 'I think I love you very much, Grandma O'Pheeley!'

He vanished, and she thought he was gone, until she heard him quarrelling with Timfy in the garden, and it came back to her with a jolt that she now had two ghowlies in the hall cupboard, one in the coalhouse, one in the toolshed, and one in the airing cupboard.

Just what her life was going to be she could not imagine, but the postman called before she had finished getting herself some breakfast, and he brought a letter from the estate agent to tell her that Major and Mrs Bodkin were going abroad, and her old house was on the market again.

Mrs O'Pheeley thought deeply for over an hour before she telephoned the estate agent and told him to give her the first refusal to buy back her old home.

Then she called all the ghostlings together and they

sat down to discuss the situation.

'First of all,' said Mrs O'Pheeley, 'do you want to go back to the old house, I mean all of us together?'

'Yes!' said Miss Willarbee.

'Yes!' said Timfy.

'Yes!' said Victoria.

'Yes!' said Beth.

'Yes!' said Winty.

'But the question is,' said Mrs O'Pheeley, 'if it was all too big and too much work for me before, how are we going to manage now?'

'I will do the housekeeping and the cooking,' said Miss Willarbee placidly.

'I will sweep the house,' said Victoria.

'I'll clean all the silver and brass,' said Beth.

'And I'll carry the coal and do the fires and the boiler,' said Timfy.

'I'll do *all* the garden *all* by myself,' said Winty. 'There will be lots of room for all of us there, like there was before, and we needn't quarrel. We need hardly ever see each other really. You can just be a lady, Granny Feeley. You can pretend *you* are a phantom and we are real! And we shall hardly bother you at all. You just see how happy we all can be!'

George and Emily, when consulted, agreed that this was the best possible answer to the situation. No ghowlies wanted to live in an airing cupboard nor even in a toolshed for ever, and it was essential to find somewhere where they could be happy and be no trouble to Mrs O'Pheeley or anybody else. There would be no immediate neighbours. The washing lines could hold real washing and not ghowlies.

George and Emily's parents thought, and said, that Mrs O'Pheeley was quite mad, and they could not think what had come over her, exchanging her beautiful new modern bungalow for the house she had been so anxious to leave. But nothing they said could shake her decision.

The ghowlies returned contentedly to their old quarters, and in their transparent way they were very helpful.

Winty managed the garden so well that there were always flowers, vegetables, and eggs from the hens. The flowers were always real, and the eggs never went off bang. Timfy was allowed to help him now and again, and they became quite good friends. The little girl ghosts fluttered about and gave the place a friendly feeling. Sometimes in the evenings Beth crept on to Mrs O'Pheeley's lap, and just occasionally Winty did too.

'Just think of those long-ago days . . . ' Miss Willarbee said, 'when everything went wrong and we had to find new homes all over the place! Now we are all together we can remember those times that will never come again! We are so happy now, but in those days we weren't!' And going about her housework she sang the song they had sung on the first evening they came to Mrs O'Pheeley:

'We are the Willarbees!
We never were!
We'll never be!
The bad old days we'll never see!
O happy, happy, happy we!'

FIRST TERM AT TREBIZON
Anne Digby

At last – a new series of boarding school stories to delight a new generation of readers. In this first story, Rebecca Mason is plunged into life at Trebizon, a famous school for girls. Lonely, afraid and anxious to prove herself, she determines to write something that will be accepted for publication in the special jubilee edition of the school magazine, but the piece that appears is not the one she intended . . .

BOSS OF THE POOL
Robin Klein

The last thing Shelley wanted was to have to spend her evenings at the hostel when all her friends were going away for the summer holidays – all because her mother, who worked there, wouldn't let her stay in the house on her own. Then, to her horror, mentally handicapped Ben attaches himself to her from the start and although he's terrified of the pool, he comes to watch her swimming. Despite herself, Shelley begins to help him overcome his fear.

ROB'S PLACE
John Rowe Townsend

Everyone Rob cares for is deserting him: first his dad left, then his best friend, and even his mum hasn't time for him now she has a new husband and baby. Just when he thinks he's got a special friend in Mike it turns out that he's leaving too. But it's through Mike that Rob learns how to escape from his everyday life – he discovers a fanastic place which is all his own and where he is master. But can he control his fantasy or will his Paradise become a nightmare?

TEMPTED TO LOVE

Four years ago, at the height of what
she had innocently thought was their
passionate love affair, Neil Dysart had
callously left Kirsty without a word of
explanation. Now he had come back
again, apparently expecting to take up
where they had left off. But he was
married now. What right had he to try
to resurrect the past like this?

Books you will enjoy
by FLORA KIDD

BETWEEN PRIDE AND PASSION

'No strings', Valentine Knight had insisted seven years ago when he and Karen had had a passionate affair; he didn't want the responsibility of marriage and a family, he told her—and she accepted it, with the result that after their parting she had never told him she had had his child. So what right on earth had he now to try and take that child away from her?

MAKEBELIEVE MARRIAGE

Mexico is not the safest place in the world for a girl to be stranded in, alone and penniless, as Daphne Thomas found when it happened to her—which was why she had accepted Carlos Reynolds' proposal of marriage. He needed a wife for a few months—purely on a business basis—and in return he would help her get back to Wales. But that was only the beginning of the story . . .

MEETING AT MIDNIGHT

When Elizabeth's husband Dugald turned up after over two years' separation, she assumed it was because he wanted a divorce, to clear things up once and for all. But the same will that had forced them to marry was now obliging them to stay together—otherwise they both stood to lose their inheritance. Or had Elizabeth got completely the wrong idea about Dugald and their marriage?

BRIDE FOR A CAPTAIN

For the sake of his young son Tim, Iseult had agreed to marry Nicholas Veryan, a man she hardly knew. And it was for the sake of the boy, Nicholas insisted that the marriage must be a real one. But surely Nicholas couldn't expect that of her, when he was so clearly still involved with Joanna?

TEMPTED TO LOVE

BY

FLORA KIDD

MILLS & BOON LIMITED
15-16 BROOK'S MEWS
LONDON W1A 1DR

First published 1982
Australian copyright 1982
Philippine copyright 1983
This edition 1983

© *Flora Kidd 1982*

ISBN 0 263 74104 4

Set in Monophoto Plantin 11 on 11½ pt.
01-0283 - 49366

Made and printed in Great Britain by
Richard Clay (The Chaucer Press) Ltd,
Bungay, Suffolk

CHAPTER ONE

UNDER the hot July sky, flecked here and there
with tiny white clouds, the silvery waters of Loch
Lannach were dulled by a shimmering heat haze.
High up on the slope of Autnoch Hill four people
walked, a woman and three men.

The men all walked ahead of the woman, in
single file as they followed a steep path which
dropped from the slope into a wooded glen made
by the Lannach River, a narrow sparkling stream,
babbling serenely over smooth ledges of basalt
rock between cliffs of reddish sandstone.

When she reached the path winding beside the
river the woman slowed down. Tall and slender,
she was dressed in pants made from a red and
green tartan, the MacGregor tartan, which she
was entitled to wear because her married surname
was Whyte, and the Whytes are a sept of the
MacGregor clan. Her blouse was a soft shade of
green and she wore an oatmeal-coloured hand-
knitted sweater tied casually by its sleeves around
her neck. On her feet were wellington boots, the
best sort of footwear for the countryside of the
Scottish Highlands.

She walked with easy strides beside the stream.
Thin shafts of sunlight slanting between the
leaves of the birches willows and hazels crowding
along the river banks glinted on her thick black

hair, which she wore coiled into a knot on top of her head. Wisps of hair escaped from the knot to twist delicately and intriguingly about her lightly sun-tanned heart-shaped face. Beneath fine arching eyebrows her eyes were a brilliant blue, their expression one of smiling pleasure as she looked at the trees. Once or twice she reached out a hand to smooth the silvery bark of a birch as if she were greeting an old friend.

The higher she walked after the men the less the stream became, until half its bed was dry and water was no more than a series of pools linked together by beds of wet shingle scattered with reddish rocks. On either side the cliffs rose high and sheer and above them steep slopes were overgrown with larch and pine, making patterns of light and dark green. The air was warm, bees and insects droned, and as always in that place she felt small but safe.

A loud shout from one of the men in front made her hurry on around a big outcrop of rock which guarded the biggest and deepest pool in the river. When she reached the narrow shingle beach edging the pool she thought she noticed a movement on the opposite shore, a slight shaking of the tiny birches, a ruffling of their heart-shaped leaves as if a wind had passed over them on that still and windless day.

'Come out of there, damn you!' roared Hamish Taggart, who was head keeper of the estate.

There was no answer to his shout and no one appeared on the opposite side of the pool, but Hamish's own voice shouted back at him in mocking echo.

'Who was it?' asked one of the other men. He was slight and slim, dressed in elegant tweeds, and his shiny black hair was brushed close to his narrow skull. His nose was hooked and his skin was sallow.

'A poacher,' growled Hamish, jerking his tweed cap forward over his eyes. A tall man, he had high square shoulders and grizzled grey hair and his tweeds had known many a soaking of fine Highland rain.

'How do you know?' asked another man. He was brown-haired and fair-skinned, and his grey-blue eyes glinted with excitement as they scanned the screen of birches on the opposite shore.

'He's left his weapon behind,' said Hamish, pointing to a ledge in the middle of the pool. 'Can't you see it?' On the ledge was a long wooden staff with a loop of wire at one end.

'What is a poacher?' asked the slim dark man. He spoke English with a strong foreign accent.

'Well now, it means someone who has no right to fish on the estate has been here and has taken a salmon from the pool using an illegal instrument, catching it by the tail with that loop of wire. He must have heard us coming. All I was seeing of him was a flash of silver in his hand which was the salmon and his bare feet and legs as he scrambled away up that bank,' replied Hamish.

'So.' The dark man's soft black eyes gleamed. 'He is a criminal, if he has no rights to fish on the estate. What is the worst you can do to him?'

'Have him fined, or put in jail if he can't be paying the fine,' said Hamish. 'But I doubt I'll be doing that now. He'll have got clean away while we've been standing here.'

He turned away and looked right at the woman. He gave a slight jerk of his head towards the opposite side of the pool and at once she began to walk back to the bank of shingle below the pool, hearing behind her the deep drone of Hamish's voice as he continued to explain to the other two men the complexities of fishing rights in the Highlands of Scotland.

Once she had crossed the bank of shingle she ducked under the branches of trees and began to climb a narrow path which twisted between broken rocks, overgrown with briar roses, blackberry vines and stunted birches, until she reached a small clearing high above the pool which was screened from the view of the men on the shore by a big boulder.

Behind the boulder a man was lying on his stomach and was watching the other men, who were just beginning to walk away down the course of the river, their departing footsteps crunching on shingle, their voices growing fainter. When she saw the man the woman stood still and stared down at him.

He was long and lean and was wearing grey corduroy trousers tucked into the tops of wellington boots, and under his heather-coloured sweater his shoulders were wide and flat. His reddish-brown hair had the sheen of a chestnut's skin and was cut in an attractively shaggy style. He lay perfectly still until the other men could no longer be heard. Then with a quick lithe movement he got to his knees and began to stuff two pairs of boots and two pairs of socks into a canvas fishing bag.

It was while he was fastening the bag that he became aware of the woman's presence. Slowly his glance lifted from the bag and slowly it drifted upwards over her boots, up over her legs and body, up to her face. His eyes, which were a clear amber brown, widened slightly in surprise and he straightened up to his full height, slinging the strap of the bag over one of his shoulders. Shoving his hands into the pockets of his pants, he stood with his legs apart returning the woman's stare, his eyes now cold and blank.

'I've been looking at the heels of your boots for quite a while, Neil Dysart,' she said mockingly. 'Shame on you for poaching a salmon in daylight when the water in the pool is low! Anyone can catch a fish like that.'

'I'm not the poacher,' he replied coolly.

'Then who is? I can't see anyone else here.' She looked round the clearing deliberately.

'They've gone, and I'm not in the habit of betraying my friends,' he said curtly.

'They must be uncomfortable walking without their socks and boots,' she remarked dryly, her glance going to the bag. She looked back at him, a slight smile curving her lips. 'I do believe you've forgotten me,' she said softly. 'I'm Kirsty Whyte. My last name used to be Ure.'

His hard glance swept over her and a slight frown brought his heavy dark eyebrows together over the bridge of his thin aquiline nose.

'I remember you.' His glance raked her assessingly again. 'You look different,' he added bluntly.

'That's not surprising,' she said with a laugh. 'I'm nearly four years older than when we last met, and I do my hair differently.' She looked at him as frankly and as assessingly as he had looked at her. 'I can see a few changes in you, too,' she added lightly.

She didn't say what the changes were. Now thirty-four, going on for thirty-five, he was still straight and lean and his hair was still quite thick, springing back vigorously from the deep peak on his forehead. But the passage of time had left marks. His eyes no longer danced with a sparkle of mischief but were cold, clear pools of yellowish light. His high cheekbones looked strangely bruised as if he had been living too hard and his mouth was set in a taut controlled line.

'I suppose you're staying at the croft on Cairn Rua,' she said, feeling chilled suddenly by his unfriendly attitude.

'I am.'

'When did you come back?'

'A week ago.'

'Oh.' She was surprised, and annoyed too, because she hadn't been informed of his return and hadn't noticed any light at night beaming out from his cottage. 'You might have let me know.'

'I'd have got round to calling on you eventually,' he replied indifferently.

'I suppose you know that Alec died four months ago,' she said.

'I had heard,' he murmured laconically, and it seemed to her his eyes narrowed calculatingly as he continued to stare at her.

'Is your wife with you?' she asked as casually as she could feeling tension building up between them.

'No.' The curt dismissing negative showed her how he felt about her curiosity. It set her back, away from him. He looked in the direction of the dark yet light-reflecting pool which could just be seen over the tip of the boulder. 'Who was with Hamish, by the pool?' he asked.

'My brother Duncan, the new tenant of Balmore, and one of his security men.'

'Tenant?' he queried sharply, turning to her again. 'You're letting it?'

'Yes, as from the beginning of this month.'

'Just the house?'

'No, the whole estate. I'm hoping that if he likes living here he'll buy the place.'

For a moment he looked stunned, staring at her, his eyes wide. Then slowly they narrowed again and his mouth curved cynically.

'I never thought a day would come when Balmore would be let to a tenant with a view to selling it. Alec and his Whyte ancestors must be turning over in their graves,' he remarked jeeringly.

'I can't help that,' she retorted spiritedly, her blue eyes flashing. 'They don't have to maintain the place and I do. Alec left a mountain of debts when he died and his lawyer suggested that I let the house and the estate to raise money to pay off his creditors. It's taken me all this time to find someone willing and able to afford the rent, and if Sheikh Hussein al Dukar offers the right price I shall certainly sell it to him.'

'A sheikh, eh?' He stepped towards her, his eyes glinting with hostility. 'You'd dare to sell property, which was granted to the Whytes nearly five hundred years ago by a king of Scotland to an Arab oil millionaire?' he exclaimed. 'My God, I would never have believed you would have turned out to be so grasping!' His breath hissed as he drew it in. 'Surely the Balmore estate should be passed on to the next Whyte, to Alec's and your son.'

'Alec and I didn't have a son,' she said stiffly.

'Your daughter, then.'

'We didn't have any children,' she snapped back at him. 'The paralysis grew worse and made it impossible for him to . . . he wasn't able to. . . .' She broke off, the colour rising in her cheeks as she realised she was betraying to him the sterility of the two and a half years of her marriage to Alec.

'Then why the hell did you marry him?' his hostile eyes challenged her. 'Was it so you could become Lady Whyte of Balmore and inherit one of the biggest estates in the Highlands and then sell it?'

'No, it wasn't!' she retorted, her head up. 'I married Alec because I liked and respected him and because he was always kind to me.'

'And no doubt because you were sorry for him,' he sneered.

'Perhaps. I felt the least I could do in return for all the help and encouragement he'd given me was to help make the last years of his life a little easier and pleasanter. Isn't that what marriage is all about?'

'If you say so,' he drawled, his manner guarded again. 'So the fishing rights belong to an Arab while he's the tenant,' he went on. 'That's going to make a number of people who live on the estate unhappy, isn't it? I mean the owners of crofts like myself who have always had the privilege of fishing its streams and lochs when Alec and the other Whytes before him were lairds of Balmore.'

'Hussein is a very pleasant man, cultured and educated, and I think he'll make a good landlord, so you don't have to sneer at him,' she rebuked him.

'Maybe he's all you say he is, but I suspect he won't have any hesitation in punishing anyone who trespasses on his rights. He doesn't belong here, so he won't know to turn a blind eye when a local lad lifts a fish from his rivers.' He rubbed his chin and looked past her. 'I think I'd best be on my way to find my friends. They went down the river path and I wouldn't like them to run into Hamish and the Sheikh.'

'Hamish won't do anything to them,' she said, hurrying after him. 'In fact he sent me here to warn whoever was in hiding.'

He turned to look at her and the corners of his mouth tilted upwards in a grin.

'I see.' His eyes lost their coldness and began to dance with devilry, reminding her of other oc-

casions when she had been with him, five years
ago, and they had hidden together behind rocks
or among bushes to avoid being caught by the
headkeeper when they had helped themselves to a
fish from a pool. 'The lads were only playing at
being poachers,' he explained. 'They were trying
to prove to me that they had the skill to lift a fish
from low water under a bright sky. No one was
more surprised than they were when they caught
it. Of course if I'd known about the tenant I
wouldn't have let them try.' He slanted her a
curious glance. 'You seem to be very friendly with
this Sheikh, calling him by his first name.'

'He asked me to,' she replied, tilting her chin.

Standing under the branches of the small
birches they were much closer to each other than
they had been. Hidden from view, shaded from
the sun, the little glade was pervaded with intimate memories for Kirsty; memories of kisses and
caresses they had exchanged on hot sunny afternoons; memories of passion which she had
deliberately banished to the cellars of her mind
but which were now breaking out of their im-
prisonment and storming her sensibilities. She
wanted to cry out, to shout at Neil, and tell him
to go away and leave her in peace. Instead she
turned on her heel and began to walk swiftly down
the twisting path towards the river.

'You should watch how you go,' behind her his
voice taunted softly. 'You'll be spraining your
ankle again if you're not careful, and we're a long
way from the house. I wouldn't like to have to
carry you there.'

The taunt was on target, reminding her of their first meeting, but instead of turning to retort Kirsty hurried on, slithering and sliding down the steep path until she reached the shingle bed below the big pools. Crossing it, she gained the riverside path and without looking back to see if Neil was following her she began to walk fast towards the loch.

It was a long time since she had felt like this, as if someone had taken hold of her and had shaken her roughly. But then Neil Dysart was the last person she had expected to see when she had climbed the rocks in search of a poacher. She shouldn't feel anything, she argued with herself. After all, she wasn't twenty-one any longer. She had been married and widowed, so she should be able to take an unexpected meeting with a former lover in her stride.

Kirsty's stride faltered in spite of her and she slowed down. Lifting her head, she looked across the loch to the slopes of Cairn Rua. Under the direct rays of the sun the spread of the moors glowed red and the rocky summit above them glinted fierily, giving the hill its name of Red Rock. Below the moors, half buried among trees and bushes, the walls of a cottage gleamed white and its windows winked with golden light.

It had been evening and the loch had been shining with a silvery light of its own as the moors had darkened to purple when she had limped to the door of that distant cottage almost five years ago. Out for a walk by herself, she had inadvertently stepped into an unseen rabbit hole and had sprained her ankle. She had noticed the crofter's house with a sense of relief and had knocked on its door confidently, knowing that the people of the Scottish Highlands are among the most generous and hospitable people in the world and would assuredly find a way to help her return to the house where she had been staying.

But the door had remained shut and she had begun to think there was no one at home when a movement to her left had startled her. Turning quickly, she had found herself face to face with a tall man who had been carrying a fishing rod.

In the mysterious violet-tinted dusk which had filled the flower-scented garden of the cottage they had stared at each other in silent surprise. He had moved and had spoken first, coming towards her with his gold-flecked amber-brown eyes gazing into hers incredulously.

'Who are you? And what are you doing here?' he had whispered.

As if she had been struck dumb she had only been able to continue to stare at him, falling in love with him on sight, seeing in his tall wide-shouldered figure, proud aquiline features and plume of chestnut brown hair the embodiment of all her romantic fantasies. He had repeated the questions in another language and the spell in which she had been caught temporarily had been broken. She had laughed and had shaken her head.

'I don't have the Gaelic. I'm not a Highlander,' she had replied. 'I'm Kirsty Ure and I'm working at Balmore Lodge for the summer. I've hurt my ankle, so I was knocking at the door thinking I might get help. Do you live here?'

'For this summer only,' he had answered briefly, and dropping his fishing rod he had gone down on one knee before her, and immediately she had been caught up again in a spell of romance, seeing him as a clan chieftain returned from the wars to pay homage to his lady. With both hands he had felt her left ankle, and his touch had been both gentle and confident.

'It does seem to be swollen,' he had said, and had straightened up. 'Let me help you into the house and I'll have a proper look at it.'

Glad of his support, she had entered the living room of the cottage and had sat down on an old ladderbacked chair beside an open hearth built of granite blocks in which a fire had been laid in the dog grate but not lit. Neil had touched lighted matches to the wicks of the two brass Aladdin oil lamps, which had been the only form of lighting in the house, and setting one of them on a small table near the chair he had knelt on one knee before her again. Lifting her left foot on to his other bent knee, he had removed her shoe and her sock. Against the bruised skin in front of the ankle bone his fingers had probed searchingly.

'Nothing broken,' he had said, lowering her foot and glancing up at her.

'How do you know?' she had challenged, aware of a strange quivering excitement fluttering along her nerves.

'I ought to know,' he had replied, flashing her a smile. 'I'm an orthopaedic surgeon. I'll bandage it for you. It needs support and you shouldn't walk on it for a while.'

'But how am I going to get back to the Lodge? I can't hop all the way,' she had complained.

'I'll take you there in my car. It's parked at the back of the house.' Again he had smiled at her. 'It isn't a Rolls-Royce and it isn't new, but it goes.' He had stood up and had gone over to an old dresser to take something from a drawer. 'Are you a friend of Sir Alec Whyte's?' he had asked casually as he had come back to her carrying a pink elastic bandage.

'No. I'm working for him. I'm studying Biology and Forestry. He advertised for a student to help him with the book he's writing about the natural history of the Highlands. I answered the advert and got the job,' she had explained while he had bandaged her ankle swiftly and expertly. 'I'll be here until the university term begins.'

'How long before you graduate?' he had asked.

'I have another year's study to do,' she had replied.

'And then?'

'I'll hope to get a job in Nature Conservancy or on an estate like Balmore. Or I might go abroad.'

By then he had been on both his knees and his hands had been resting on the arms of the old chair. Slowly he had leaned towards her, his hands sliding along the arms until she had been trapped against the back of the chair.

'You have the bluest eyes I've ever seen,' he had murmured, and his own eyes had glittered with a rich tawny light like topazes. 'They're as blue as speedwells, the tiny flowers which grow among the grasses at the edge of the forests. And when I first saw you standing at my doorway in the twilight with your hair hanging like a wimple about your face I thought for a moment you were the ghost of some Highland lady come to haunt this place.'

'And when I saw you with your rod in your hand I thought you were a clan chieftain with your sword, come to claim me as your lady,' she had whispered back.

'It seems we share similar fantasies,' he had replied, and as a strange indefinable longing to share more with him had swept over her she had placed her hands on his shoulders and had lifted her face to his. He had hesitated, his eyes clouding with doubt, then with a sound, half groan and half sigh, he had bent his head towards hers.

When his lips had touched hers she had shivered, not with cold but with delight, because his lips had been cool and firm yet sweet and seductive, just as she had always imagined her lover's lips would be. His tongue had flickered tantalisingly against her lips, and she had been surprised and a little shocked by its intimate touch and by the sensations it had aroused in her, because no man had ever kissed her like that before. Slowly but willingly her lips had parted, learning from his. The kiss had deepened and her arms had gone round him to hold him closely. . . .

A whaup called with sudden sharp sadness as it winged its way above the moors, and Kirsty was jolted back into the present to find herself at the place where the path met the road which curved beside the loch, the parting of the ways for her and Neil. She would take the road which sloped up to Balmore Lodge and he would take the lower part of the road to walk the mile or so to the other shore and up Cairn Rua to his cottage. The distant hill, the glinting house, the shining loch all swam into focus before her eyes again, but her skin was filmed with sweat, her mouth was dry and her heart was pounding as remembered passion continued to pulse through her.

Her hands clenched at her sides, she was cursing Neil Dysart silently for having come back and was turning to walk up the road when he spoke behind her.

'Kirsty.'

His hand touched her arm. Immediately she flinched away and swung round to face him, her chin up, her face pale and stiff, her eyelids drooping haughtily over her eyes.

'Well?' she snapped. 'What is it now?'

Faced with her hostility he changed. His eyes went blank, his nostrils flared slightly and his mouth twisted cynically.

'I was only going to ask you where you're living while the Sheikh is staying in the Lodge,' he said curtly.

'I'm living in the factor's house,' she replied. 'Alec hired me to be the factor of the estate after I graduated and I continued to do the job after we were married. I'm still doing it, and if I sell the estate to Hussein I'll make it a condition of the sale that he employs me as his factor.'

His eyes narrow, their expression hostile, he looked beyond her at the house whose pale walls sparkled through the green foliage of shrubs and trees.

'You mustn't sell it,' he said harshly, glaring at her. 'You mustn't sell it to the Sheikh.'

'I can do what I like with it,' she retorted. 'And perhaps I should remind you that you have no right to tell me what to do with Balmore—no right at all. Alec left it to me and once I've got probate it will be mine to do what I like with.'

'And I have to remind you, Lady Whyte, that I have the same rights as anyone else who holds a croft on the estate. I have the right to object if you dare to sell the property to a foreigner,' he retorted.

'Then maybe I won't sell,' she said lightly and mockingly. 'Maybe I'll marry Hussein instead and use his millions to turn Balmore into the show-place of the Western Highlands.'

'You'd marry for money?' he exclaimed, frowning at her.

'Why not? You did. So why shouldn't I?'

If her taunt about his marriage to the daughter of a wealthy American business tycoon found its mark he didn't show it but continued to stare at her in a cold calculating way that made her feel uneasy.

'No sheikh is going to be master of Balmore while I'm alive,' he muttered threateningly.

'My goodness, you sound as if you're declaring war on Hussein!' she said flippantly, but she backed away from him, disturbed by the flicker of violence now showing in his eyes. More than ever he reminded her of a fiercely proud Highland chieftain determined to defend his heritage to the death.

'I am,' he replied succintly.

They stared at each other like enemies; enemies who had once been lovers. Searching his taut angry face, Kirsty wondered if he remembered what had happened between them four years ago and guessed that what had meant so much to her when she had been twenty-one, vulnerable and a little naïve, in love for the first time, had meant little, possibly nothing, to him. For him she had been merely a passing fancy, a brief summer affair in which he had indulged his own physical desires, an entertaining deviation from the path he had been following at the time in pursuit of a career as a surgeon and of a wealthy wife.

Footsteps sounded on the road behind her. Neil looked past her. She turned to see who was coming. Her older brother Duncan appeared round a bend walking fast. His usually good-humoured face was wearing an anxious frown.

'Och, here you are,' he said, coming up to her. 'I was just looking for you. There's hell to pay up at the Lodge.' He became aware of Neil and glanced at him curiously. 'I don't think we've met,' he said bluntly.

'Neil Dysart,' said Neil, holding out his right hand.

'Duncan Ure, art dealer.' Duncan's curiosity deepened. 'You look familiar, for some reason.

You're not related to the artist Morag Dysart, by any chance?'

'She was my mother,' said Neil.

'Well now, if this isn't a coincidence!' exclaimed Duncan. 'Only this morning I was looking at two watercolours painted by her, both of them views of the scenery around here. I found them in a room in the turret. Both of them are dedicated to someone called Ian.'

'Sir Ian Whyte,' murmured Neil. 'He was my father.'

'Good God!' said Duncan excitedly. 'That's it. You're like him about the eyes and the hair grows in the same way. Of course,' he added with a grin, 'I've only seen his portrait.'

'Where? Where have you seen it?' demanded Kirsty.

'In the turret room.' Duncan jerked his head towards the house. 'It was with the watercolours. What's the matter with you? Didn't Alec ever tell you he had a half-brother?'

'No. No one ever told me. You didn't tell me.' Kirsty glared accusingly at Neil.

'I thought you knew. I thought Alec had told you,' he said coolly. 'Not that he had any reason to acknowledge my existence. As far as he was concerned I was born the wrong side of the blanket.'

'You should have told me,' was all she could say. He shrugged indifferently and turned to Duncan.

'What's going on at the Lodge?' he asked.

'Och, that Sheikh of yours is going to be more

trouble than he's worth, Kirsty,' Duncan
grumbled.

'Why? What's he done? What's happened?' she
demanded. She was feeling more than shaken
now. She was feeling as if she had been turned
upside down and she couldn't stop staring at Neil,
who was deliberately ignoring her and looking at
Duncan. Why had Alec never told her that Neil
was his illegitimate half-brother? Why had he kept
her in ignorance? Why?

'That big bodyguard of his, the one who walked
up to the pool with us, spotted two lads crossing
the river. They were without socks and shoes and
had obviously been fishing.'

'Did they have a salmon?' asked Kirsty
sharply, dragging her gaze away from Neil's aquiline features to look at her brother and attend
better to what he was telling her.

'No. They had only fishing rods. I pointed out
to the Sheikh that they didn't have a fish when he
insisted they must be the poachers, but he
wouldn't listen. Anyway, to cut the story short,
he had them brought to the Lodge, and because
they refused to answer his questions or to give
their names he's locked them up in one of the
garages until the police arrive to deal with them.'

'Has he called the police yet?' snapped Neil
sharply.

'Not yet. Hamish and I managed to put him off
by telling him that Kirsty should call the police
because she is the factor as well as the owner of
the estate, then I came to look for her,' said
Duncan. He turned again to Kirsty. 'You're going

to have difficulty in talking him out of bringing the police in. He's determined that they should be punished for what he calls "their serious crime against his person".'

'Oh, no!' groaned Kirsty, feeling suddenly irritated with the antics of supposedly adult men. 'This is all your fault,' she complained, swinging round to glare at Neil, but he wasn't there. Not by a quiver of a leaf did the shrubs betray that he had pushed his way through them. Shading her eyes against the glare of the sun, she looked down the road, but he hadn't gone that way either. Nor was he on the shore of the loch. She looked at Duncan.

'Where did he go?' she demanded angrily.

'How should I know?' His blue-grey eyes were bland, and she guessed he knew exactly which way Neil had gone. He had guessed also that Neil had something to do with the poachers and with typical Scottish clannishness he had closed ranks with his own countrymen to present a united front to the 'incomer' who was Hussein. 'Are you coming to see the Sheikh now?' he asked smoothly.

'Oh, I suppose so,' she snapped, wiping her brow with the back of one hand in an unconsciously weary gesture. Duncan's face softened and he pulled her arm through his as they began to walk up the road to the house.

'You got a shock just now when Dysart admitted to being Sir Ian's illegitimate son, didn't you?' he said.

'Yes. I wonder why Alec never told me?'

'Well, you know what old Alec was alike—a bit

of a puritan. I don't suppose he really approved of his father and was ashamed of the old man's behaviour with the opposite sex. He probably didn't want you to know Sir Ian had a fairly torrid love affair with Morag Dysart. I expect that's why her paintings are hidden in the turret room. You know, they should fetch a good price. Her paintings have become very popular recently. Some of the other original paintings in the house are worth a lot too.'

'Thanks for coming up from Edinburgh and looking at them,' said Kirsty, giving his arm an affectionate squeeze. 'I wish you'd brought Jean and the girls with you, then you could all have stayed for a few days with me. There's just one thing that puzzles me. How did you know there were some paintings in the turret room?'

'Mary Taggart, the housekeeper, told me when I asked her if she knew of any paintings other than those on show in the gallery and the lounge,' he replied, giving her a sideways glance. 'When did you first meet Dysart?'

'When I first came here, five years ago. He was living then in the croft which had belonged to his mother. Soon after I met him he left and went to New York to work with a famous surgeon there. He married the heiress to the Gow millions.'

'*Whew!* He did well for himself, didn't he?' remarked Duncan. 'What's he doing back here?'

'I don't know. He didn't tell me.'

'Perhaps he's going to contest Alec's will. As Sir Ian's younger son he might think he has more right to the property than you have.'

'That did cross my mind,' said Kirsty with a sigh. 'But I don't see how he can contest the will. I mean, he said himself he was born the wrong side of the blanket, so he can't really prove he's Sir Ian's son, can he? I don't think there's anything he can do to claim Balmore as his.'

'I wouldn't be too sure about that,' warned Duncan thoughtfully. 'I got the impression he's a man who'll fight for what he believes is his and what he believes is right, regardless of consequences.'

CHAPTER TWO

BALMORE LODGE was a simple but elegant two-storey house built from limestone quarried from a nearby hillside. Mullioned windows glinted on either side of a gracious front entrance and at one end of the building there was a round tower or turret with a pointed roof.

In front of the house a smooth green lawn rolled down to the shore of the loch. At the back of the house, enclosed by tall hedges, were the famous gardens where Sir Alec Whyte had once supervised the cultivation of many species of plants. Behind the gardens a wood of mixed coniferous and deciduous trees climbed a hillside. Above the trees the moors, a mosaic of purple bell-heather just in bloom, black bog and green bracken, spread, rolled and lifted to lavender grey rocks.

Duncan and Kirsty went straight to the courtyard beside the house and he pointed to the old stable buildings which had long been used as garages. Standing on either side of the double doors of one of the garages were two swarthy-skinned, black-haired Arabs, dressed neatly in white shirts and light grey suits.

'The lads are in that one,' Duncan whispered.

'Did you see them?' asked Kirsty.

'Of course I did. Both of them were about twenty-five or six and both of them were stubborn

Scots, refusing to speak. I warned the Sheikh that he was breaking the law by detaining them, but he wouldn't listen to me or to Hamish. Maybe he'll listen to you.'

'They're friends of Neil's,' Kirsty told him.

'Then they're probably medics; perhaps house surgeons from some hospital,' Duncan guessed.

'He said they were only playing at poaching. You're quite sure they didn't have a salmon?'

'Quite sure.'

'Then even if the police are called in nothing can be done to them without evidence,' mused Kirsty. 'I'll go and tell Hussein that. We can't expect him to know or understand the law of the land yet. He hasn't been in Scotland for very long.'

They entered the house by a side door and walked along a passage to the big entrance hall which was panelled in golden pinewood and had a wide staircase going up to a gallery where paintings hung. Outside the double carved pinewood doors of the lounge another Arab stood on guard. Kirsty asked him if she could see the Sheikh. The man nodded, asked her to wait, opened the door, entered the room and closed the door behind him.

'All this security and formality makes me angry,' muttered Duncan. 'Anyone would think you were a visitor in your own house!'

'I am while Hussein is paying rent for it,' Kirsty replied.

'But why does he need so many bodyguards?'

'He has to be careful about the people who

approach him. His father was assassinated only a few months ago by a young terrorist who was allowed to enter the palace in Dukar somehow. Since then there has also been an attempt on Hussein's life,' explained Kirsty. 'It isn't fun being wealthy or the ruler of a country these days, with so many terrorists roaming the world.'

The door opened again and the Arab security man indicated that Kirsty could enter the wide, high-ceilinged room. As soon as he saw her Hussein sprang to his feet from the chair behind the delicate antique writing desk where he had been sitting and writing. He came across to her, his right hand outstretched in greeting as if he hadn't seen her for a long time.

'Ah, Christina, I'm glad you have returned at last. Has Duncan told you we have caught the poachers?' he said.

'Yes, he has.'

'And now we must punish them.' Hussein's eyes gleamed with a cold cruel light.

Although she knew he was a couple of years younger than she was Kirsty always felt he was older. There was about him an indefinable sadness, as if he had been forced to grow up too quickly; as if he had had no time in his life for mischief or the typical wild oats behaviour of most young men. She knew he was going to have great difficulty in understanding what she had to tell him about the easygoing relationship that had always existed in Scotland over hundreds of years between clan chieftain and clansman, between landowner and crofter. Equality between men, equality between men and women too, was something Hussein had never known.

'We can't punish them,' she said.

'But they have done wrong,' he exclaimed. 'They have broken the law and stolen a fish from the river.'

'How do you know they've stolen a fish? Did they have a fish when Ahmed caught them?'

'No. But your head keeper saw one of them leaving the pool and they had no shoes and socks on,' he replied sharply, frowning at her. 'I would like you to call the police now, if you please, Christina,' he continued autocratically. 'I want them arrested.'

'The police will only arrest them if there's some evidence that the young men you've locked in the garage have stolen a fish,' she explained as patiently as she could. 'But there is no evidence. There's only Hamish's word that he saw a man leaving the pool in a hurry. That's what's called hearsay, and it isn't enough. The police won't accept it and they won't make an arrest.'

'It is very puzzling.' He shook his head from side to side.

'And when the police know that you've forcibly detained two men and have locked them up your bodyguards could be charged with assault and you could be charged with illegally arresting them.'

'I do not understand,' he said, and shook his head again. 'I thought the police in this country existed to enforce the law of the land.'

'They do. But the laws are made to protect the

citizens ... *all* the citizens,' Kirsty was saying when there was a commotion at the door. One of the security men who had been standing guard outside the garage doors came into the room. He came right up to Hussein, salaamed briefly and began to talk very fast in Arabic. Hussein listened attentively, his expression varying from irritation to anger chasing across his narrow sallow face.

'They have escaped!' he exclaimed, turning to Kirsty when the bodyguard finished explaining. 'And they have stolen my Rolls-Royce. We must go after them. Ahmed, my man here, will go after them. Please, Christina, will you lend him your car?'

'Yes, yes ... of course. The keys are in the glove compartment,' said Kirsty. She glanced appealingly at Duncan. 'Please go with Ahmed,' she whispered. 'I don't want any more violence. I wouldn't like anyone to be hurt.'

'All right,' he said. 'I'll go. Although how we're expected to catch up with a Rolls-Royce in your beaten-up old Sunbeam I don't know,' he added grumblingly.

He left the room with Ahmed and Hussein turned to Kirsty.

'How can this have happened?' demanded Hussein.

'I don't know,' she said with a sigh. But she had a good idea that Neil Dysart was the master-mind behind the escape of the poachers, re-membering how he had disappeared so suddenly after Duncan had told her how the poachers had been caught and locked up.

'Ahmed is very strong. They could never get past him,' mused Hussein. 'He says they must have been able to get from the garage where they were locked up to the garage where my car was. How could they do that? Do you know?'

'If they could have got up into the hayloft through the trapdoor they could have reached the other garages. The loft runs the full length of the stables above them,' replied Kirsty.

'Then they must know the buildings very well, better than my men know them,' remarked Hussein shrewdly.

Or they had help from someone outside who had known the buildings well, thought Kirsty. Someone like Neil. Or had Hamish helped them? No, the head keeper wouldn't have done anything to help anyone whom he suspected of trying to poach one of his salmon.

'So now you do have good reason to phone the police,' Hussein said. 'My car has been stolen. Do you know the number of the police station?'

'The nearest station is in Fort William, about forty miles away from here,' said Kirsty, going over to the writing desk. 'The number is in the directory.'

'Please find it for me,' ordered Hussein, and for one wild rebellious moment she was tempted to refuse, to tell him to find the number himself, because she wasn't one of his servants to be bossed about in such a peremptory manner. Then she remembered she needed the money he was paying for renting the estate and she subdued her rebellious feelings quickly. Taking the directory out of the desk drawer, she looked up the number and wrote it down on a pad of paper for him. He looked at it, looked at the telephone, then looked at her. A slight diffident smile curved his lips, making him look younger.

'Please, Christina, will you phone them for me?' he asked, and the autocratic manner had gone. He was appealing to her charmingly. 'I have difficulty in understanding what your fellow countrymen say over the phone. Their accent is so different.'

'Oh, very well.' Kirsty picked up the receiver and dialled. In a few seconds she was talking to a police sergeant. She explained what had happened and listened to the questions he asked her. At first he sounded very sceptical when she told him that the Rolls-Royce belonging to His Excellency the Sheikh Hussein al Dukar had been stolen, but he seemed more disposed to believe her when she provided him with the registration number of the car.

'Ye wouldn't have any idea now which way they were travelling, would ye?' asked the sergeant.

'Well, there's only one way to go from Balmore estate and that is to the village of Balvaig. From there they could go either north to Ullapool or south to Fort William.'

'Thank you. I'll inform any of our men who happen to be on duty in the vicinity to keep a look out for it. That's all I can do.'

'Please let me know as soon as you hear anything of it,' said Kirsty.

'Just let me have your name and phone number and I'll do that,' replied the sergeant.

She supplied the information and rang off. Turning to Hussein, she told him what the sergeant had said.

'And that's all we can do for now,' she added. 'I'm really sorry this has happened, your Excellency. . . .'

'Hussein, please, Christina,' he pleaded.

'But if you hadn't decided to take the law into your own hands. . . .'

'They wouldn't have taken the law into their hands,' he finished for her dryly. 'I understand now, I think,' he went on in a low voice. 'It is not your fault. There is so much I have to learn about this country and about the estate. But you can teach me much. I hope we become good friends while I stay here.' He moved towards her, smiling a little, his dark eyes warm. 'Would you like for us to be friends?'

His appeal for friendship touched her generous heart. She saw suddenly how lonely he was in the high position into which he had been thrust by the unexpected death of his father.

'Of course I would like to be your friend,' she replied impulsively.

'I have never been able to have a woman friend,' he continued. 'When my father was alive he forbade me to have women friends.'

'But surely he wanted you to marry and to have children,' she exclaimed.

'Oh yes, he wanted that for me. But he would only approve of marriage to women of my own country, simple girls who would accept without question a position in my harem in the Islamic tradition. It was the Western women I met when I was a student in Paris and then at Oxford that he worried about. He was afraid I might fall in love with a Christian foreigner and want to marry her.' His charming, shy smile appeared. 'But until now I haven't had any desire to marry. What about you, Christina? You are young to have been left a widow. Would you ever consider marrying again?'

'I might, if the right man came along,' she replied noncommittally.

'And how will you recognise the right man?' he queried, laughing a little. 'Do you have a list of the qualities he must possess? If so please tell me what they are and then I'll be able to tell whether I have them or not.'

'No, I don't have a list, and even if I did, I wouldn't tell you,' she replied teasingly, feeling lighthearted suddenly. It seemed a long time since she had been able to indulge in such a conversation with a young man. Her marriage to Alec, who had been so much older than she, had tended to cut her off from relationships with her peer group. 'You'll just have to take your chance with all the others.'

'So,' Hussein's smile widened into a grin which showed his beautiful teeth, 'you have many admirers? I am not surprised. You are very pretty, with your pink and white skin, your black hair and your blue eyes. But I also admire your competence in looking after this huge estate. And your independence of spirit, your refusal to be domineered over is extremely attractive to me. I'm glad I have competition. It always brings out the best in me, and I'll take my chances as you suggest. To begin with I'd like to invite you to dinner here in the Lodge this evening. Some friends of mine from France will be arriving in half an hour and I'd like them to meet you. Will you come, please, Christina?'

'I'd like to. But Duncan is staying the night with me and he'll be expecting me to provide his dinner,' she said.

'Then bring him to dinner with you. He can entertain us with his opinions of the paintings he has been evaluating for you and we shall have a very pleasant party,' replied Hussein, his mood more lively and more cheerful than she had ever known it to be. 'I'll expect you both at about seven o'clock.'

It was almost six-thirty and Kirsty was changing in her bedroom at the factor's house when she heard Duncan come in. He called to her and with a last glance at her reflection in the mirror she left the bedroom and went downstairs. In the small hallway his blue-grey glance took in the dress she was wearing. A soft shade of blue, it had a pleated skirt and a softly draped bodice with a frill at the neckline and frills at the cuffs of the long sleeves.

'Why are you all dressed up?' he asked with brotherly directness.

'We're invited to have dinner with Hussein at the Lodge. He expects us at seven. Did you find the Rolls?'

'No.' His glance was derisive. 'Did you expect us to?'

'Which way did you go?'

'Beyond Balvaig and then part way along the road to Fort William. Then your car started to behave badly. It took me a while to get it going again.'

'What was wrong with it?'

'Och, this and that,' Duncan said evasively. 'By the time it was going again Ahmed agreed with me that there was no point in pursuing the Rolls, so we came back here.' He glanced down at his hands. The fingers were marked with motor oil. 'If we're expected at seven at the Lodge I'd better get cleaned up,' he added, turning towards the stairs.

'Now wait a minute, Duncan Ure,' said Kirsty, purposefully stepping in front of him. She could tell by his blandness that he had been up to some sort of mischief. 'I don't believe there was anything wrong with my car. It had its monthly check-up only last week. I think you pretended there was something wrong with it.'

'Now why would I be doing something like that, Kirsty?' he asked, rounding his eyes in an expression of innocence.

'Because you didn't want to give chase to the poachers that's why,' she accused.

'Och, I was never able to get away with lying to you,' he grumbled. 'All right—there wasn't anything wrong with the car, but I wasn't going to chase the Rolls as far as Fort William when I knew damned well it was still here on the estate.'

'Still here?' she gasped in puzzlement. 'How do you know?'

'When I left here with Ahmed in the Sunbeam I noticed the Rolls climbing the road to the croft on Cairn Rua,' he said.

'Neil took them to his cottage?' she exclaimed.

'So, like me, you guessed Dysart sprang the lads free from the garage,' said Duncan with a pleased and knowing grin. 'I didn't tell Ahmed I'd spotted the Rolls and I drove part way to Fort William to give the lads long enough to collect their gear and be on their way.'

'Conspirator!' Kirsty hissed at him, but he only grinned again. 'Oh, you and Neil Dysart make a nice pair of mischief-makers!'

'I agree with you,' he said equably. 'And I think we'd have done well together dodging the Redcoats after the Forty-Five Rebellion,' he added. 'My trick to divert Ahmed and the other bodyguard worked too. We were just coming back through Balvaig when a small car passed us going the other way. I recognised the driver as one of the poachers, but Ahmed and the other fellow never noticed them. They'll be well on their way past Fort William by now.'

'Thank God,' said Kirsty with feeling. 'I wasn't looking forward to hearing from the police that they'd found the Rolls and had arrested the thieves.'

'You didn't phone the police?' exclaimed Duncan, scowling fiercely at her.

'I had to—Hussein insisted. And it did look as if his car had been stolen, didn't it?' she retorted defensively. 'Where is it now?'

'Still at Dysart's cottage, I suppose,' said

Duncan, beginning to go up the stairs. 'I expect
he'll return it sooner or later. At least his friends
got away.' With one hand on the banister he
turned to look down at her, suddenly very much
her bossy older brother. 'Now you're not to tell
Hussein about any of this, Kirsty, do you hear?'

'I hear,' she replied with a sigh of exasperation.
'Hurry up and wash, Hussein has guests from
France and he wants us to meet them.'

The elegant oval dining room of the Lodge
looked its best that evening with candlelight
gleaming softly on Royal Doulton china, fine
silver cutlery and delicate Stuart crystal. If
Hussein was still worried about the theft of his
car he made no mention of it to his French guests,
Monsieur and Madame Delacroix and their
daughter Camille, and neither Kirsty nor Duncan
made reference to the afternoon's events. The
evening passed pleasantly with good food, good
wine and stimulating conversation, and at eleven
o'clock Kirsty and Duncan said goodnight to their
host and his guests and returned to the factor's
house.

'A very interesting day,' remarked Duncan with
a yawn. 'I'd have liked to have gone over to have
a word with Dysart to tell him his friends got
away, but I think I'll leave you to pass on that
piece of information.' He glanced sideways at
Kirsty. 'I suppose you'll be seeing him.'

'I might,' said Kirsty shortly. 'Are you going to
tell me how much you think the paintings might
bring before you go?'

'I'll make out a list of them with the prices I

think they'll fetch and leave it with you.' He gave her another thoughtful glance. 'You know, it would be a nice gesture on your part to give those two Dysart paintings to Neil.'

'I'll think about it.' She spoke shortly again.

'You don't like him, do you?'

'Don't like whom?' she queried, being deliberately obtuse.

'Neil Dysart.'

'Not at the moment I don't,' she replied, going towards the stairs. 'One way and another he's caused me a lot of trouble today.'

'And it's my guess he and other local people are going to cause you more trouble while this place is let to the Sheikh,' Duncan warned seriously. 'It's a pity you didn't think of selling some of the paintings or the antiques before you leased Balmore to a tenant. They might have brought in enough money to pay part of Alec's debts.'

'Letting Balmore was a much quicker way of raising money,' Kirsty argued. 'Hussein has paid six months' rent in advance. What time are you leaving in the morning?' she added.

'About nine.'

'We'll have breakfast at eight, then. Goodnight.'

' 'Night, Kirsty.'

She didn't sleep well that night. The unexpected meeting with Neil, his sardonic confession that he was Sir Ian Whyte's illegitimate son and his mischievous rescue of his friends from the garage had set her nerves on edge, so that every

time she started to slip into sleep thoughts of him
would prod her cruelly into wakefulness again. He
had leapt back into her life to torment her and
she knew she wouldn't regain her peace of mind
until she confronted him again and demanded
why he had come back to Balmore.

Next morning Duncan was unkind enough to
comment on the lines sleeplessness had scored
under her eyes, but before he left he gave her a
hug and a kiss.

'Let me know if you want to sell any of the
paintings,' he said.

'I will,' she promised. 'And next time you come
bring Jean and the girls and stay longer.'

She was clearing the breakfast table when she
heard him come back into the house. She hurried
out into the hall thinking he had forgotten
something. Standing just inside the front door, he
was grinning delightedly.

'The Rolls is back,' he said. 'I told you he'd
bring it back—must have brought it at dead of
night when there was no one around to see or
hear him. The Sheikh and his bodyguard are
dancing around it, exclaiming and looking for
damage.'

'I'd better go and have a word with Hussein,'
said Kirsty, whipping off her apron. 'And I'll
have to phone the police to ask them to call off
the search.'

Although he was pleased that his favourite toy
had been returned to him unscratched Hussein
was plainly puzzled by its stealthy reappearance
and had soon come to the conclusion that the two

poachers must have had a friend living on the estate who had helped them to escape.

'I shall interview everyone who lives on the estate,' he announced to Kirsty after she had phoned the police at Fort William. 'Please will you invite all of the people who work for you or who have farms or crofts to come here tomorrow afternoon for tea? It will be an "at home" party and will give me the opportunity to meet them and for them to meet me. A good idea, don't you think?'

'Yes, it's a good idea,' agreed Kirsty cautiously. 'I'll go and find Hamish now and ask him to pass the invitation on. What time would you like everyone to come?'

'At three o'clock. And if it is a fine day we'll have tea served on the terrace.' Hussein smiled with pleasure. 'I like to entertain,' he confided in her. 'Especially do I like to entertain people who work for me. I enjoy being . . . what do you call it?' He snapped his fingers together.

'A benefactor?' she suggested.

'Exactly.' He beamed at her. 'I like to be kind, to do good, and I can afford to.'

'But don't you think it's rather hypocritical to give a party . . . or to do good . . . just so you can find out who borrowed your car to help the young men to get away?' she argued.

'Can you suggest any other way I can find out?'

'No, not really. But supposing you do find out who took the car. What will you do to him?'

'I don't know,' he said with a laugh. 'It will depend on what he is like.' His eyes narrowed.

'You look worried, Christina. Is it possible you
know the culprit and are afraid I might have him
put in jail?'

'I'm afraid of what you might do to whoever
borrowed your car, but not on his behalf. I'm
afraid that if you punish him severely you will
become unpopular with the people who live on
the estate and that they will then make your stay
here very uncomfortable,' she said very seriously.
'And I wouldn't like that to happen to you.'

'Thank you, Christina,' he said, coming to
stand close to her, so close that she could smell
his strongly scented aftershave lotion. 'I am glad
that it is on my behalf you are afraid.' He reached
out and took her hand in his and raised it to his
lips. 'Already we are becoming friends,' he whispered, his dark eyes glowing sensuously as he
fondled her hands with both of his. 'I wish we
could. . . .' He broke off as the door behind her
opened. He dropped her hand, his head tipped
back haughtily and he spoke sharply in Arabic to
the man who had entered.

'Excuse me,' said Kirsty, glad of a chance to
escape from what might have become a difficult
situation to handle, and with a nod and a smile at
the security man Ahmed she left the room.

She found Hamish in the byre at the back of
the garages. He wasn't impressed when she told
him about the tea party.

'Ach, I'm thinking no one will be wanting to
have tea with yon Sheikh,' he complained.

'And I'm thinking they will want to have tea
with him out of sheer curiosity, if nothing else,'

Kirsty retorted. 'Now you be sure to tell every-one.'

'Ye want me to tell himself over at Cairn Rua?' he asked, cocking a shrewd grey eye at her.

'No, I'll tell Mr Dysart,' she said coolly. 'By the way, why didn't you tell me he'd come back?'

'Well now, ye might say it slipped my mind,' drawled Hamish, looking past her, his eyes taking on the distant dreamy expression that meant he wasn't telling the truth.

'Do you know why he's come back?' she asked sharply. In all the time she had lived at Balmore she had never been able to get a straight answer out of Hamish, yet of all the people who lived and worked on the estate he probably knew the most about the Whyte family. He probably knew that Neil was Sir Ian Whyte's younger son, but he would never have admitted to anyone that he knew.

'Ach, he's come for a wee bit of a holiday, I'm thinking,' he replied, still vague. Then he looked at her suddenly, his expression no longer dreamy but sharp with hostility. 'And why shouldn't he come here? The croft is his. He inherited it from his mother. And he has as much right as anyone to live on the estate; more right than some.' He gave her another piercing glance, then hunching one shoulder, turned away from her. 'Ach, well, if I'm going to be delivering that invitation to everyone I'd best be off. It's likely to be taking me all day to get round the estate, so it is. As if I didn't have enough of me own work to do.'

He clumped away across the courtyard. For a

few moments Kirsty stood thinking. The sun was growing warmer. It was going to be another fine day. She glanced towards the loch. Blue, satin-smooth, it stretched away to the slopes of Cairn Rua. Slowly she began to walk out of the court-yard to the road.

She should really have gone the other way, back to the factor's house to attend to estate business, but it was too pleasant a morning to spend indoors. She would walk round the head of the loch and find out how the stand of pines and birches which had been planted the previous year on the lower slopes of Cairn Rua were progress-ing.

The road was dry and dusty, splashed with bright yellow light where the sun shone through the foliage of the trees which edged it on her right. To her left the loch dimpled and glittered among the reeds and a heron, disturbed by her approach, took to the air with a great flapping of its wings.

How often she had walked this way that August four years ago! Every afternoon she had come. She had walked slowly as she was walking now, taking pleasure in all that was around her; in the play of light and shadow, the flash of brilliant blue as a kingfisher dived to the loch, the soft gurgle of the water as it lapped among the reeds. Sometimes she had stopped to examine and admire some wild flowers growing in the grasses at the side of the road, just as she was stopping now. But wherever she had looked her glance had always been drawn back to the slopes of the hill before her; to the white walls of the small cottage glinting in the sunlight as they were glinting now, beckoning to her.

Her meetings with Neil had happened every day for over four weeks and had apparently been accidental, although she had always walked this way on purpose, hoping to meet him. She had done all the seeking out. He had never come looking for her. Yet when they had met on the hillside she had always been so shy and tonguetied in his presence that he had then taken the initiative and had made the next moves.

Young and hopeful, she had really believed he had been as emotionally involved with her as she had been with him. She had expected their affair to have continued after the summer and to have grown and developed into a serious romance which would have led ultimately to marriage. The daily meetings, her whole relationship with him, had become during those weeks her sole reason for living. Other people had ceased to be important to her, but she had never asked him if he had had relatives and he had never told her about them or about his plans for the future.

That was why she had been so upset when he had left Balmore suddenly without telling her he would be leaving. Even now she could remember the hollow feeling of desolation she had experienced the day she had found the cottage door locked and his car gone. Thinking that he had gone only to Balvaig, she had lingered about the cottage for a long time, leaving only when hunger had driven her down the road towards the loch.

She had been halfway down the hillside when she had met Hamish Taggart on his way up. Lifting his cap to her, he had greeted her with his usual Highland courtesy, showing no surprise at meeting her there.

'Have you seen Neil Dysart?' she had asked, pushed into asking the question by the aching need to know that Neil would be returning soon.

'No. And I'm thinking we won't be seeing him here for a long time,' Hamish had replied.

'Oh. Why? Where has he gone?'

'Today he's away to Glasgow.'

'Well, that isn't far away, and I'll be going there myself in a few weeks' time,' she had replied, feeling hope surge back. Then remembering she had had no idea where Neil lived in the city she had asked, 'Do you know his address in Glasgow?'

'You could be asking Sir Alec,' Hamish had said in his vague way. 'Good evening to ye.' And he had lifted his cap and walked on up the hill.

It had taken Kirsty all next day to pluck up the courage to ask Alec about Neil, because she had been reluctant to admit to her employer that she had been meeting the doctor who had been holidaying on one of the Balmore crofts, but eventually she had found a way to ask him if he had known where Neil lived in Glasgow.

They had been sitting in Alec's study relaxing after working all afternoon on annotating the book he had written about the natural history of the Highlands. Alec had been sitting in his wheelchair behind the desk and he had given her a frowning glance.

'Why do you want to know where he lives?' he had asked.

'I'd like to get in touch with him when I go back there,' she had replied. Trying to appear casual, she had shuffled papers together pretending to tidy the desk.

'He doesn't live in Glasgow,' Alec had replied.

'But Hamish told me Neil went there yesterday,' she had retorted, looking across the desk at him. He had been looking at her an expression of sadness in his pale blue eyes.

'He went to Glasgow to catch a plane to London and from London he flew to the United States today.' Alec had looked at his wrist watch. 'He'll be in New York now,' he had added. 'He's going to work in a clinic there with a famous orthopaedic surgeon, and I doubt if he'll come back to this country once he's established as a surgeon over there. They make a lot of money, you know, in the States.'

Kirsty remembered feeling as if all the life had drained out of her. Her legs had shaken and she had sat down suddenly on the nearest chair. Her face had felt dry and taut and her eyes had burned.

Vaguely she had been aware of the swishing sound of the wheels of Alec's chair as it had skimmed over the floor and around the side of the desk towards her.

'Kirsty, what is it? What's wrong?' he had asked in a concerned voice.

Pride had come to her aid. Blinking back tears, she had forced her lips to smile and had said jauntily.

'Nothing.'

'Come now, my dear. *You* know that isn't true, and *I* know that you've been seeing Neil Dysart every day for the past four weeks.' Alec's voice had held a note of mockery.

'How do you know?' she had exclaimed. With his silvery fair hair, his almost round face and his blue eyes, he had always seemed to her to have been a middle-aged cherub, kind, gentle, helpful and understanding, but at that moment there had been something sinister in the way the pale eyes had stared at her.

'Even though I can't get about easily I know everything that goes on on the estate,' he had said softly.

'Did Hamish tell you?' she had asked.

'Hamish tells me only what he feels like telling me, unfortunately,' he had snapped, his lips thinning. 'But I know you've been visiting Neil Dysart because I've watched you walking in that direction every afternoon. I've seen you climb the hill and I've seen you go into the cottage. You've always stayed there a long time, all evening and sometimes all night.'

Her cheeks burning, she had stared at him, feeling the hairs prick at the back of her neck as for a moment she had had the wild fantastic idea that he had possessed occult powers. Then she had looked beyond him at the telescope on its tripod in the big window behind the desk. The window had a view of the loch and the heather-covered moors of Cairn Rua.

'You've been spying on me!' she had cried accusingly, and had sprung to her feet, revolted by the idea of him watching her through his spy-glass.

'Not spying, my dear. No, not spying. Just keeping watch over you,' he had replied, his face softening into an affectionate smile. 'You see, having brought you here to work for me I feel responsible for your welfare.' He had sighed heavily and had frowned as he had also looked at the telescope. Then he had shaken his head. 'Several times I've thought of warning you and then I've decided that you wouldn't listen to an old fuddy-duddy like me, that you'd think I was making a fuss about nothing.' He had looked at her again and had smiled. 'Young women are so sensible these days, and not easily fooled.'

'Warn me about what?' she had asked, sinking down on the chair.

'About Neil.' He had sighed again. 'He's a handsome lad, clever too, and very ambitious. I promised his father I'd keep an eye on him, see that he had a good education and followed a career. He's done well and now he has a chance to do better, and I don't blame him for taking that chance. In fact I've encouraged him to take it.' He had frowned down at his hands which were playing with a paper knife. 'I'm not sure of the best way of putting this,' he had continued. 'I've known Neil a long time and he's ... well, he's like his father, and where young women like yourself are concerned his morals are not of the best. He likes to ...' He had broken off, looking rather embarrassed.

'Play around?' Kirsty had suggested in a cool voice.

'You put it very well,' he had said, nodding his head.

'Oh, I knew he's like that.' Now, she didn't know how she had managed to sound so careless.

'Did you?' Alex had looked up in surprise. 'Oh, then that's a relief. I was afraid, you see, that you'd be hurt by his abrupt departure.'

'I am a little,' she had confessed. 'I mean, we've been quite friendly and you'd have thought, wouldn't you, that he'd have said something about going away.' She had stood up again and had begun to collect more papers together. 'But I'm not going to fall into a depression about it,' she had added with a lightness she had not been feeling. 'He's gone, and his way of going tells me that he feels about our brief friendship the same way I feel about it.'

'And how do you feel about it?' Alec had asked, looking at her curiously.

'It was fun while it lasted,' she had replied with a shrug and an impish smile. 'But I'm really glad it's over. Now I can concentrate better on helping you to finish the footnotes for this book before I go back to university.'

She had really meant what she had said to Alec that day, Kirsty thought now as she approached the stand of tiny trees, dark green feathery pines alternating with the slender silvery trunks of young birches. She had really believed that by saying she had been glad Neil had gone away and their affair had ended she would feel glad.

But it hadn't worked out that way. The wound he had inflicted had gone very deep, and in spite of being a sensible, practical young woman, not easily fooled, she had yearned desperately for Neil, hoping that he would write to her explaining why he had left so suddenly. She had hoped he would write to tell her he missed her, that he loved her and would be returning soon to Scotland to ask her to marry him. She had hoped he would write and ask her to fly out to New York and join him there after she had graduated.

A month after he had left Balmore she had left too, after promising Alec she would return the following summer to work for him on the estate. No letter had come from Neil and none arrived in the following months, and after a while Kirsty had accepted the fact that her first love affair was over.

With acceptance came a certain cynicism about young men. She had vowed secretly that she would never believe anything a man said to her. Never again would she let a man make love to her without making some sort of commitment to her and to her alone. Applying herself wholeheartedly to her studies, she had managed to achieve a brilliant degree and after she had graduated she had returned to Balmore. Alec had generously offered her the position of factor of the estate, an unusual appointment, because rarely had women been land stewards. Not long after she had taken the job he had told her one day, quite casually, that he had heard of Neil's marriage in the United States to Barbara Gow, heiress to the Gow millions. Six months later Alec had asked her to marry him, and the ceremony had taken place quietly in the old stone church at Balvaig.

CHAPTER THREE

An hour after leaving the Lodge Kirsty emerged
from the stand of new trees to find herself half
way up Cairn Rua. She felt hot and her brow was
beaded with drops of sweat. Pulling her sweater
off, she tied the sleeves around her waist and
flipped undone another button of her shirt. Far
below her the loch was as still as a puddle caught
in a rut and its earlier brilliance was dimmed by a
heat haze. Behind her bees hummed ecstatically
in the bell heather which had just bloomed in
splashes of purple all over the moors. She glanced
upwards. From among its sheltering drystone
walls and tangled bushes Neil's cottage glinted at
her.

Now she was so near she might as well go to
see if he was there and deliver Hussein's invitation
to tea, she thought, and she began to follow a
narrow sheep path which twisted through the
rough brown bushes of real heather which was
not yet in flower. The path was steep and she
walked slowly, feeling the sun's heat beating down
on the back of her head and filtering through the
thin stuff of her shirt.

When she reached the green level grass in front
of the cottage she stopped to get her breath.
Before the open door of the house Neil was sitting
in an old deck chair, one leg bent, its foot resting

on the knee of his other leg. Against the frame made by his bent leg he had rested a pad of paper and seemed to be drawing or writing on it.

Standing and staring, Kirsty had an uncanny feeling that four years hadn't gone by and that this was the day after the day when she had found the cottage locked and his car gone. The feeling was so strong that it pushed her forward through the opening in the low grey drystone wall which surrounded the cottage garden and along the path towards him.

The words 'Where were you yesterday?' were on the tip of her tongue and she was about to say them when he looked up, probably having heard her footsteps, and he wasn't the young man she had known, with mischief dancing in his clear amber eyes and laughter curving his lips. He was an older man; older, tougher and as wary as a wildcat, his eyes narrowing between dark lashes when he saw her and his lips curving sardonically.

She pulled up short bit back the words she had been going to say, schooled her face to smoothness and thrust her hands into the pockets of her pants.

'Good morning, Neil,' she said calmly.

His glance lifted to the sun, then returned to her face.

'It's just about afternoon,' he said. 'I wondered how long it would be before you came.' He tossed aside the pad of paper and rose to his feet.

'You can be sure I wouldn't have come if I hadn't a good reason,' she replied sharply, thinking he was implying that she couldn't stay away now that she knew he was at the cottage. 'I've come with an invitation. Hussein al Dukar would like you to have tea with him at the Lodge tomorrow afternoon.'

'Just me?' His eyebrows lifted in surprise.

'No. He's invited everyone who lives or works on the estate.'

'Why?'

'Because he wants to meet everyone, of course.'

'Is this your idea?'

'No. His own. He wants to find out who helped the two young men who were caught poaching yesterday to escape.'

'Really?' This time the tilt to his eyebrows was mocking. 'Doesn't he know? Haven't you told him?'

'How could I tell him? I didn't see who it was.'

'And that's your only reason for coming all this way, to issue an invitation from him?' he queried.

'Yes,' she snapped, suddenly irritated by his mockery.

'You could have sent Hamish,' he suggested.

'I could, but I happened to be over this side of the loch inspecting the new plantation of trees on the lower slopes. You must have noticed them.'

'I have. They're growing well.' His glance drifted over her and again she sensed he was laughing at her. 'I guess you're good at your job and Alec made a good choice when he hired you to be factor,' he added.

They stood facing each other in the same way they had stood the day before on the road to the Lodge, and again Kirsty had the impression that they were enemies more than they were friends.

She searched her mind for something to say, anything to bridge the sudden awkward silence.

'My brother asked me to tell you that he saw your friends in their car going towards Fort William when he was returning to Balvaig yesterday afternoon,' she said. 'He'd noticed the Rolls coming this way and so he drove in the opposite direction with the security guards Hussein sent after you, to give your friends time to collect their gear and make a getaway.'

'That was helpful of him. Please thank him for the lads and for me when you see him again,' he replied coolly.

'I asked him to go with the security guards when Hussein ordered them to chase the Rolls,' she added.

'Then my thanks to you too,' he said, his eyebrows lifting again in surprise. 'I had a feeling you would disapprove of what I did. And that's why I thought you'd come here today, to give me a piece of your mind.' The glint in his eyes challenged her.

'Well, I have to admit I wasn't exactly pleased by what you did,' Kirsty retorted spiritedly. 'Hussein was very upset when he found his car had been taken. Why couldn't you have taken mine, or even Duncan's?'

'Because the Sheikh's was there in the garage when we climbed down from the hayloft and the keys were in it. It was just asking to be taken. And also I guessed it would hurt him if his expensive status symbol went missing for a few hours.'

'But you didn't have to rescue them,' she argued. 'I could have talked Hussein into letting them go, I know I could—I'd already persuaded him not to send for the police because there was no evidence that they were the poachers. They didn't have a fish or a weapon when they were caught.'

'How was I to know whose side you were on?' he asked. 'As factor you had every right to call in the police and I had to get my friends away from here before you did, so I acted accordingly. You see, my friends were unknown to Hamish or to anyone else on the estate and as long as they remained unknown there was a chance for them. I didn't want the affair investigated by the police or their names would have appeared in the local papers. They're both training to be surgeons, so their professional reputations had to be protected. That more than anything else moved me to do what I did.' He paused and devilry glinted again in his eyes. 'Although I also wanted to teach the Sheikh a lesson and to show him he can't play the tyrant here like he can in his own country.'

'Hussein wasn't playing the tyrant,' she retorted hotly. 'He's ignorant of the way the law works in this country, that's all, and he hasn't been here long enough to understand some of our customs. But at least he's showing he's willing to learn by inviting everyone to tea. Will you come tomorrow?'

'Will you be there?'

'Of course.'

'Then I might come.'

Another silence. She supposed Neil was waiting for her to leave, since he hadn't invited her to sit down and hadn't offered her any hospitality. But now that she was there it seemed wrong to leave and much more natural to stay, to linger in the flower-scented, bee-loud garden with him as she had often lingered four years ago, to talk lazily of this and that and eventually . . . to make love.

Kirsty glanced away from him quickly, down at the sketchbook on the grass.

'I see you still draw,' she murmured.

'I haven't done any sketching since I was last here,' he replied. 'I've almost forgotten how.' He shrugged indifferently.

'I wondered . . . I mean, Duncan suggested that you might like to have the two watercolours your mother painted and gave to your father.' She saw him stiffen and added hurriedly, 'Neil, why didn't you tell me you're Ian Whyte's younger son?'

'I've told you why I didn't. I thought you knew, that Alec had told you.'

'You should have told me yourself,' she insisted.

'It wasn't important at the time.' He looked right into her eyes. 'You and I had other things on our minds, if you care to remember,' he added softly.

To her surprise her heart leapt with sudden joy because after all he had remembered too that time of loving companionship they had known. The heat of passion pulsed through her unexpectedly as if she had been in his arms, moulded against his lean muscular body, lying among the heather on a hot August afternoon, his lips searing her throat, his hands sliding over her from shoulder to thigh.

'I remember,' she whispered shakily. 'But I thought you'd forgotten. You left so suddenly, without a word, and you didn't write to me.'

He stepped back from her, his eyes narrowing warily, his eyebrows slanting in a frown.

'There didn't seem much point in writing to a two-timing cheat who hadn't meant a word she'd said and who'd only been interested in having a sexual fling with me while she made up to her employer, a man with a title and an estate,' he retorted, his lips thinning to a cruel taut line.

Kirsty saw red. Her arm swung up and the flat of her hand struck his face. The loud sound of the slap brought her to her senses. She stepped back and stared at the red marks left by her fingers appearing on his tanned cheek.

'Feel better now?' Neil asked tauntingly.

'You deserved it,' she retorted breathlessly.

'For telling the truth?' he jeered.

'For calling me a cheat!' she flared, anger boiling up within her again as she recalled how unhappy she had been after he had left four years ago, the long dreary months of hoping and waiting for a letter from him; the cold raw ache of disillusionment when no letter had come. 'I wasn't the cheat—you were. You were the one who didn't mean what you said, and you were too much of a coward to tell me you didn't want me any more, so you left.' Her breath hissed as she drew it in sharply. Now she was angry with herself for letting him see how much he had hurt her. With a great effort she controlled her feelings and glanced deliberately at her watch. 'I must get back to the Lodge,' she said as coolly as she could, 'I haven't time to stay and rake over dead ashes with you.'

'No one was asking you to,' he retorted nastily. 'I didn't ask you to come here today.'

It was the last straw. Turning on her heel, Kirsty didn't run away, she marched, her head held high. Right through the opening of the gate she went and turned left to take the rough road which slanted down to the lochside road. It was a good thing she knew the way without looking, she thought with self-mockery, because she was so angry she could hardly see.

By the time she reached the other road she was feeling more calm, but she was wishing she hadn't gone to see Neil. She had been foolish to let herself be tempted into going to his cottage, into hoping that they could at least be friends again even if they couldn't be lovers. Cautiously she glanced back over her shoulder to see if he had followed her as he had followed her the day before. But he hadn't. And why should he? One way and another he had made it very clear that he didn't like her.

But where had he got the idea that she had been cheating four years ago? As she walked along Kirsty frowned at the spurts of pale dust churned up by her leather brogues. Who had suggested to him that she had been making up to Alec at the same time she had been visiting him at his cottage? Who, apart from Hamish, had known she had been friendly with Neil? Only Alec, and he had warned her against him. Oh, Neil must have invented the whole story to excuse his own cowardly behaviour.

Tossing back her head, she strode along, pretending she didn't care that Neil believed she had been two-timing him four years ago. What did it matter now anyway? He was married and he probably had a son or a daughter by now, perhaps both. She frowned again. She didn't really know if he had a family or not, because after informing her that Neil had married Barbara Gow Alec had never mentioned him again. Nor had she.

There was a lot Alec hadn't told her. He'd been a very secretive man. For instance, he hadn't told her that Balmore was mortgaged to the hilt. He had taken out the mortgage apparently when he had begun to employ her as factor. He had done it to finance the re-afforestation of the estate and to renovate the house.

Balmore had been his obsession, and everything and everyone had been subservient to that obsession. He had only asked her to marry him because he had known she could run the estate exactly as he had wanted it run but had been too incapable of doing as the dreaded multiple sclerosis had eventually overwhelmed him. And she had married him, as Neil had suggested yesterday, because she had been sorry for him and had wanted to help him. She had never thought for a moment that he had intended to leave Balmore to her in his will.

In leaving the estate to her had he really bypassed Neil, to whom it should have been left? And why hadn't Alec told her Neil was his half-brother? Perhaps he had thought she had known. Or perhaps he had thought she would guess there was some relationship between him and Neil when he had told her he had promised Neil's father he would keep an eye on him.

'He's like his father,' Alec had said. Had that been a hint? If it had she hadn't taken it, because she hadn't known what Sir Ian Whyte had looked like. His portrait didn't hang in the gallery with the portraits of the other Whyte baronets and there had been no photographs of him about the house. And since there had been no resemblance whatsoever between Alec and Neil she couldn't have possibly guessed that they had been fathered by the same man.

As soon as she could she was going to the room in the turret to look at the portrait Duncan had mentioned. Kirsty put on speed and almost ran along the road to the Lodge. After a quick lunch in the factor's house she sat down at her desk to open letters and to answer some of them. Once the correspondence was done she went over to the Lodge to find Mary Taggart.

'I'd like to have a look at the upstairs room in the turret,' she said to the housekeeper. 'My brother said you told him there were some paintings up there. I'd like to see them.'

'Ach, have ye never been up there?' exclaimed Mary, her reddish-brown eyes rolling expressively.

'No, I haven't. Sir Alec said it was just full of old junk.'

'Now, fancy him saying a thing like that,' remarked Mary. 'It was his father's favourite room, so it was. Sir Ian had his bed there and all his favourite paintings. Come along then and I'll be showing it to you myself. Perhaps ye'd like to be opening it up and having it used now that Sir Alec has gone?'

The turret was really a separate building from the Lodge and was all that remained of an old castle which had once been situated on the green hill which commanded a view of Glen Lannach. There were two entrances, one from the courtyard and another from the kitchen which had been put in during Sir Ian's time, Mary explained, so that he could go to his room without going outside the house.

'There are only two rooms in the tower,' said Mary breathlessly as they walked up the circular flights of stair set into the thickness of the walls of the turret. 'You can only get into the lower room from the outside, and that's the one that's full of old furniture and junk. Sir Ian once told me it was the place where the servants would live and cook, and the room upstairs would be where the clan chieftain and his lady and their children would sleep. Ach, it must have been very overcrowded to my way of thinking, as well as insanitary, and I'm glad I didn't live in those times.'

'I hadn't realised before that you knew Sir Ian,' said Kirsty as she followed Mary up the next spiral of stairs. Sunlight shafting in through the narrow slits of windows struck diamond sparks from the rough stone from which the tower had been built.

'It was Sir Ian himself that asked me to be housekeeper, soon after his wife died, Lady Constance, that was,' replied Mary.

'What was Sir Ian like?'

'He was a fine man, handsome and generous, some might call him extravagant. He was a surgeon and spent most of his time in Edinburgh and only came to Balmore for his holidays. Aye,' sighed Mary, 'it was a sad blow to him when his wife died before she could have any more children. He loved her dearly and never married again.' Mary stopped outside a stout oak door set into the curving inside wall and inserted a key in the lock. 'Not that he didn't have a few affairs after Lady Constance died, if ye ken my meaning,' she added with a sly wink. She opened the door and pushed it wide. 'So here ye are. Step inside and see for yerself if I'm not telling the truth when I say Sir Ian was handsome.'

The room was, of course, round, and surprisingly light, having a wide curved window which looked out over the loch towards Cairn Rua. It was furnished not with junk but with a wide comfortable bed covered with a brocade cover, a big wardrobe, a chest of drawers and a dressing table and two armchairs. The floor was completely covered with a thick blue and pink Chinese carpet. Against the end of the bed a large painting in a gilt frame, like the frames surrounding the portraits in the gallery, was resting, put there presumably by Duncan.

Standing in front of the portrait, Kirsty stared at it in amazement. Only a few hours ago she had stood and stared at a man who had looked very like the man in the portrait. The hair was a different colour, it was true. Ian Whyte's hair had been dark brown, not chestnut, but the deep peak was there, the haughty arching eyebrows were the same and the clear amber eyes seemed to glance at her down the aquiline nose in the same way Neil had glanced at her so many times. Perhaps the mouth and chin were different, Neil's mouth being wider and his chin more angular than those of the man in the portrait, but any stranger knowing one of them and then seeing the other would know at once they were related. Of Alec there was nothing in the painted face.

'Sir Alec must have looked more like his mother,' Kirsty murmured.

'Well now, I'm not so sure. Lady Constance was a small thing, black-haired and blue-eyed. She was a dainty wee thing and not given to childbearing, I'm thinking. Sir Alec now was always fair-haired and big-boned.'

'Do you know why this portrait is here and not in the gallery?' asked Kirsty, walking over to the window and looking across the loch to Cairn Rua. The weather was changing. Heat had caused big clouds to build up and the sky was no longer blue but had taken on a yellowish tinge. The water of the loch was a sullen grey and even as she looked out she heard the distant growl of thunder and a few raindrops spattered against the windowpane.

'Sir Alec had it put up here when the gallery was redecorated,' replied Mary. 'Everything else belonging to his father was up here, so I suppose he thought the portrait should be here too.'

Or he didn't want anyone to see how like Sir Ian the son of Morag Dysart looked, thought Kirsty with a sudden flash of insight into the workings of Alec's mind. He hadn't wanted her to come up here in case she had seen the portrait. He hadn't wanted her to know that Neil was his half-brother. Why?

'And these are the paintings I was telling your brother about,' Mary was saying as Kirsty swung away from the window to look round. The paintings were small, about eighteen inches by fourteen inches, framed simply and covered with glass. They were exquisite delicate colour washes of the view across the loch from the high turret room and of the view from the cottage on Cairn Rua of the loch and the tower. Lifting them off the wall, Kirsty examined the backs of them. The dedication was written on the back as Duncan had described. She looked at Mary Taggart.

'Morag Dysart was Sir Ian's mistress. wasn't she?' she said.

'Aye, aye, just so, just so,' sighed Mary, nodding her head. 'He gave her yon croft to live in when he knew she was expecting his child. She stayed there until he died and then she went away to Edinburgh to be near the boy while he was at school there. She died just over four years ago.'

Four years ago Neil had come to stay at the croft which he had inherited from his mother.

'I didn't know. Oh, Mary, I didn't know about her and Sir Ian. No one told me,' she muttered, and laid the picture down on the top of the chest of drawers. 'Sir Alec never told me he had a half-brother. Do you know why he didn't tell me?'

'If you want my honest opinion,' said Mary in her blunt matter of fact way, 'I think Sir Alec was jealous of Neil Dysart. And why shouldn't he be? Neil had everything Sir Alec didn't have. Neil was strong and clever, not pulled down by that awful creeping paralysis. Neil was handsome and popular with women, and most of all he was the constant reminder of Sir Ian's close association with Morag Dysart, the young woman Sir Alec had always fancied for himself.'

Kirsty looked up sharply from the paintings to stare at the housekeeper.

'Mary, you're not saying that Sir Alec and Morag Dysart were once lovers?' she gasped.

'No, I'm not saying that. I don't think she gave Sir Alec another thought once she had met his father. But it was Sir Alec who introduced her to Sir Ian when he brought her here one summer. That would be when he was about nineteen, just before the paralysis began to show itself. He met her in Edinburgh when he was studying at the university there. She was three or four years older than he was, tall with long red-gold hair and dark brown eyes, a lovely-looking lass, but a wee bit strange and wild, ye ken.'

'My brother says she was a very good artist, and her paintings are worth a lot of money now.'

'Then you could be selling those two and some of the others and paying off those debts instead of letting the place to yon Sheikh,' said Mary tartly. 'Ach, that Arab cook and those bodyguards are enough to drive me out of my mind! They're forever watching everything I do. As if I'd be wanting to poison him.' Mary folded her arms across her ample bosom and glared at Kirsty. 'I may as well be telling you while I've got you to myself for a few minutes, this letting of the estate to foreigners with outlandish names and queer customs isn't at all popular with the people on the estate or in the village.'

'So I've gathered,' replied Kirsty, stiffening up. 'But perhaps I'm not popular either because I've inherited the estate; because I'm not the natural heir.'

'Aye, you could say that,' said Mary with brutal frankness. 'And if you really belonged to the Highlands you would never have considered letting the place to an outsider.'

'I suppose everyone had known except me that Neil Dysart is the natural heir to Balmore,' Kirsty muttered miserably.

'Not everyone, but most of the older folk know,' said Mary, her reddish-brown eyes hard and hostile. 'What are you going to do about it now that you know?'

'I don't know. I . . . I'm not sure that there is anything I can do,' replied Kirsty, wishing now that she hadn't said anything to Mary. Finding out the truth had made her feel suddenly very insecure and she had a strong desire to turn and run far away from Balmore and its responsibilities. She wanted to be Kirsty Ure again, young and free, single and lighthearted, not Christina, Lady Whyte, widowed and bowed down with the burden of debts her late husband had left to her.

'Have ye seen all ye want to see now?' asked Mary.

'Yes, thanks. But I'd like the portrait taken down to the gallery and hung there . . . over the hearth . . . before the tea party tomorrow. From the look of the weather now we'd better be prepared to serve tea in the gallery. I wouldn't be at all surprised if it doesn't rain for a few days now that it's started.'

Her prediction was right. Next morning was grey and wet and the rain continued into the afternoon so the tea-party could not be held on the terrace as Hussein had hoped. He was very disappointed, but cheered up when Kirsty told him tea would be served in the long gallery instead.

A fire was lit in the great stone hearth and a long refectory table, covered with a white cloth, was set with plates of tiny sandwiches, cream cakes and biscuits, all made by Mary Taggart who presided over the tea urn and the cups and saucers. The flickering firelight, the soft rosy glow from various table and standard lamps did much to create a warm almost festive atmosphere, setting at bay the grey gloom of the day outdoors.

From their portraits the Whyte baronets of the past looked down their aquiline noses in haughty surprise at the gathering.

As Kirsty had guessed, everyone who lived or worked on the estate and even a few villagers came to tea to meet Hussein out of sheer curiosity, and from three o'clock onwards she was busy at the top of the stairs greeting and introducing farmers, crofters, gamekeepers, gardeners and foresters and their wives to the Sheikh. Soon the gallery was echoing to the sing-song hum of many Highland voices and the tinkle of china cups against china saucers.

She was talking to Monsieur and Madame Delacroix and watching how Camille was never far away from Hussein as he chatted with perfect courtesy and amiability to one of the gardeners when Neil walked into the gallery.

Looking every inch the successful doctor and surgeon in a well-tailored suit of fine greenish tweed, his chestnut-coloured hair smoothly brushed and shining with reddish lights, he paused at the top of the staircase to look round and the aquiline cast of his features, the straight proud set of his shoulders, the cool amber glance of his eyes were so like those of the man in the portrait which hung over the hearth that Kirsty was sure most people in the gallery would notice the strong family resemblance and comment on it.

His glance alighted on her and he moved towards her. Excusing herself to Monsieur and Madame Delacroix, she walked across to meet him, aware that her colour had heightened and that her heart had begun to pound excitedly.

'I was beginning to think you wouldn't come,' she murmured when she was close to him.

He gave her a mocking glance and held out his right hand. For the sake of appearances Kirsty put her right hand in his. At once he raised her hand and bending his head brushed the back of her hand with his lips. At their touch hot colour ran up into her cheeks and it took all her self-control to stop herself from snatching her hand from his grasp.

'Did you have to do that?' she whispered through tautly smiling lips.

'I always like to show my appreciation of feminine beauty, and you're looking remarkably elegant this afternoon, Lady Whyte. This is, I believe, the first time I've ever seen you in a dress.' His eyes gleaming with wickedly blatant admiration he looked her up and down insolently. 'And you should wear blue more often. It enhances the colour of your eyes.' He paused, then added with a sardonic grin, 'Are you still angry with me?'

'Was I angry?' she retorted, arching her eyebrows at him in mock surprise.

'If you weren't you gave a good impression of being angry yesterday, and my cheek still stings.' He fingered his left cheek. 'I've only come this afternoon to seek my revenge.' He leaned forward suddenly and whispered right into her ear so that his breath tickled the skin, 'No woman, not even you, my dear, slaps my face, calls me a coward and gets away with it!'

Her cheeks now blazing red, Kirsty stepped back quickly glancing sideways hoping that no one had noticed how closely he had approached her and finding, to her chagrin, that several people were watching them, including Camille who, for once, wasn't with Hussein, but was with her mother, and who began to sidle back to Hussein to draw his attention to Neil.

'I'll fetch you a cup of tea,' Kirsty muttered to Neil, and would have stepped away from him, but he caught hold of her arm and said,

'Whose portrait is hanging over the hearth?'

She gave him a surprised glance. He was staring at the painting in puzzlement.

'Don't you recognise him?' she said. 'He's Sir Ian Whyte. That's the portrait Duncan found in the turret room——' She broke off, aware that Hussein and Camille were approaching.

'I do not think we have met,' said Hussein politely. Beside Neil he looked slight, very dark and, for once, very boyish. 'I am Hussein al Dukar.'

'Neil Dysart,' replied Neil, shaking hands. 'I'm the tenant of the croft on Cairn Rua.'

'Forgive me for being personal,' said Hussein charmingly, 'but you do not seem to be like the other crofters here.'

'Neil is a surgeon,' said Kirsty quickly. 'He comes to the croft only for holidays.'

'Aren't you going to introduce me?' Camille said, in her attractively deep husky voice, and reminded of his duty, Hussein turned to her quickly.

'*Excusez-moi, mon amie,*' he murmured. 'Mr Dysart, this is Mademoiselle Camille Delacroix, a friend of mine from Paris.'

Camille was looking very lovely and chic, Kirsty thought, in a dress of brilliant emerald green silk with a plain tunic-type top fitted over a knife-pleated skirt. Neil greeted her in French with a suave gallantry which Kirsty realised he must have inherited from his father and Camille responded charmingly, showing more animation in her face than she had all the time she had been at Balmore.

'I cannot 'elp but notice, Monsieur Dysart,' the French girl said, 'that you are very like the man in the portrait which 'angs over the 'earth. You are related perhaps to the family which own this *château*?'

Above Camille's shining blonde head Neil sent Kirsty a murderous glance. Returning it with a mocking smile and a nod, she excused herself to Hussein, having noticed that Ahmed, the big bodyguard, was coming across the gallery, his sharp black eyes fixed on Neil. As she walked over to the table to talk to Mary Taggart Kirsty couldn't help laughing to herself. Not only would Neil have to explain his likeness to the portrait over the hearth, he would very soon have to answer Ahmed's charges that he was the person who had helped the poachers to escape the previous day.

Standing behind the table with Mary, she served tea and talked with various people, occasionally sparing a glance at the group of four

standing near the hearth, half expecting to see
Ahmed seize hold of Neil and march him out of
the room to lock him up somewhere. She could
see that Neil was talking and that both Camille
and Hussein seemed to be entranced by what he
was saying to them. Particularly did Camille seem
to be entranced, thought Kirsty waspishly, and
suddenly she saw Neil through the eyes of the
eighteen-year-old French girl.

· He was the handsome older man, impeccably
dressed, with the aura of success glowing about
him, experienced with just a touch of cynicism in
his attractively tanned lean face to hint at a mysterious and possibly outrageous past, sexually
magnetic to a woman of Camille's tender age . . .

No, no! Kirsty found herself wanting to rush
across the room to Camille and to warn her against
Neil, but at that moment he stopped speaking and
Ahmed stepped forward to say something.
Camille and Hussein both burst out laughing.
Ahmed looked embarrassed and Neil looked
wickedly amused. Hussein placed a hand on the
arm of his bodyguard and turned Ahmed away
from Neil and Camille to speak to him confi-
dentially. Left to themselves, Camille and Neil
chatted for a few moments, then linking her arm
through one of Neil's Camille guided him towards
her parents, presumably to introduce him to
them.

'No!' said Kirsty loudly and vehemently, and
actually stamped her foot on the floor.

'Is it to yourself you're after talking or to me?'
asked Mary Taggart amiably.

'To myself,' muttered Kirsty, glancing across to the Delacroix family again. Camille and her parents and Neil were leaving the gallery by way of the stairs and again she felt she wanted to run after them, to butt in on their conversation, to insert herself somehow between Camille and Neil.

'Everyone seems to be leaving now and the Sheikh is saying goodbye,' Mary said, 'so I'm thinking we could be collecting up the cups and saucers and taking them back to the kitchen. Ye'll no mind helping me?'

'No, not at all,' sighed Kirsty.

An hour later, when she was thinking of leaving the kitchen after having helped Mary to wash up and put everything away, Neil walked into the room. Mary greeted him cheerfully and with obvious affection.

'Ach, it's grand to be seeing ye again, so it is. Hamish was telling me ye're staying at Cairn Rua. Ye'll be seeing a lot of changes in the glen, I've no doubt.' Mary sent a sly glance in Kirsty's direction. 'Lady Whyte here is responsible for many of them. There isn't anything she doesn't know about planting forests and looking after the land. Was there something you were wanting, now?'

'A few words with Lady Whyte, that's all,' said Neil coolly.

'Then I'll be away to my own house now before that Arab cook starts making a mess of my kitchen,' said Mary. 'I'll be seeing you tomorrow, my lady,' she added, putting on her tough

Burberry raincoat and slipping her feet into wellington boots. 'Good day to both of you.'

She left the room, and Kirsty began to take off the apron she had worn to help with the washing up.

'Why did you hang my father's portrait in the gallery?' demanded Neil.

'I decided it should be restored to its proper place,' she replied. 'I was surprised you didn't recognise him.'

'How could I recognise him? As far as I know I never saw him when he was alive.'

'But surely he visited you and your mother when you lived at the croft.'

'Possibly he did visit my mother, but not when I was capable of remembering him or when I was present.' His mouth twisted. 'I didn't even know he was my father until my mother told me, four years ago just before she died. I came back here then to stay at the croft and to see Alec.' He gave a short mirthless laugh. 'He was furious with me for turning up, and now I've seen that portrait I can understand why. He didn't like having his father's bastard staying here. Did you see the other paintings when you were in the turret room, the ones painted by my mother?'

'Yes, I did.'

'I'd like to see them, and I'd also like to accept your offer of them. Is the turret open?'

'No. But the key to the room is here.' Kirsty went over to the wall board where all the keys for various parts of the house were hung and took out the bunch of three large keys for the turret doors. Turning round, she offered them to Neil. He looked down at them, then slowly took the keys from her hand. 'The door to the turret is over there,' she added, pointing. 'And when you've finished up there please lock both doors again and put the keys back on the board.'

'I'd like you to come with me, Kirsty,' he said, stepping in front of her as she started to leave the kitchen.

'I really don't have the time. Excuse me,' she replied briskly. She made to step around him, but he sidestepped in front of her.

'No, I won't excuse you,' he said. 'As the lady of the house you should be there when I take the paintings, a witness to the event.'

She stared up at him searchingly, trying to guess what was behind his request. The amber-brown eyes looked back at her coolly, not a flicker of mockery in them.

'Oh, all right, I'll come,' she sighed. 'This way.'

He unlocked the door, but she led the way through and up the winding stairway. Compared with the day before the light slanting through the slit windows was full and they seemed to go upwards through a grey mistiness as if they were moving in a dream. The round upstairs room was also full of misty grey light and the view from the window of the loch and Cairn Rua had almost disappeared behind a curtain of drizzling rain.

Kirsty snapped a switch and two lamps came on. The blue and pink carpet glowed softly and the brocade bedcover glinted with gold threads. Neil closed the door. The key clocked in the lock and Kirsty turned quickly from the window in time to see him put the bunch of keys in his jacket pocket.

He leaned against the door in the shadow cast by the bedside lamps and there was something vaguely menacing about his casual stance that tripped her nerves, causing them to tingle with apprehension.

'Why have you locked the door?' she demanded, going across the room towards him.

'To keep you in here and other people out,' he replied softly, stepping towards her. They met at the end of the bed. His eyes glowed yellow like a cat's in the dark as they looked right into hers and there was savagery in the sensual curl of his slightly parted lips. 'It's time you and I had a heart-to-heart talk, in private, Lady Whyte,' he murmured. 'And I think this is as good a way as any to begin.'

Kirsty stepped back too late. His hands gripped her shoulders mercilessly. She was jerked forward. Her head swung back and as she opened her mouth to protest against the pain which shot through her neck his mouth came down to cover hers in a hot hungry kiss.

She could have resisted. She could have hit at him with her fists and kicked him in the shins with the pointed toes of her shoes. But she did neither, because at the touch of his lips against hers all the hungry physical yearnings she had been suppressing over the past few years exploded upwards, shattering her defences against invasion.

Her arms went around his neck to hold him closer. Her body, taut and twanging with desire, pressed against his in shameless self-surrender. Being close to him was like arriving home after a long and lonely journey. It was like entering a warm and candlelit room after being outside in cold darkness, and when his arms closed strongly about her and he lifted her to carry her to the bed and lay her down upon it, it seemed to her the most natural thing for him to do.

Mouth to mouth, heart to heart, legs entwined, they lay while their fingers sought to undo buttons and fastenings and stroke away clothing. His kisses were like dark red wine going to her head and under her fingertips his warm skin was like velvet. She became almost delirious with sensuousness and moved against him provocatively and appealingly, knowing instinctively how to arouse and increase his desire yet uneasily aware that to give in to her desire to love him again might lead to some sort of disaster.

CHAPTER FOUR

ROUND and round, down and down, she seemed to be falling, spinning into the dark depths of sensuous pleasure where there was no coherent thought, only the tingle of titillation and the sweet joyous leap of passionate response, where there were no sounds save the thud of her excited heart in her ears and her sighing moans of entreaty.

Then suddenly Neil moved away from her, although his hands still clung to the soft curves of her breasts.

'Hell and damnation,' he whispered.

'What's the matter?' Kirsty asked, sitting up, the straps of her underslip sliding down her arms.

'I think I heard someone come into the tower,' he replied his hot glance arrowing in the direction of her half-exposed pink-tipped breasts. 'But I could have been mistaken.' With a hand on her shoulder he pulled her down against him again and dragged her head back so he could ravage her mouth in arrogant demand.

Her senses were beginning to reel again when someone turned the doorknob and tried to push the door open. Kirsty froze where she was, her whole body going stiff. Neil lifted his mouth from hers and grinned at her, his eyes glinting with unkind amusement.

'Are you afraid someone will come in and find

you in bed with one of your tenants, Lady *Chatterley* Whyte?' he scoffed. 'Don't worry—the door is locked. No one can come in.'

He had hardly finished speaking when the person outside the door thumped on it and rattled the doorknob.

'Who is in there? I can hear you speaking. Open the door at once or I will break it down!'

'It's Ahmed,' Kirsty gasped, sitting up again, and suddenly the whole door shook as the weight and strength of Ahmed's massive body was thrust against it.

'To hell with him,' growled Neil, and rolling off the bed he began to pull on his shirt. 'Who does he think he is, going round trying to break down doors?' Picking up his jacket, he took the bunch of keys from his pocket. Immediately Kirsty jumped off the bed and began to dress quickly.

'No, no,' she whispered desperately, 'don't open the door yet. Wait until I'm dressed.'

'Who is there?' shouted Ahmed, and thumped on the door again. 'Open the door!'

Neil thrust the tails of his shirt into the waistband of his trousers, raked tousled hair back from his brow and advanced to the door. The lock clicked back and the door swung open just as Kirsty finished fastening the belt of her dress.

'Oh, it's you,' said Neil unpleasantly as he faced up to Ahmed. 'What do you want?'

Ahmed's black eyes widened in surprise. It seemed he had not expected to see Neil. Then he looked at Kirsty, who was standing at the end of the bed without shoes on her feet, her usually coiled-up hair hanging like a curtain of black silk about her face and shoulders.

'I am sorry, my lady,' Ahmed said stiffly. 'I see a light shining out from the tower window and I wonder who is in here.' His glance wandered from Kirsty, to the rumpled bed, and then down to the floor where Kirsty's dark filmy nylon tights lay close to her black shoes.

'Mr Dysart and I are just looking through the contents of this room,' Kirsty explained, drawing herself up to her full height and trying to look every inch the lady of the manor. 'Some of them belong to him and he is deciding what to take away with him. We won't be here much longer.'

Ahmed frowned uncertainly, then gave Neil a suspicious look.

'Well?' said Neil sharply. 'What are you waiting for? Didn't you hear what Lady Whyte said? We won't be here much longer. And we don't need a bodyguard watching over us.'

Ahmed hesitated for a few more seconds, his glance flitting from Neil back to Kirsty.

'You will be sure to lock the door to the tower, my lady,' he said. 'We cannot be too careful after what happened yesterday. We do not want any more strangers finding their way into the buildings.'

'I understand,' said Kirsty placatingly. 'And I'll be sure to lock up. Please go now.'

Ahmed inclined his head politely, gave Neil another suspicious glance and turning away went down the stairs. Neil shut the door and locked it again.

'Ahmed knows you helped the poachers to escape,' said Kirsty. She picked up her tights and leaning against the bed began to roll them on to her feet.

'I know he does,' said Neil. 'He told his lord and master he recognised me as the driver of the Rolls when we were all in the gallery.'

'So what did you say?'

'I didn't have to say anything. Camille Delacroix came to my rescue.'

'Oh. How?' Kirsty felt an unusual prick of jealousy at the mention of the young Frenchwoman's name.

'I'd just told her and Hussein that I'm the second son of Sir Ian Whyte and half-brother of your late husband. They were most impressed, and when Ahmed made his accusation they laughed at him and Camille said she couldn't possibly believe that I could have anything to do with poachers. Fortunately the Sheikh was more inclined to agree with her than with Ahmed.' He paused, then added roughly, '*God*, it infuriates me to see those security men snooping around Balmore! I wish now I'd locked the other door from the inside and then we wouldn't have been bothered by him.'

'Ahmed was only doing his job, making sure that Hussein is safe,' said Kirsty, slipping her feet into her shoes.

'Oh, sure,' Neil jeered. 'But I'm willing to bet he's gone now, hotfoot, to inform the Sheikh that you're not the prim and proper lady you seem to be.' He laughed and gave her a glance which was brimful of mockery as he approached her. 'He'd only have to take one look at you to guess what we've been doing.' Raising a hand, he pushed back a swathe of hair from her throat and his fingers lingered lightly but dangerously against her skin. 'You look as if you've been very thoroughly made love to, my raven-haired, blue-eyed lady,' he added softly, and bent his head to kiss her lips again.

'No!' Kirsty sprang away from him. 'Keep away from me! I'm not going to let you have your revenge.'

'Revenge? What revenge?'

'You said you'd only come today to get your revenge for what I said to you yesterday about being a coward, and I suppose that was what was going to happen there on the bed. You thought you'd punish me by taking me against my will.'

Neil stared at her for a moment in surprised silence. Then he began to laugh.

'So it was going to be against your will, was it?' he mocked. 'Somehow I don't think so. You were very willing, far more willing than I'd expected. In fact I got the impression that my kisses were most welcome and that you'd been longing to be made love to for a long time.' He stepped towards her again. 'Remember the first time we kissed, Kirsty?' he whispered, his eyes taking on that dark topaz glow. 'You looked so lovely and untouched as you sat in the old chair at the cottage that I couldn't believe you were real. I had to kiss you to find out if you were flesh and blood or merely someone I'd dreamed up, a fantasy lover. Your lips were as soft and delicate as thistledown and they didn't know how to kiss.' His mouth twisted cynically. 'But they soon learned. By God, how soon they learned!' His voice grated with bitterness. 'Yet still I believed you to be innocent.'

'I was!' she cried in outrage. 'You were the first one who'd kissed me like that.'

'I doubt it,' he sneered.

'Oh!' Furious with herself because she had been betrayed into telling him something she had had no intention of telling him, Kirsty swung away from him and collecting her long hair in one hand to hold it back at her nape she went over to the dressing table to look for something to tie her hair back with. 'Anyway,' she raged on, 'your kisses were suspect too. They had nothing to do with love, just as what you were doing a few minutes ago on that bed had nothing to do with love either, even though you call it "making love!" '

She opened the tiny drawers in the base of the old-fashioned mirror on the dressing table and to her surprise found it full of feminine knick-knacks, hairpins and slides, and some pieces of coloured ribbons. Taking a length of red ribbon, she tied her hair at the back of her neck. When it was done she turned to face Neil again.

'You don't know what love is. You wouldn't be here if you did,' she accused. 'You'd still be in New York with your wife.' She gave him a scornful glare. 'Oh, you haven't changed really. You still like to play around and to lead a woman on into believing you love her so you can take what you want from her. Well, this afternoon I was going to turn the tables on you if Ahmed hadn't interrupted us. I was going to lead you on and make you believe I was willing to make love, so that I could take what I wanted from you!'

His face went white under the summer tan and between their dark lashes his eyes glittered murderously. Muttering something virulent, he raked a hand through his hair and turned away. Going over to the window, he stood there looking out, his hands in his trouser pockets. After a while he said in a cold clipped voice,

'There's a good view of Cairn Rua from here, on a clear day, that is. Better than the view from the study where Alec used to work and where he had his telescope.' He looked over his shoulder at her. 'Did you know he used to watch you going over to the cottage?' he asked.

'Yes, he told me. But how do you know he used to watch me?'

'Because he told me too.' He paused, then added in a lower tone, 'He hated me. My mother knew he did, and that's why she took me away from Balmore when my father died. She didn't trust Alec. But I had to come back here after she'd died. Something drew me here. Perhaps it was the Highlander's attachment to his heritage. Who knows?' He shrugged and turned to face her again, his eyes dark and brooding as their glance lingered on her face. 'I came here. I met you. I fell in love with you one evening at twilight.'

'No, you didn't. You only pretended to be in love with me,' Kirsty retorted. 'You didn't really care about the real person who was me. You were in love with a fantasy woman.' She drew a shaky breath and held out her hand. 'Give me the key, please. I'd like to go now. I promised Hussein I would dine with him and his guests this evening and I'd like to change my clothes.'

'He invited me to dinner too,' he replied coolly. 'At seven, and it's now only five-thirty. We have plenty of time to finish this heart-to-heart talk, and at the risk of boring you I have to repeat that I fell in love with you and was foolish enough to believe you fell in love with me. I was even crazy enough to think of asking you to marry me one day when I'd become established as a surgeon in New York and you had graduated.' Kirsty made a short exclamation of disbelief and his eyes narrowed. 'Don't you believe me?' he queried sharply.

'No, I don't. How can I believe you? You went away without saying anything. You didn't write to me. There was nothing, only silence, blankness. It was as if you'd never existed,' she retorted stubbornly. 'If you'd cared, really cared about me, you wouldn't have left like that without saying anything, without even leaving a message for me.'

'But I did leave a message for you. I left a letter for you with Alec.' Neil stepped towards her, his eyes searching her face. 'I had to go away—suddenly, I admit, to New York, for an interview. It was the chance of a lifetime, one I couldn't pass up. I went to the Lodge to find you, to tell you I was leaving. You were out somewhere on the estate. I saw Alec instead. We had an interesting conversation.'

'What about?'

'About the fickleness of women in general and of my mother and you in particular,' he said dryly.

'Me?' she exclaimed. 'Alec said I was fickle? Oh, how ridiculous! You're making it up.'

'No, I'm not. I'm telling you exactly what we talked about. I told him of the interview in New York and of how I hoped to work with Carl Weingarten, the famous American orthopaedic surgeon. Alec was very enthusiastic and encouraging and said it was what my father would have wanted for me. Then I told him I wanted to marry you.' His lips twisted wryly. 'That was when he delivered his lecture on how fickle women could be. He told me that he hoped to marry you too and that you'd given him every reason to believe that you would once you'd graduated.'

'Every reason? What do you mean by every reason?' gasped Kirsty.

'You know damned well what I mean,' he retorted scornfully. 'You made love to him, made him think you loved him, just as you made me think you loved me. He said he'd thought of warning me about your fickleness but had hesitated.'

'I don't believe you,' she whispered, staring at him in horror. 'I don't believe Alec would say that about me.'

'But he did,' said Neil, his voice drawling wearily as if he were tired of trying to explain to her. 'Although I didn't believe what he said about you at the time and I said so to his face. He became angry then and challenged me to leave a letter proposing marriage to you since I didn't have time to see you before I left. He said he was sure you would turn me down. I wrote the letter then and there, sitting at his desk. He called Mary Taggart in and instructed me to give the letter to her to give to you. Then I left.'

'I didn't receive it. Mary didn't give it to me,' she moaned. 'Oh, I wish you'd stop telling lies! I wish you'd stop!' she cried, her hands holding her head as she shook it from side to side.

'I am not telling lies,' he snapped. 'Oh, come on, Kirsty, if Mary didn't give it to you she must have put it in your room at the Lodge. She's as honest and straightforward as anyone I know. She would make sure you got it somehow.'

'I'm not pretending—I didn't receive it,' she insisted.

'Okay, have it your own way if it makes you feel better, takes the edge off your guilt,' he sighed wearily, turning away from her again.

'I'm not guilty of anything,' she stormed. 'How do I know you wrote a letter to me? This is the first I've heard of it. Alec never told me about it. You could be pretending you wrote it to clear your conscience.'

'Hell!' Neil swore viciously, and paced towards the window, then swung round and paced back to her. His face was pale, his eyes glittered and he was breathing hard. 'For the last time I'll tell you. I wrote a letter to you proposing marriage and asked you to write to me at an address in New

York. When you didn't answer my letter I decided
that Alec had been right about you after all and
from then on I put my career first always. Women
went way down to the bottom of my list of priori-
ties.' He shrugged, his lip curling. 'It's paid off—
I've been successful and made money.' He
laughed shortly. 'I've never thought about it
before, but I could say I owe my success and my
wealth to you. You turned me down and helped
to make me what I am now.'

'No, no,' she muttered, not wanting to take the
blame for his hard cynicism where women were
concerned. 'I didn't turn you down, because I
didn't receive your letter. If I'd received it I'd
have replied to it and then everything would have
been different.' Her voice faded away to a whisper
as the cold chill of regret crept along her veins.
'Oh, what's the use of talking about it, if neither
of us believes what the other is saying and the
only person who might have known the truth is
dead?'

He looked up sharply as he slid his arms into
the sleeves of his jacket.

'Alec, you mean?' he queried.

'Yes.' She sighed. 'When I asked him if he
knew where you'd gone he said he'd almost
warned me about you. He said you were like your
father and that your morals where women were
concerned were not of the best. He said you
wouldn't come back and that I wouldn't hear from
you again. And he was right. You didn't come
back and I didn't hear from you again, and whatever there was between us soon died. It can't have

been much, because it didn't stand the test of time and distance, did it? It's over.' She laughed a little, shrugging her shoulders. 'Once you were out of my sight you were soon out of my mind, Neil,' she lied. 'Could I have the keys now, please?'

He came towards her slowly and dropped the bunch of keys into her hand. She turned and inserted the key in the lock.

'But I did come back,' he said quietly behind her. The lock clicked as the key turned. She pulled the door open. 'I've come back, and it isn't over, whatever there was between us,' he added.

Kirsty glanced at him warily. There was an enigmatic slant to his lips and his eyes gleamed with his intention as he looked at her mouth deliberately.

'It's begun again,' he said softly, leaning towards her so that his breath caressed her lips tantalisingly. 'It's begun again in this love-nest where my father used to bring my mother.'

He slid an arm around her waist to draw her closer to him, yet still his mouth didn't touch hers but hovered tormentingly, and it came to her than that he was well aware of the power he possessed to rouse her to delirious abandoned passion. The realisation gave her strength and she pushed free of him.

'No, it hasn't begun again. It's dead, cold as ashes,' she said defiantly.

'Not quite dead. There are still a few embers left.' He touched her cheek lightly, his fingers sliding down to crook under her chin. 'And it'll be better this time, Kirsty, because we're both older, more knowledgeable. We're two consenting adults free to love where we wish.'

She knocked his hand away and backed out through the doorway.

'I'm not consenting to do anything with you,' she retorted, 'so you needn't think you're going to have an affair with me to pass the time this summer while you stay at Cairn Rua. You can find some other woman to be unfaithful to your wife with!'

'You're on the wrong track, Kirsty,' he said warningly, his eyes beginning to glitter angrily again. 'I wish you'd listen to me. . . .'

'I'm tired of listening to your lies, and I wish you hadn't come back!' she almost shouted at him. 'The sooner you leave again and go back to New York the better I'll feel. And don't forget to take the paintings. They're over there.'

She pointed across the room to the chest of drawers where she had put the paintings, and when he turned to look she left the room and ran down the winding stairway.

The kitchen was bright with light and noisy with the jabber of Arabic as Hussein's cook issued instructions to his helpers. Ahmed was leaning against the wallboard where the keys were hung watching all that was going on, but when he saw Kirsty he straightened up and came towards her.

'Have you locked the door?' he queried.

'No. Mr Dysart is still up there. I left the keys with him. Excuse me,' she said.

She slid past him and went out of the kitchen to leave the house by the side-door. Across the courtyard she walked, lifting her face to the soft drizzle of rain. There were two other cars in the yard, a big black Cadillac limousine which she presumed had brought Hussein's new guests and a sleek grey Jaguar which she guessed belonged to Neil. It was quite different from the battered little car he had driven four years ago, she thought with a bleak smile of remembrance. Quite different.

But then he was not successful and wealthy. *You turned me down and helped to make me what I am today*, he had said, and the bitterness in his voice had seared her. Kirsty's footsteps quickened and she hurried towards the factor's house, eager now to reach its quietness and privacy, to be alone for a while and sort out her thoughts. Neil had accused her also of being on the wrong track. But then hadn't he been wrong about her too?

In the house she went straight up to her bedroom intending to change her clothes, but once she had closed the door she gave way to her feelings. Flopping down on the side of the bed, she covered her face with her hands. Her heart was beating so hard it seemed to fill her throat and she felt sick. Sick at heart? Oh, God what was she going to do?

Moaning, she swayed back and forth in an agony of frustration and regret; regret for what might have been for the long-lost years when she and Neil could have been together if only she had received his letter, because if she had received his

letter she would have answered it. Immediately.
And she would have accepted his proposal of
marriage. She would have given up all idea of
getting a degree and of having a career. She would
have flown to New York to live with him there,
married or not.

She groaned again. Had he really written a
letter to her? Only one person could verify the
truth of his statement—Mary Taggart. The
housekeeper might also know what had happened
to the letter. Kirsty's hands slid from her face
and she rose to her feet to move heavily and
lethargically over to the wardrobe. In the long
mirror she watched curiously as she approached
her reflection.

With her hair down and tied at the nape of her
neck she resembled the young woman she had
been four years ago, Kirsty Ure, shy and sensitive,
warm-hearted and romantic, longing to be loved
and in love with a handsome rakish doctor. It was
only when she got close to the mirror that she
could see the droop to the corners of her mouth,
the pinched look about her nose, the lack of
sparkle in her eyes. She looked unhappy, down-
right miserable, in fact. Unhappy Christina
Whyte, who knew all about planting trees and
looking after the land and who had done what her
crippled husband had wanted, made Balmore the
perfect example of how an estate should be
managed. Oh, yes, she had been successful too, in
her own way. But at what a cost!

She covered her face again and leaned against
the wardrobe, her whole body shaking as forgot-

ten emotions and sensations tore her apart. She wanted Neil with a hunger that frightened her. She ached for him and she could have had him. She could have found the physical satisfaction she had denied herself during the years of marriage to Alec with Neil this afternoon gloriously and tumultuously, and the embers of their love might have been rekindled into a new blaze.

So why hadn't she? Because Ahmed had interrupted them? No, that wasn't the reason. She and Neil could have continued to make love after Ahmed had gone. Then why had she rejected Neil's attempts to kiss her again?

She didn't trust him, that was why. She was afraid he would hurt her again. After all, he was married and would probably return to his wife once his holiday at Balmore was over. Feeling calmer, Kirsty pushed away from the wardrobe, and opened its door to flick through her clothing, her mind busy with new questions.

Why had Neil returned to Balmore alone? Had he really been drawn by something stronger than his will, by that primitive historic urge of the Highlander to return to his heritage? She paused in her search for another dress to wear, feeling exhausted suddenly, wondering whether she should send a message to Hussein asking to be excused because she had a headache so that she could avoid meeting Neil again that evening.

No—she braced her shoulders and lifted her chin—to do that would be to admit she was afraid of the power Neil possessed to disturb her. She must pretend she didn't care if he were there or

not. She would put on the plain red silk
jersey dress, make up her face, coil up her hair,
tilt her lips into a smile and go over to the Lodge
as if nothing unusual had happened to her that
day.

She was a little late arriving in the lounge and
she apologised politely to Hussein, who greeted
her warmly, taking her hand in both of his while
his dark eyes gleamed with admiration of her
appearance. Keeping hold of her hand, he drew
her into the room where his guests were sipping
sherry.

Neil was there talking with one of the new-
comers, a tall stately man with a lean swarthy face
and a hooked nose who wore the traditional Arab
headdress with his beautifully tailored pearl grey
suit. Camille stood beside Neil looking up at him
in blatant adoration. In a dress of apricot-coloured
chiffon, which had an uneven petal-like skirt, she
managed to look both childlike and sophisticated
at the same time, and Kirsty felt envy crawl
through her.

'I am wondering a little, Christina, why you
did not tell me that your late husband's half-
brother is a highly respected surgeon in the
United States,' said Hussein as he handed her a
glass of sherry.

'To tell the truth I'd forgotten about him,' she
replied.

'You did not know, then, that he was coming
here this month?'

'No. Alec, my husband, and Neil did not
correspond with each other and I was very sur-

prised when Neil walked into the gallery,' she said. And it was partly true. She had been surprised because she hadn't expected Neil to come to the tea party after their quarrel in the cottage garden.

She sipped sherry and glanced again at Camille and Neil. Was it her imagination or was Camille standing even closer to him?

'Who is the gentleman talking to Neil now?' she asked. 'He looks important.'

'He is my uncle, Said al Dukar, and he is a religious leader in my country,' replied Hussein. 'I will introduce him to you presently. But first I would like to know if you and Neil Dysart are good friends?'

She gaped at him in surprise. He was watching her closely, almost possessively, as he stood very close to her.

'No. We hardly know each other and I haven't seen him for years,' she said.

'Yet when he entered the gallery and you went to greet him this afternoon he kissed your hand and whispered in your ear. Camille noticed too. "They have been lovers," she said to me.' Hussein gestured with his hands. 'The French have a way of sensing such things,' he added.

Kirsty's hand shook a little as she raised her glass; but she managed to keep her colour under control.

'Camille has a vivid imagination,' she retorted lightly. 'And she's only eighteen, at an age when a woman sees romance everywhere and believes in it.'

'What is this?' queried Hussein mockingly. 'Are you trying to tell me that you don't believe in romance or that you are too old for it? I do not believe you are, Christina.'

'But it's true. I don't believe in romance any more.'

'So why did you go with Neil to the turret and spend more than an hour with him there, behind locked doors if you are not good friends with him?' he queried jealously, and for a moment she was tempted to tell him sharply to mind his own business.

'Oh, I suppose Ahmed told you,' she said, forcing a laugh. 'Poor Ahmed, I'm afraid Neil was rude to him. You see, Neil isn't used to having every move he makes watched. I tried to explain to him that Ahmed was only doing his job when he came up to find out who was in the turret room. Neil and I were going through the contents of the room. Some of the things up there belonged to his mother and I feel he should have them.' She looked down at her empty glass. 'The sherry is good. Do you think I could have some more, please?'

'Of course.' He had the grace to look a little flurried because she had apparently caught him out being bad-mannered. 'And come with me,' he added, taking her arm. 'I'll introduce you to my uncle, now.'

Half an hour later, seated at the dining table between Said al Dukar on her left and Madame Delacroix on her right and directly opposite to Neil who was sitting between Camille and another elderly Arab who had come with Said, Kirsty wished she had sent her excuses to Hussein after all and had not come. Trying to ignore Neil while he and Camille whispered and laughed together was more difficult than she had anticipated. It meant she had to give her undivided attention to either Said, whose English was not of the best, or to Madame Delacroix who preferred to converse with Said's secretary, a tall slim Arab who had been educated in France.

After a while her neck began to ache from turning her head first this way and that and keeping it turned so that she didn't have to look at Neil. But in spite of her efforts her glance kept sliding surreptitiously across the table to him, drawn as if by a magnet, only to flit away from him as soon as he became aware of her stare and withdrew his attention from Camille to look across at her.

He and Camille were getting on together far too well, she thought, and remembered uncomfortably that she had told him to find another woman to be unfaithful to his wife with.

But surely he wouldn't choose a girl hardly out of her adolescence? Kirsty looked up sharply and across at Camille as if to warn her only to encounter Neil's hard mocking eyes. With slow deliberation he turned his head to look at Camille's pretty oval face, which was turned up to his as she talked to him. Kirsty's lips thinned. Her question seemed to be answered. Neil had chosen to encourage Camille!

At last the meal was over and they all strolled back to the lounge to have coffee, thick and black,

served in tiny cups. All of them except Camille
and Neil, Kirsty realised with a stab of jealousy,
and looked round at the others, wondering if
anyone had noticed the absence of the other
two. Only Madame Delacroix seemed to have
missed them and was frowning anxiously at the
wide-flung double door of the lounge as if willing
her daughter to appear. After a while there came
the sound of dance music from the record player
in Alec's study. Madame Delacroix's face relaxed
slightly. She came across the room and sat down
beside Kirsty.

'Camille loves to dance,' she said. 'And she has
missed her disco friends while she has been here.
I think perhaps she has found a partner in Dr
Dysart.'

'Perhaps,' replied Kirsty stiffly.

The music being played on the record player
was certainly not disco. Nor was it rock and roll,
nor punk rock. It was an old-fashioned slow fox-
trot, a sentimental ballad played on a trombone
backed by a big band, one of Alec's collection of
music from the forties and fifties.

Body contact dancing? Kirsty's lips curled in
self-derision. How cynical she was becoming! And
it was taking her all her time not to leap to her
feet and march into the study to see what was
going on there.

'If I'd known Camille likes to dance I could
have arranged for her to go to Balvaig. There are
often dances held in the village hall, especially in
the summer for the summer visitors,' she said as
pleasantly as she could.

'Thank you,' replied Madame Delacroix politely. 'But we do not allow Camille to mix with strangers, you know,' she added snobbishly. She glanced at the group of men who were standing before the fire-place obviously arguing about something. 'I am glad to have a few minutes to talk to you privately, Lady Whyte,' she continued. 'I think it is time you were told why Jacques and I have brought Camille to stay here. It is to arrange the marriage between her and Hussein.'

'Oh,' said Kirsty weakly, her hand going to her forehead. Hadn't she had enough surprises for one week? 'I didn't know that they are engaged to be married.'

'They are not engaged yet,' said Madame Delacroix. 'They have known each other for a long time, six years in fact, and we have hopes, Jacques and I, that one day they will marry. Before he was assassinated Hussein's father was beginning to show leniency towards the match, and Camille has agreed to adopt the Islamic faith.'

'But what about Hussein? How does he feel?' asked Kirsty, whose free-thinking attitude to love and marriage caused her to be amazed by Madame Delacroix's cut-and-dried approach to her own daughter's marriage.

'He is fond of her and we think he would have proposed marriage to her before this if he hadn't been plagued with political and business problems ever since his father was killed.' Madame heaved a sigh. 'It has been an anxious time for him and we were relieved when he invited us here. We hope that he has at last come to a decision.' Madame gave Kirsty a sidelong glance from beneath lids which were painted green. 'But we cannot be sure. He seems to be fascinated by you, now.'

'Oh,' said Kirsty again, opening her eyes wide.

'I tell Camille and my husband that Hussein's infatuation with you will not last,' Madame Delacroix went on. 'I tell them all,' here she waved a plump white hand, on which many rings glittered, in the direction of the other groups of people, 'that he is only temporarily attracted to you because you are different from any other woman he has known before.'

Madame's toothsome smile was worldly-wise. 'As I'm sure you know, it is not uncommon for a young man to be attracted to an older experienced woman, especially if he is a little shy, as in the case of Hussein.'

'But I'm not that much older than he is,' retorted Kirsty indignantly, her eyes flashing. 'About two years at the most.'

'But you have been married already,' Madame reminded her dryly. 'You are not innocent like Camille is. *Ça ne fait rien,*' she made a dismissing gesture. 'What matters is this. Hussein will get over his infatuation more quickly if you show a little less appreciation of his attentions.'

'And how can I do that, Madame?' Kirsty asked silkily. She was becoming more than a little irritated by the French woman's patronising, snobbish manner.

'You could refuse his invitations to dinner and

refrain from holding long conversations with him. You could hold yourself aloof. It should not be too difficult for you.'

Kirsty was silent for a few moments as she struggled to control an urge to tell Madame Delacroix where she could go with her advice. At last she managed to say,

'I think the music has stopped.' She almost laughed at the anxiety that flashed across the other woman's face. 'I suggest you go and see what Camille is doing. My husband's half-brother has a reputation for dalliance and it could be that Camille's chances of marrying Hussein are much more endangered by any friendship she forms with Neil than they are by me.'

She didn't wait to see what Madame Delacroix would do but walked over to the group of men who were not arguing any more but were listening to an impassioned speech by Said al Dukar, who was looking very stern. Hussein was looking sullen and defiant and Monsieur Delacroix was looking as if he were at the end of his patience. Said's secretary and the elderly Arab were both still and quiet, seeming very interested in the pattern on the carpet while they listened.

'Excuse me, your Excellency,' Kirsty said quietly to Hussein. 'I must leave now. Thank you for a pleasant evening.'

'It was my pleasure,' he said stiffly, bowing slightly to her, his eyes avoiding hers. 'Goodnight, Lady Whyte.'

'Goodnight.' She smiled generally in the direction of the other men and they all nodded to her,

barely polite, and all her antennae quivered warningly. They were behaving towards her as if they
had heard something about her they didn't like.

She walked across the room towards the doorway feeling rather than hearing the silence behind
her. In the hallway she almost walked into
Madame Delacroix who was hurrying towards the
lounge breathlessly.

'They aren't there,' she exclaimed. 'The record
was going round and round and they were not
there. Do you know where they have gone?'

'No, I'm afraid I don't,' snapped Kirsty, and
turning away walked down the passage to the side
door of the house.

The drizzle had stopped and clouds were being
blown across the sky by a warm breeze. In the
east the moon was rising. In the west light from
the sun which had just set still lingered. There
were only two cars in the courtyard now, her own
and the Cadillac limousine which had brought
Said al Dukar to Balmore. The grey Jaguar had
gone.

A movement drew Kirsty's attention to the
shadows by the garage doors. The tall massive
figure of the ever-watchful Ahmed appeared.

'You are looking for Mr Dysart, my lady?' he
asked smoothly. 'He had left. Mademoiselle was
with him.'

'Thank you,' she replied coolly. 'Goodnight.'

On the still damp stone flags of the courtyard
her high heels made a sharp skittering sound as
she walked once again towards her haven, the
factor's house. The pines behind the house made

a soft soughing noise as the breeze ruffled them. Above the curve of the dark moors behind the trees a star twinkled in a band of pale green sky still lit by the setting sun. It was going to be a lovely moonlit summer night in the Highlands; a night to be spent with a lover not alone.

Where had Neil taken Camille? Had he taken her to the dance in the village where he had sometimes taken herself? where they had often danced to the music of the fiddle and accordion?

> 'Now the fiddler's ready let us all begin,
> So step it out and step it in,
> To the merry music of the violin,
> We'll dance the hours away.'

The words and music of *The Dashing White Sergeant* the well-known Scottish choral dance jangled through Kirsty's mind as she entered the house. But her heart wasn't dancing, nor was it singing. It felt heavy in her breast, like a lump of lead, as she yearned for the times she had danced with Neil and then had ridden with him in his old car back to the cottage on Cairn Rua, and she wished she was with him instead of Camille.

CHAPTER FIVE

THE afternoon was warm and sunny, with a fresh breeze ruffling the loch making the water glitter with specks of silver light. High in the sky puffy white clouds blown over from the sea sailed above the summits of purple-grey mountains and away from the glen.

Kirsty drove her car up the road to the Lodge and into the courtyard. She parked it neatly, got out and took her shopping bags from the back seat. She had spent all morning in Balvaig, visiting the bank and buying necessities from the few small shops. Then she had had lunch with her friend Jessie Craig, who had also been recently widowed when her husband, the local veterinary surgeon, had died in a car accident.

Almost a week had passed since the day of the tea-party in the gallery, and during that week Kirsty had managed to stay aloof from the people who were staying in the Lodge, not because she had wanted to please Madame Delacroix, but because of an innate desire not to become involved with Hussein's problems.

It hadn't been difficult to keep clear of Hussein and the others because she hadn't been invited again to dinner, nor had she been asked to accompany Hussein and his guests on any of the fishing trips Hamish had organised for them or on any of their other outings. But she had been aware of the comings and goings of the Rolls and the Cadillac, and only that morning she had seen Said al Dukar depart in the big black car to return to London.

She hadn't seen much of Neil either, at least not to talk to him, but she knew he was still at the croft of Cairn Rua because she had seen the grey shape of the Jaguar streaking along the lochside road several times and had passed it one day when she had been driving back from Balvaig. He had honked his horn and had raised a hand in greeting as his car had flashed past hers. She hadn't waved back, but she had caught a glimpse of a shining blonde head close to his shoulder. Camille had not waved either.

The knowledge that the French girl had been with him had bothered her for the rest of the day in spite of her attempts to shake it out of her mind. She had a feeling Neil was deliberately trying to cause trouble with Hussein. Several times she had been tempted to go over to his cottage to remonstrate with him and to tell him Camille was more or less engaged to marry Hussein.

But she hadn't gone because she was afraid of what might happen if she did go. She was afraid he might try to make love to her again as he had in the turret room and, if he did, she might not be able to control her own desires. She might 'give', as he had called it, and if she did that she would have no self-respect left. She would hate herself for behaving no better than she had behaved four years ago, when she had believed he had been in love with her and she had been so sure she had loved him.

It wasn't as if she was in love with him now, she thought as she put away the groceries. How could she possibly fall in love with a man who behaved the way he was behaving? Who was openly unfaithful to his own wife by making love to another woman? And who told lies about Alec, her late husband?

She slammed the cupboard door closed to give vent to the strong hostile feelings memories of Neil's behaviour in the turret room had aroused in her. She despised him. She hated him and she wished he would go away, go back to New York.

'Hallo there, Lady Whyte. Do you have a wee minute to spare?'

Mary Taggart's lilting voice broke in on her thoughts and leaving the kitchen she hurried out into the small hallway. Mary was standing just inside the front doorway.

'I thought I'd just drop by to tell you what's going on at the Lodge today,' Mary said, her reddish-brown eyes sparkling with excitement. There was nothing she liked better than to be the bearer of gossip. 'Ach, there's been such a fuss over there this morning, so there has!'

'Come into the office,' said Kirsty, leading the way into the small room at the front of the house. 'And sit down while you tell me. I hope the fuss isn't to do with anything you and Hamish had done.'

'Ach, no,' said Mary, settling down into the only armchair in the room. 'Ye ken that young

French woman, Miss Delacroix? Well, she's gone off.'

'Gone off?' exclaimed Kirsty, with visions of cheese which had gone mouldy or meat that had become high. 'What do you mean?' She leaned against the desk.

'She's gone off somewhere without telling her mother. Mind you, it's the third time in a week she's gone out without telling anyone where she was going,' said Mary. 'But this time she's packed her bags and taken them with her. Now, what do you think of that?'

'I don't know what to think,' said Kirsty vaguely, but she felt her heart sink as she remembered again seeing Camille sitting in the front of Neil's car when it had passed her on the road, two days previously.

'If you ask me what I think ... which you're not doing ... I think she's found a friend,' said Mary importantly. 'Someone near her own age she can have fun with. And I can't blame her for going. She must have been sick to death with being cooped up here with her parents, yon Sheikh and his Arab friends, having to mind her manners all the time and to dress up in her best clothes. It's not natural for a young woman of her age to have to behave like that. I wouldn't have liked it when I was that age. Nor would you.'

'No, I wouldn't,' murmured Kirsty, thinking back to when she had been eighteen. Free and independent she had been in her first year at university, enjoying her studies and making friends where she wanted to. Marriage had been far from

her mind and she had never spared a thought for
the future. She had been much too busy making
the most of the present.

'If ye canna have fun while ye're young ye'll
never have it or ye'll always be hankering after it,
to my way of thinking,' Mary philosophised. 'I
mind I didn't take too kindly to being at home
with my parents when I was that age. I used to go
out every evening to meet my friends. We'd go to
the flicks or to dances. Ach, we had a fine time,
so we did. Anyway, Mr and Mrs Delacroix were
in a terrible way this morning and I wouldn't be
surprised if you'll be hearing about it now that
it's known you're at home. They'll be wanting to
see you to find out what you know about it.'

'But I know nothing. I've hardly seen Miss
Delacroix for a week. In fact, I haven't spoken to
her since I was at dinner with the Sheikh and his
uncle when she. . . .' Kirsty broke off frowning.

'When she what?' prompted Mary, leaning forward curiously.

'Nothing much. She disappeared after dinner
and her mother didn't know where she'd gone.'

'She went to the dance in Balvaig with himself
of Cairn Rua,' said Mary, looking self-important
again.

'How do you know?'

'Archie Thornton was playing the fiddle at the
dance as he always does, and he told his wife
Maggie that he was so surprised when he saw Neil
Dysart that he nearly fell off the stage. But he
was pleased too when Neil remembered him and
had a few words with him. Archie said Neil had a

young woman with him and told Maggie she was very pretty and had a lot of shining blonde hair. I guessed at once who she was when Maggie told me that.' Mary nodded again with an air of satisfaction with her own powers of deduction and rose to her feet. 'Ach, it's time I was off to my own place,' she said.

'Wait a minute,' said Kirsty as she followed the housekeeper into the hall. 'There's something I've been wanting to ask you. What's your memory like?'

'Fair to middling, I'd say,' replied Mary. 'I've a good memory for faces, but I'm not good at remembering names.'

'What about events, happenings? Could you remember something that happened four years ago, for instance?'

'Ach, now that might depend on what it was that happened if it was out of the usual run of things, ye ken.' Mary cocked her head to one side and looked at Kirsty out of the corners of her eyes. 'Four years ago, hm? What time of the year?'

'In the late summer. About the end of August.'

'You were here then, weren't you?'

'Yes, it was the first summer I had come to help Sir Alec. He was writing his book on Natural History.'

'Aye, I remember you arriving. Ye were a wee bit shy and didn't have much to say. Looked as if you wouldn't say bo to a goose,' Mary laughed. 'Who would have thought you'd turn out to be so clever and become Lady Whyte of Balmore? Aye, ye've done well, so ye have, and ye were a good wife to Sir Alec, God rest his soul. I mind him saying to me once he never regretted the day he married you, even though you were half his age.' Mary's expression became sardonic. 'I didn't like to tell him *he* was the lucky one when you agreed to marry him because he didn't have that many women to choose from. But ye didn't say anything like that to Sir Alec. Very sensitive about his handicap, he was.'

'You'll remember perhaps that Neil Dysart was also staying at his croft that summer,' said Kirsty, quickly getting a few words in edgeways while Mary paused to draw breath.

'Aye, I remember that too.' Mary gave Kirsty another sly sidelong look. 'You and he were awful friendly, I'm thinking.'

'He left at the end of that August, went away to New York,' persisted Kirsty stonily.

'So he did, so he did.' Mary's eyes narrowed as she seemed to look into the past. 'I mind he came to see Sir Alec before he left. I showed him into the study. They had an argument. I remember being a wee bit worried hearing Sir Alec shouting. I thought he might bring on another heart attack.' Mary's eyes focused on Kirsty's face. 'He'd had one before that summer, ye ken. That was when the doctor re-commended he should employ someone to help him with his books and his plans for the estate.'

'But he didn't have a heart attack the time he was arguing with Neil, did he?' said Kirsty, determined to put Mary back to that particular moment in time.

'No. He quietened down and they parted

friends. I was in the room at the time and saw them shake hands. Neil gave me a letter for you and asked me to give it to you. Then he left.'

'But you didn't give me the letter,' said Kirsty. She felt suddenly short of breath with excitement as if she was on the verge of making an important discovery.

'I didn't need to. Sir Alec said he would give it to you when you came in. Aye, that's so—I remember him taking it from my hand.' Mary sighed. 'Now what was it you were wanting me to remember?' she asked.

'Oh, I just wondered if you could remember when Neil was here last, that's all. I wasn't sure whether it was that summer four years ago or whether he'd visited Balmore again, later that year, perhaps.'

'As far as I know he hadn't been back until now,' said Mary, opening the front door. Kirsty followed her out into the breezy sunny day. 'Ach, here comes the bodyguard,' she added. 'He'll be coming to summon you to appear before the Sheikh, I shouldn't wonder, so I'll be off. See you tomorrow.'

Mary hurried away and Ahmed approached, a dark alien figure.

'His Excellency would be pleased if you would agree to have tea with him on the terrace this afternoon,' he said, bowing slightly.

'Will anyone else be there?' Kirsty asked cautiously.

'I do not know, my lady. His Excellency said to tell you it is most important that you come.'

'Please tell him I'll be there in a few minutes,' she said, and with another bow he turned and walked back to the Lodge.

Fifteen minutes later, having changed from the suit she had worn for shopping into a flower patterned cotton skirt and a thin white cotton blouse, Kirsty stepped out of the French windows of the lounge on to the stone terrace.

'His Excellency won't be a moment,' Ahmed explained. 'Please take a seat.' He pulled out one of the wrought iron garden chairs from the small round table.

Sitting down, Kirsty tried to relax and enjoy the view. She had sat in this place on sunny afternoons sometimes with Alec but mostly by herself, and she would miss the view of the loch and the hills beyond if she ever had to leave Balmore; if she ever had to sell the estate, and the likelihood of her having to sell it once Alec's will had passed probate was looming larger and larger, judging by the letter she had received from his lawyer that week which had informed her that the mortgagers were threatening to foreclose if the debt was not paid off before the end of the year.

Why had Alec left such a financial mess? Why hadn't he told her he was so much in debt? What had she ever done to him that he had had to punish her in this way? Had he known she hadn't loved him? Had he guessed she had married him only because she had been sorry for him?

Her parents and her brother Duncan hadn't approved of her sudden marriage. Her mother in particular had been very much against it, and ever since relations between them had not been comfortable.

'It won't be normal, that's why,' Catherine Ure had replied when Kirsty had asked her why she hadn't approved. 'Don't you see? There's more to marriage than being a companion to a man old enough to be your father—much more. By tying yourself to Alec Whyte you'll miss a lot. You'll miss the joy of loving a man properly, of making your own home with a loving partner and of having children.'

'From what I've seen of some of my friends' marriages making a home, keeping house and coping with children aren't joy,' Kirsty had pointed out dryly. 'And some of them are wishing they hadn't opted for marriage but had stayed single and had continued with their careers. And their partners have turned out to be not all that loving. By marrying Alec I'll be able to continue with my career.'

'Marriage is a joy if you love your husband sincerely and he loves you,' Catherine had argued determinedly from the security of knowing that her own marriage had been successful and happy. 'By working together you can make it a joy.' Her blue eyes had expressed deep concern. 'Kirsty, I wish you would take more time to think about this. Leave Balmore, come home, or better still, look for a job somewhere else where you'll be with people your own age. You've been cut off from the reality of life, living up there in that romantic glen.'

'I like living there,' Kirsty had argued. 'And it's not true that I've been cut off from reality.

And I'm not going to leave and look for a job somewhere else. I'm going to stay there and I'm going to marry Alec.'

'You'll be sorry,' Catherine had remarked quietly.

'I don't think so,' Kirsty had retorted stubbornly.

'Isn't there another man you know whom you could marry, someone younger, someone you're in love with?' Catherine had queried shrewdly. 'I had a feeling last year that you'd met someone.'

'I did, but he went away and he's married to someone else now,' Kirsty had replied stiffly. 'And . . . and I don't think I'll ever be able to trust a man again. At least I won't be worried about Alec ever looking at another woman,' she had added miserably. 'He . . . he won't be unfaithful to me ever, for the simple reason that he's too crippled now. I'll always know where he is.'

'Kirsty, that's a terrible thing to say!' Catherine had remonstrated sharply. 'And not a good reason for marrying him.'

'I also admire and respect him, Mother,' she had retorted. 'Surely you approve of that? Oh, don't worry about me. I'll make it work out all right.'

And her marriage to Alec had worked out all right, she thought now. She couldn't say she had been unhappy during the two and a half years they had been married. She couldn't say either that she had been ecstatically happy. But then she had not expected to be, nor had she wanted to be. In her limited experience ecstasy was only followed by an aftermath of deep depression. She had known ecstasy briefly with Neil, then he had left her and for a long time afterwards the world had been a grey dull place where she had moved about like a robot, without feelings.

Alec had loved her in his own way, she was sure. Then why hadn't he told her about his debts? And why hadn't he told her about Neil's letter? She didn't doubt that Mary Taggart had told her the truth. It had all come out so naturally and it meant that Neil had been telling her the truth too. He had left a letter for her, a letter in which he had asked her to marry him even though Alec had told him she was fickle.

'Ah, forgive me, Christina. I did not intend to keep you waiting.'

Hussein had stepped out on to the terrace. Slim and dark, as neatly dressed as ever, he pulled out another chair from the table and sat down. A young Arab, one of the helpers from the kitchen, appeared with the tea tray and set it down. When that was done he stood waiting politely until Hussein dismissed him.

'Please pour the tea, Christina,' Hussein said. The tray was set only for two.

'No one else is coming?' she asked, lifting the silver pot.

'No. I wished to see you alone. It seems a long time since we talked last. There have been too many people, too many problems.' He sighed. 'I have missed you and it is good to be with you again. In your presence I always feel I can relax, be myself.'

'I noticed that your uncle left this morning,' she said, placing a cup and saucer before him.

'Yes. And I am glad he has gone.' Immediately he bit his lip. 'I should not say that because I realise he has only been trying to do what he sees as his duty.' He sighed again. 'Since my father was killed Uncle Said feels he must advise me on all matters, not just political and business matters but personal and religious ones too.' He picked up the tea cup and sipped from it. 'He did not like me being friendly with you, Christina, and so while he was here I did not invite you to come to the house again or to go out with me. You understood, I hope.'

'Yes, of course I did. I suppose he didn't like you being friendly with me because I'm a Christian,' she said. 'I remember you saying that your father didn't like you to associate with women who are not of your faith.'

'No. It was not that.' His dark glance wavered away from her. 'Uncle Said was with me when Ahmed told me about finding you in the turret with Dr Dysart. He could not help overhearing what Ahmed said to me and I'm afraid he got the impression that you are. . . .' Hussein broke off, dull red staining his sallow cheeks. 'I do not like to say this, Christina, but my uncle felt that perhaps you are a woman who is too free with her favours.'

Hussein flushed even more with embarrassment and Kirsty sat perfectly still, staring at him.

'What exactly did Ahmed tell you?' she asked after a while, her voice dangerously smooth.

'He said that it looked very much to him as if you and Neil had been lying on the bed together,' muttered Hussein.

'Is that all he said?' asked Kirsty, quelling an urge to burst out laughing suddenly.

'Yes.'

'And you believed him, of course.'

'I didn't want to, but my uncle did,' he murmured. 'But let us forget what Ahmed said and what my uncle inferred from it. I have to tell you that Monsieur and Madame Delacroix are now very upset. You know, of course, that last week when you came to dinner, Neil took Camille to the dance in Balvaig.'

'I did hear about it.'

'And every day since then Camille has left the house without telling anyone and has gone either to his cottage or out in his car?'

'How do you know this?' Kirsty asked. 'Has Camille told you she'd been meeting Neil?'

'No. She has told me nothing. She has been strange, a little wild, and when her mother has remonstrated with her, she has answered insolently, refusing to say where she has been or to give the name of the person she has been meeting. She has not been like Camille at all, but like a woman who has been suddenly bewitched.' Hussein shook his head slowly from side to side. 'I do not understand her any more.'

'She could have been meeting someone else, a young man she met at the dance, perhaps,' said Kirsty, wondering whom she was trying to convince, Hussein or herself, that Camille had not been meeting Neil, 'It isn't unusual for a girl of her age to want the company of people of her own age. It must have been dull for her staying her, especially after Paris.'

'She has been meeting Neil,' insisted Hussein. 'She has been seen walking up to his cottage and has been seen in his car.'

'Have you seen her with him?'

'No, but Ahmed. . . .'

'Of course,' said Kirsty scornfully. 'Ahmed. He sees everything, doesn't he? He makes it his business to see everything and report back to you. He's nothing but a spy and a busybody, and I'm still angry with him for telling you I was with Neil in the turret for an hour behind a locked door and for implying what he did. It was none of his business what we were doing. It was none of yours, either.'

'Please, Christina,' Hussein said reproachfully, 'do not be angry with me. I didn't want to believe what he implied. I didn't want to believe my uncle either. I like you.'

He broke off with a muttered imprecation and springing to his feet paced over to the stone balustrade which edged the terrace. For a moment he stood staring out at the loch, then he turned to face her, resting his hips against the balustrade. Even at that distance she could sense the tension which was in him.

'Can you deny what Camille suspects?' he asked tautly, his dark eyes seeming to burn into hers. 'Can you deny that you and Neil Dysart were once lovers? And can you deny that you and he were making love in the turret room when Ahmed knocked on the door?'

His questions caught her off guard. Pink colour suffused her face, but pride and a certain hard-won dignity came to her aid.

'As I've said, it's none of your business,' she replied coolly, and rose to her feet. 'I think it's time I left, if that's all you have to say to me.' She turned towards the window.

'No, please, Christina—wait!' He hurried to her side. 'That isn't all I have to say to you. In fact that isn't what I wanted to say at all. Ah, in the name of Allah, will you please listen? This morning Camille left the house very early before anyone was awake and she took all her belongings with her in her suitcases.'

'Has she gone back to France?' Kirsty asked, turning obligingly to face him.

'We do not know where she has gone. But we know with whom she has gone,' he replied grimly. He pushed a hand into his jacket to an inside pocket and brought out a single sheet of thick writing paper. He handed it towards her. 'Read it,' he ordered.

Kirsty took the note, opened it and looked down at the sloping writing. She recognised only three words: Hussein, Neil and Camille. She handed it back to Hussein.

'It's in French,' she said. 'I can't read it. Please tell me what it says.'

He took the note from her, his face set in grim lines.

'It says, "My dear Hussein. I can't stand it any longer. Please try to understand. I have gone with Neil Dysart. My love to you always. Camille." That's all. Not a word of where they have gone.'

Kirsty felt suddenly the need for support and

put her hand out to the back of the chair she had just vacated. In the silence she could hear the lap of water on the shore, the sigh of wind in the trees, the sound of a lawn mower from the back of the house.

'You do not seem very shocked or surprised,' Hussein said. 'Did you know? Did your "lover" Neil tell you he was taking Camille away with him?' he demanded hoarsely.

'No. I knew nothing about it. And Neil is not my lover and I have no knowledge of his plans,' she retorted.

'So you do not know where he might have taken her?'

'No.' She paused, then added more gently, 'Hussein I'm really sorry this has happened.'

'In the way perhaps that you were really sorry when he stole my Rolls and helped his friends to escape?' he replied viciously. 'You knew all the time he had helped them, yet you said you were sorry.'

'They weren't real poachers,' she objected. 'They were two young men on holiday, enjoying themselves. And they put the fish back. They were only trying to prove to Neil that they could catch a fish by that method.'

'But you knew they were his friends and you pretended you were sorry my car was stolen,' he accused her.

'I didn't pretend,' she said. 'I was sorry at the time because you were so upset. And I'm sorry now because you're obviously upset Camille has left with Neil. I wish I could do something to help, but I can't. I don't know what to do.'

'Aah!' Hussein clutched his head between his hands. 'I think I will go mad,' he muttered wildly. 'Your calmness will drive me mad! You do not seem to understand. The woman I am considering for marriage has gone away with another man who is your erstwhile lover. Why aren't you furiously angry as I am? Do you not care for Dysart?'

'Look, I am a little worried, I must admit, on Camille's behalf,' she said. 'I mean, she's so young and has led such a sheltered life. But she's old enough to make her own decisions, to choose what she wants to do, and perhaps she has chosen to have a little fun before she settles down to marriage with you and life in your harem. I can't say I blame her. Living in a harem must be like living in prison.'

Hussein's face went red again and the veins stood out on his forehead while his black eyes glared at her.

'I will not have a harem,' he said through gritted teeth. 'I loathe the institution. I shall have only one wife. But she must be innocent, untouched, when I marry her, as I know Camille to have been until now.' He gasped as if short of air and made a few rapid paces back and forth in front of her. 'But now,' he muttered as he stopped to face her again, 'now she has gone with Dysart I cannot be sure of her any more. You yourself told Madame Delacroix he has a reputation for amusing himself with women, and who should know that better than you?'

'Oh dear, yes I did say that, didn't I?' said Kirsty, biting her lower lip. She was experiencing again a desire to burst out laughing in reaction to Hussein's excitability. He seemed to be making such a fuss about very little. 'I'm so sorry,' she began again. 'No, you don't like me to say that, do you? But what else can I say? What are you going to do? I'm surprised you haven't sent Ahmed after them?'

'By the time I had found the note and we had realised Camille had gone it was too late,' said Hussein, calming down. 'Monsieur and Madame Delacroix have gone to Fort William this afternoon to the police station to lay charges against Dysart.'

'Charges of what?' exclaimed Kirsty.

'Kidnapping.'

'Oh, no! They can't do that!' All desire to laugh had gone. She was really worried about Neil. 'Camille has gone with him of her own free will. The fact that she's taken all her belongings with her proves that.'

Hussein gave her a dark suspicious glance.

'I suppose it does,' he muttered grudgingly. 'But, in the name of Allah, what am I going to do? My uncle, who is the chief leader of the Islamic faith in my country, has just given me permission to ask Camille to marry me because she had promised to change her religion, and now she has run away!'

'Go after her,' suggested Kirsty brightly.

'But I don't know where they have gone. If I knew I'd have followed them by now.'

'Then you'll just have to wait won't you? I'm sure she'll let her parents know where she is sooner or later.'

'That is all you have to say?' he whispered.

'That's all.'

He stared at her, his face working with conflicting emotions, then stepped forward and grasped her hands in his to hold them close to his chest.

'Christina, I love you,' he whispered. 'I love your eyes, your skin, your hair. I love your soft musical voice. I love the way you laugh, the way you sigh. I love your cool clear mind. I love you more than I love Camille, so what are you going to do about it?'

Amazed, she stared up into the soft black eyes for a moment, then tried to free her hands, afraid that Ahmed or one of the other security men might appear.

'Hussein, you're distracted with worry and you don't know what you're saying,' she replied. 'Please let me go.'

'No. And I do know what I'm saying. And if circumstances were different I would ask you to marry me now that Camille has gone.'

'Circumstances? What circumstances? What do you mean? Are you sure you're using the right word?' she asked.

'You have been married. You are a widow. You are no longer a virgin, and the woman I must marry must be. . . .'

'Innocent. Untouched,' she said dryly. 'I see.'
She tried again to free her hands, but his grasp
tightened.

'Wait,' he ordered. 'Hear me out. I cannot
marry you, but we could be lovers. You could be
my mistress, live here all the time, and I could
visit you. Ah, Christina, please say you will!'

Astounded by his suggestion, she stared at him
again, recalling her own mocking remark that she
might marry Hussein and use his money for
Balmore.

'You mean you'd continue to pay rent for
Balmore and allow me to live here if I agree to be
your mistress?' she whispered.

'That is exactly what I mean. Or if you would
prefer it I will buy Balmore from you and give it
back to you as long as I could visit you here and
be assured of a welcome when I come.' He pressed
closer to her, his dark face hovering just above
hers, his dark eyes blazing. 'I love you and I want
you to be mine. Never have I felt like this about a
woman. Christina, you must say yes,' he pleaded.
'You must say yes!'

'I can't. I can't give you an answer, not yet. I
. . . I'll have to think about it. Now please let me
go. Someone might come and find us like this,
see you holding me like this.'

'Ahmed might come, you mean.' His mouth
twisted wryly. 'I wish he would come and find
you in my arms. But he isn't coming, so I will
continue to hold you like this, and now I am going
to kiss you.'

His lips were hot, moist and soft. They pleaded

for her response rather than demanded it, and Kirsty kissed him back because she felt sorry for him and also because she thought that if she did he would release her.

'You see, you like me a little bit,' he said with a flicker of triumph as he let her go. 'You returned my kiss. But I will give you time to think about my proposition. Tomorrow you will give me an answer.' He looked past her and he frowned. 'What is it, Mohammed?'

Kirsty turned quickly. One of the bodyguards was standing just within the French window, his dark face impassive. He spoke to Hussein quickly in Arabic.

'It is my uncle phoning me from London,' Hussein explained to Kirsty. 'I tried to reach him earlier, but he was not at his hotel. Now he is returning my call. You will please excuse me while I talk to him?'

'Of course.'

'And you will wait here until I come back?' he asked. 'Have some more tea?'

'No. I have work to do. I'll see you tomorrow,' she replied, and turning, she walked away along the terrace and down the steps at the end.

She needed something a lot stronger than tea to soothe her, thought Kirsty wryly as she entered the factor's house again. A good tot of straight whisky wouldn't have done any harm, only she didn't drink and there was no whisky in the house. She possessed no means of seeking oblivion from her tumultuous thoughts.

But she couldn't spend the evening by herself.

She had to get out of the house, go somewhere. There was only one place where she knew she would be welcome. She would go to Jessie's house and tell her friend about Hussein's surprising proposition. She might even tell Jessie about her anxiety about Camille's apparent elopement with Neil.

Over an hour later, sitting in an armchair in Jessie's house on the outskirts of Balvaig, she told her everything.

'Well!' gasped Jessie. 'To think of you being asked to be the mistress of a real live Sheikh! It's like a story out of the Arabian Nights. Or a novel by Elinor Glyn or Ethel M. Dell.' Her dark brown eyes narrowed shrewdly. 'I can understand, though, why you're in a bit of a tizzy over that French girl running away with Neil Dysart. And you were right to come here and tell me about it. No good you bottling all that up inside yourself. Ach, some men are never happy unless they're causing trouble!'

'I'm only worried in case . . . in case he takes what he wants and then drops her,' sighed Kirsty, trying to ignore the feelings of jealousy which kept swelling up inside her. 'In case he hurts her.'

'As he hurt you, you mean, four years ago. I thought you'd got over that?' remarked Jessie.

'I had,' whispered Kirsty.

'Then forget him and her.'

'I can't. I keep wondering where he's taken her and what they're doing. Oh, Jessie how could he do it? How could he do it?' she groaned.

'Now you can stop that!' said Jessie sharply.

'No man is worth all this self-torture you're putting yourself through. You're not responsible for anything he does. And you're not going back to Balmore tonight. You can come with me to the party at the sailing club.'

'But I haven't been invited and I'm not a member.'

'That won't matter. You're coming with me and we'll have a good time. The fact that you're Lady Whyte of Balmore will be enough to open the doors wide to you.'

'Yes, but you know I don't like using the title. . . .'

'Shut up!' said Jessie, laughing. 'It's time you had some fun. Ever since Alec died you've been turned off. God knows why, because we all know you and he didn't. . . .'

'Didn't what?' Kirsty interrupted her threateningly.

'You know what I mean,' retorted Jessie with a knowing grin. 'Anyway, it's time you got into circulation again. You don't want to be a widow for ever, do you? So we'll go to the party, have a few drinks, get a little squiffed and maybe someone will ask us to dance. And don't worry about having to drive back to Balmore. You can stay the night here.'

'All right,' Kirsty capitulated suddenly, thankful that for the next few hours she wouldn't have a chance to worry. 'Do you think this skirt and blouse are suitable to wear?'

CHAPTER SIX

ALTHOUGH she hadn't gone to bed until the early hours of the morning Kirsty woke early next day and lay for a while drowsily looking around the small bedroom at the back of Jessie's house. Sunlight slanted in around the edges of the brightly coloured curtains which covered the dormer window. It was time she got up and went back to Balmore to find out if Hussein had heard from Camille.

Quickly she sat up, then groaned, her hands going to her head as pain twisted through it. Remembering how she had come by the headache, she grinned ruefully. She had drunk too much at the party, not a lot but too much for her because she wasn't accustomed to drink. But it had been a good party. She had enjoyed it. And she had met some pleasant people of all ages, mostly summer visitors who owned houses and cottages in or near Balvaig which they had renovated and had turned into comfortable holiday residences.

'Kirsty? Are you awake? I've brought some tea.'

Jessie pushed the door open. She came in carrying a tray on which there were two mugs and a teapot. She was wearing a flower-patterned quilted housecoat and her curly hair was tousled. She set the tray down on the bedside table, then perched on the edge of the bed. Her dark brown eyes quizzed Kirsty's face.

'How do you feel this morning?' she asked.

'Not bad, but I have a headache.' Kirsty reached out and lifting the teapot poured tea into the mugs. Picking up one of them, she drank some of the clear brown liquid without sugar or milk. 'Mmm, it tastes good,' she said, and glanced at her friend's round good-humoured face. 'I hope I wasn't silly or anything last night. I think I had too much to drink.'

'You had a bit more to say than usual, that's all,' said Jessie. 'Otherwise you were your normal lively self. And you were certainly a hit with some of the lads. I'm thinking they fall for those big blue eyes of yours.' Her glance swept over Kirsty. 'You know, you have all the makings of a *femme fatale*. There's an aura of mystery about you. No wonder the Sheikh has fallen for you and asked you to be his mistress! Have you decided what to do? Are you going to accept his offer?'

Kirsty finished her tea and set the mug down on the tray. Leaning back against the pillows, she folded her arms behind her head. She was wearing one of Jessie's nightgowns and it was several sizes too big for her. The bodice had slipped down to give a tantalising glimpse of her uptilted white breasts.

'No, I'm not,' she said firmly. 'Knowing me, can you imagine me as the mistress of a wealthy Arab, my favours bought and paid for?'

'No, quite frankly, I can't,' said Jessie, and her face expressed relief. 'You're too much of a puritan like me. And too damned independent. It has to be marriage or nothing for both of us.' Jessie laughed as she poured more tea. 'And the way things are going for me it looks as if it's going to be nothing! Not one of the men I've met recently can compare with Jamie.' She sighed, her eyes darkening with sadness. 'Oh, Kirsty, I do miss him,' she whispered, her eyes filling with tears.

Touched by her friend's distress, Kirsty spent the next few minutes comforting her. As she expected, Jessie soon cheered up and left the room to go downstairs to prepare breakfast.

It was nearly ten o'clock when Kirsty left the house and set off for Balmore. She drove fast along the winding road to Glen Lannach, hardly sparing a glance for the beauty of the scenery; the lush green meadows dotted with shaggy golden-brown Highland cattle; the light and dark pattern of larch and pines; the purple-tawny sweep of moorland; and towering over all the naked rain-scoured rocks of the mountains seeming to touch the clouds which were fast covering the sky.

The nervous agitation from which she had suffered the previous afternoon was back. She was worried still about what had happened. Why was she so anxious? She had told Jessie that it was on Camille's account she was worried, in case Neil hurt the girl, but she knew deep down that she didn't care what happened to Camille at all. It was on Neil's account she was worried. She was afraid of the damage he might do to himself by running away with Camille.

Since Camille came from an important French

family and had been staying with a well-known Arab there could be publicity about the elopement. In their attempts to find their daughter she guessed that the Delacroixs would have no hesitation in using the media to draw the attention of the British public to what had happened.

And adverse publicity would damage Neil's reputation as a surgeon. It would disrupt his marriage. It might destroy him!

Oh, why should she worry about him? Why should she care what happened to him? He had meant nothing to her for the best part of four years, so why feel deeply concerned about him now? Why did she have this urge to rush to his defence, to protect him against the consequences of his own mischievous behaviour? Surely she wasn't in love with him again? No. She shook her head in quick negation. It took time to fall in love, and she hadn't seen much of him since he had returned. It took time ... yet four years ago it had taken her only ten minutes!

By the time she reached the Lodge rain had begun to spit down from the grey clouds. Yet the yard was full of people coming and going, Hussein's Arab servants hurrying to and from the side door of the house, carrying out cases and boxes, packing them into the van in which they had travelled up from London and which had been parked in the middle garage ever since it had arrived.

Seeing Ahmed, Kirsty went over to him.

'What's happening?' she asked.

'We are leaving, my lady. His Excellency wishes

to see you as soon as possible. He is in the lounge.'

Hussein was sitting at the desk in the lounge talking on the phone. When he saw her he said a few more words, then put the receiver down. Rising to his feet, he did not approach her but waited for her to go to him. His face was serious, his dark eyes sad.

'Good morning, Christina,' he greeted her. 'All morning I have been looking for you. I looked for you last evening too, but you were not at your house.'

'I went to Balvaig to visit a friend, and stayed the night with her. Why did you want to see me?'

'To tell you I am going to look for Camille.'

'Oh, have you heard from her? Do you know where she is?'

'No, we haven't heard from her, but we think she is in London. Yesterday evening the Delacroixs received an anonymous phone call. The person who spoke to them said that Camille was safe and well and was staying with a friend near London, then hung up. They left immediately for London in their car. I said I would join them there today and help them to search for her.' He twisted his hands nervously together. 'I hope you understand why I must go.'

'Of course you must go and look for her. I understand.'

His hands stopped twisting. He looked at her, and relief shone in his eyes. His glance seemed to caress her.

'I knew you would understand,' he said. 'You

are a very generous and understanding person. A man feels comfortable with you and that is important. It is why I have fallen in love with you.' He stepped closer to her. 'Have you thought about my suggestion? You promised to give me an answer today.'

'Yes, I have thought about it,' Kirsty replied steadily. 'The answer is no. I couldn't do it. I'm not that sort of woman.'

To her surprise he nodded, although it seemed to her that tears glistened suddenly in his eyes.

'I expected you to answer in that way,' he said. 'As you say, you are not that sort of woman. You are the sort of woman who should be comfortably married to a kind, supportive husband, who should be bearing and rearing children.' He broke off, his face twisting with pain. 'I wish to Allah that I could be your husband. I wish I had the courage to run away from my responsibilities, turn my back on the Sheikhdom of Dukar, stay here and marry you, live with you here always. But I don't have the courage. I am afraid to offend my people, my uncle, the leaders of my religion.' He held out a slim dusky hand to her. 'This is goodbye, Christina. I will not be coming back to Balmore.'

'But you've paid the rent for six months!' she exclaimed.

'I know, but I will not be coming back. Now that I know I cannot have you I will not come back. You see, I could not bear to be here, to see you almost every day and knowing that I cannot ever give expression to my love for you.'

'I could be away when you want to stay here. You wouldn't have to see me,' she offered.

'No.' He shook his head. 'It is my destiny to marry another woman, if not Camille, then some other innocent girl who probably would not like this place any more than Camille does. This is the parting of our ways.'

'But you must let me refund the rent you've paid,' said Kirsty anxiously, knowing that the money had already been used to pay off some of Alec's debts. 'It's so wasteful to pay rent for a place you're not going to live in.'

'I can afford it,' he said with a shrug, then added in an agonised whisper, 'Please will you say goodbye and go, Christina. I can't bear being with you any longer.'

'Goodbye,' she said softly, and kissed him quickly on the cheek. 'I hope you find Camille none the worse for her adventure and are able to marry her.'

Leaving the lounge, she went to the kitchen to make sure Mary Taggart was there and supervising the departure of the Arab cook and his equipment. But the cook and his minions had already gone and Mary was alone, humming cheerfully to herself as she cleaned the big electric range.

'Well, I can't say I'm sorry they're leaving,' she said. 'And I won't be singing "Will ye no come back again" to them, either. Good riddance to them all!' she glanced sideways at Kirsty. 'Ach, ye're looking a wee bit pale this morning. I'll put the kettle on and we'll have a good cup of tea by way of celebration.'

Through the rain-spattered window Kirsty watched the van reverse into the space of the yard and then go forward and out of sight. A few seconds later the Rolls-Royce followed, driven by Ahmed with Hussein sitting beside him. Then that had disappeared too and there was only the soft tinkle of raindrops falling on the old grey cobbles of the yard and against the window pane.

'So that's that,' said Mary prosaically as she poured tea. 'And I'm thinking you won't be in a hurry to let the place to a foreigner again after that experience,' she added sharply.

'I'll have to let it to someone,' retorted Kirsty. 'Mary, do you have any aspirin? I've got an awful headache.'

'Ach, sure I have.' Mary went to a closet to find her handbag and rummage in it.

Kirsty sat with her shoulders slumped and her head in her hands, staring at the cup and saucer in front of her but not seeing it. Hussein had gone. The Delacroixs had gone. Neil had gone. Balmore was back to normal. She could move back into the Lodge if she wished, take up the usual routine, behave as if nothing strange had happened; as if the place hadn't been overrun with Arabs; as if Neil hadn't come back.

Where was he now? Was he in London with Camille? Oh God, she hoped not. She couldn't bear the thought of him making a fool of himself over an eighteen-year-old blonde. She ground her teeth and glared at the cup and saucer. She hadn't thought it possible to be so jealous. And possibly it was her own fault Neil had taken Camille away with him. He might not have done it if she herself had not rejected him in the turret room; if she hadn't thrown a taunt at him.

You can find some other woman to be unfaithful to your wife with. She groaned softly with regret, wishing she had never said that. It had been a mistake to taunt Neil like that. She should have known better than to throw down a challenge in front of him. Neil was the type of man who would always take up a challenge. Descended from a long line of stubborn, fighting Highlanders, he would enjoy nothing better than to pick up the gauntlet tossed before him and to throw it back in his enemy's face.

'Here you are,' said Mary, plonking down a small bottle of aspirin. 'Take some with your tea and then be off with you for a rest. You look worn out. It's been too much for you, the worry of this place, and I for one wouldn't blame you if you did get rid of it. You're too young to be saddled with the responsbility of it. You should be off and away, working with people your own age, enjoying yourself.'

'But you wouldn't like me to sell it to a foreigner,' said Kirsty dryly after swallowing two aspirin.

'No, not to a foreigner,' replied Mary wisely. 'To someone who belongs to this country, even an Englishman would do. There must be someone who can afford to buy it.'

'Yes, there must be,' said Kirsty with a sigh, rising to her feet. 'I'm going to spend some time this afternoon in the study. I have to look for something in there.'

The study, which had once been the hub of the house, had a musty unused atmosphere now. Pausing in the doorway, Kirsty tried to imagine what Alec had been doing the day Neil had come to look for him nearly ten years ago.

Alec would have been sitting as usual behind the big desk in his wheelchair, near to the window and his telescope. Slowly she closed the door and walked over to the desk. Alec would have watched anyone approaching him in silence, looking over the tops of his dark-rimmed reading glasses, his blue eyes wintry, his small mouth tightly pursed, his intention to reduce the person coming towards him to a state of awe and possibly fear. It had taken her a long time to find out that his rather bulldoggish, Churchillian pose had been just that, a pose; a defence behind which he had hidden his weakness and caused by his handicap.

But she doubted if Neil had been afraid of Alec. Neil would have advanced into the room as if he had owned it and would have marched right up to the desk and said outright what he wanted without waiting to be asked. And that day he had asked to see her.

Going over to the desk, Kirsty sat on the side of it, away from the window. The top of it was neatly set with a blotting pad, a sheaf of writing paper and some envelopes, put there for the use of the tenant of the house. In Alec's day the top would have been scattered with books and papers and he would have moved some of the books to give Neil room to write the letter to her.

When the letter had been written Neil had given

it to Mary Taggart. Then he had left. At Alec's request Mary had given the letter to him. Where had Mary put it? On the desk? Or into Alec's hand? If she had put it on the desk the chances were it had been covered up and forgotten, perhaps collected up with some papers and put somewhere else. Or it might have been thrown in the waste-paper basket and destroyed before Alec had remembered to give it to her.

She hoped that was what had happened. Now that she was sure that Neil had written the letter she didn't want to believe that Alec had deliberately withheld it from her.

Yet Alec had rarely mislaid anything. He had always tidied his desk himself at the end of the day, sorting out the correspondence he had received, filing the personal letters himself, putting the business letters in a pile to be filed later by her in the big filing cabinet.

She knew he had kept the few personal letters he had received in a locked box in his room. It was still there and several times she had thought she should go through it since he had died. But an innate dislike of prying into other people's privacy had kept her from unlocking the box. She should really open it, though, because there might be something in it of importance. *The letter Neil had left for her, perhaps?*

Oh, no. That was just wishful thinking. The letter was lost, gone for ever, swept away. Springing to her feet, she left the study and returned to the factor's house. The postman had been and there was a pile of bills on the doormat.

Kirsty picked them up and flicked through them quickly. Electricity, the half-yearly rates, a note from the Inland Revenue, and a letter from Dawson, Pettigrew and Tanner, family solicitors.

Going into the kitchen, she dropped the bills on the table and ripped open the letter from the solicitors. The letter was very short and to the point. It asked her to meet with a Mr Douglas Pettigrew at his office in Fort William at her earliest convenience to discuss the will of the late Sir Alec Whyte.

Chewing her lower lip, Kirsty re-read the note, wondering what lay behind the uncommunicative statement. Why should she discuss Alec's will with another lawyer? As far as she was concerned the will was quite straightforward. Alec had left everything to her. It was a proper legal document and had been drawn up with the help of Alec's own lawyer, Mr Robert Rankin, of Tweedie, Rankin and Peat, Glasgow.

She pushed the note back into its envelope, made herself some lunch and then went to the office. It was a good day to catch up on the correspondence and involving herself in estate work would as usual take her mind off personal problems. First of all she phoned the office of Dawson, Pettigrew and Tanner and made an appointment to see Mr Douglas Pettigrew, the next day. Then, sitting down, she pulled the rack where the letters she had received recently had piled up and began to go through them.

Two hours later she leaned back in her chair and stretched her arms. It was time to stop and do something else. Going to the window, she looked out. The rain had stopped and the clouds were clearing. Patches of blue sky showed. She would have her tea and then walk around the estate and call in to see some of the farmers as she usually did on a fine evening.

The sun had long been set and the moon was rising, peering above the summit of Cairn Rua when she walked up the slope to the dark and silent Lodge. As always the long walk had soothed her. She felt at peace with her world to-night and knew she would sleep well.

Before turning into the courtyard she paused to look down at the ghostly glimmer of the loch. Out of habit her glance lifted to the dark slopes of Cairn Rua and her heart skipped a beat. Narrowing her eyes, she stared intently. No, it wasn't her imagination. A yellow gleam of light twinkled through the bushes that surrounded the cottage. Someone was there. Neil? Had he come back? Or had someone broken in?

Almost before she realised it Kirsty was running down the road, her rubber boots clumping on the surface. Along the lochside road she hurried, her glance still held by the twinkle of light until it disappeared as she approached the far side of the loch and the cottage was hidden by the curve of the lower slopes of the hill.

Up the rough gravel road she walked, her speed slowing down as she reached the top of it. Breathless, she paused at the opening in the dry-stone wall, staring at the light slanting from the window and hearing the loud clamour of her heart in the soft still silence of the night.

Cautiously she approached the window. It was set low enough for her to see inside the living room. At the plain wooden table Neil was sitting. There was a sketch pad in front of him and a piece of charcoal between his fingers. But he wasn't sketching. His head supported by his left hand, his left elbow resting on the table, staring at the pad of paper as if thinking.

Relieved that it was he who was in the house and not an intruder, Kirsty stepped back from the window. She stepped on one of the stones which formed the edge of the flower bed under the window. Her ankle twisted and she lost balance. The large stone clattered against another stone, and she fell, knocking other stones together. The sound of them seemed unnaturally loud in that very quiet place.

Although she was jolted Kirsty didn't cry out. She gritted her teeth together against the pain that shot up through her ankle, the same one she had sprained four years ago. Staying in a crouching position close to the ground, she waited, hoping that Neil hadn't heard the rattle of stones when she had fallen.

She hoped in vain. The door opened, and yellow light shafted across the grass, missing her by inches. Neil's figure loomed darkly in the doorway.

'Who's there?' he demanded sharply, and when he didn't get an answer he stepped out and looked around the garden. He saw her and came towards her. Quickly he crouched before her. 'Kirsty!' Surprise lilted through his voice. 'What the hell are you doing here?'

'I saw the light from the other side. I thought someone might have broken into the cottage, so I came to look. I tripped over and fell.' She began to get to her feet. Neil straightened up too.

'Why did you think someone might have broken in?' he asked.

'I knew you'd gone away,' she replied. Tentatively she put her left foot to the ground. Pain shot through her ankle and she couldn't help gasping. 'Oh, dear,' she muttered. Faintness came over her and she swayed. 'I think I've hurt my ankle again.'

'Then you'd better come in and let me look at it . . . *again*,' he said dryly, and moving to her side put an arm about her waist.

'No, it's all right. It'll be all right,' She began to limp towards the opening in the wall. 'I'll go home now. Goodnight,'

'Kirsty, stop being so bloody stubborn,' he growled taking hold of her arm. 'You known damn well you can't walk back to the Lodge. I'll drive you there. But first come inside for a few moments, catch your breath.'

His mood wasn't of the best, she could tell by the abrasive note in his voice. Maybe it hadn't worked out with Camille the way he had hoped and that was why he had come back. Perhaps the flighty French girl had hurt his feelings, had found that he was not to her liking after all, had left him and skipped back to Paris.

'No, I. . . .' she began, and put her left foot to the ground again. The pain was worse. Everything whirled about her. Her arms went out instinctively towards him to hold on to him as the only substantial support she could find and she fainted.

The faint didn't last long. She came to as Neil was carrying her through the doorway into the living room of the cottage.

'I'm sorry,' she mumbled into the soft Shetland wool of his sweater. 'I've never fainted before. I didn't mean to. I ... what I'm trying to say is that I didn't faint deliberately.'

'No one ever does,' he remarked as he set her down in the big ladderbacked chair by the hearth. He pushed her back against the cushion which was tied to the rungs and looked down at her with narrowed assessing eyes. 'I'll get you a drink of water,' he said curtly. 'Then I'll look at your ankle.'

'Neil, I don't want you to think I fainted just so you would bring me in here,' she said urgently, leaning towards him.

'But I don't think that,' he retorted. 'You fainted because the pain in your ankle got to you. It's not unusual. Now sit back and relax, I'll be back in a minute.'

He stepped through an open doorway at the back of the room into the small kitchenette. Kirsty leaned back with a sigh and looked around the room. It hadn't changed much in four years. The furniture was the same simple and sturdy, the floor was still covered by woven, brightly coloured rugs. The same books stood on the bookshelves by the hearth. The only different things were the curtains at the window and the electric light. Hamish Taggart had looked after the cottage well in the absence of its owner and it had been let each summer, until now, to families who liked to take a holiday in a Highland croft.

'Here you are,' Neil handed her a glass of water. Hooking a foot under a small three-legged stool, he dragged it over and sat down on it in front of her. 'Now for your boot. This will probably hurt, Kirsty. Ready?'

She nodded. She set the glass of water down on the high stone curb of the hearth and gripped the arms of the chair. Holding the heel and toe of her wellington boot, Neil slowly eased it from her foot. There was more pain, but it wasn't sharp and she didn't feel faint again. Next Neil peeled the short sock from her foot and with their heads almost touching they both peered at her ankle. Neil stroked it with his forefinger and Kirsty shuddered, not with pain, but because he had touched her.

He looked up right into her eyes. Their faces were so closed they could have kissed easily. His glance drifted down to her mouth and his lips parted. Kirsty drew back to lean against the cushion again and closed her eyes. Her heart was pounding and her throat felt dry.

'Feeling faint again?' he mocked, and she opened her eyes quickly. He was still sitting before her, his elbows on his knees, his chin in his hands, and was watching her sardonically, the lines from his nostrils to the corners of his mouth very pronounced, his eyes half-closed.

She nodded again and reaching for the glass of water picked it up and sipped from it.

'The sprain isn't bad,' he said. 'Want me to bandage it for you?'

'No, thank you,' she said quickly. Bandaging would mean him touching her again. 'I'll do it myself when I get home.' She licked her lips, sat up straight and asked coolly, 'Why have you come back?'

His eyebrows tilted and he gave her a glance of amused surprise.

'Why shouldn't I come back? This is my place. I like being here and I intend to stay here for the rest of the summer.' His eyes narrowed again. 'Did you think I'd returned to New York?'

'I didn't know what to think,' she murmured, avoiding his penetrating stare and looking down at the half-full glass in her hands. 'Why did you go away with Camille?' she forced herself to ask.

There was a short tense silence. When he didn't answer Kirsty looked at him. He was still staring at her with narrowed eyes.

'I didn't go away with Camille,' he said at last. 'She went away with me.'

He rose to his feet and went over to the dresser with the willow pattern plates on its shelves. Opening the bottom cupboard, he took out a bottle and two glasses. He picked them up and came back to sit on the stool, handing her one of the glasses. 'Here, this might help you to relax a bit,' he said. 'Thaw you out.'

'I'm not cold,' she retorted, but took the glass from him and placed the glass of water back on the hearth curb.

'You may not feel cold, but your attitude is, to say the least . . . frigid,' he replied nastily, and drank half his whisky.

'That's because I'm not young and innocent or easily deceived and seduced any more by a man experienced in romancing women,' she retaliated forcefully. 'I'm not like Camille.'

'You can say that again,' he jibed, his eyes blazing with anger, and tossed off the rest of his whisky. He stood up again, stalked over to the dresser and sloshed more whisky into his glass. He didn't come back to the stool but leaned his hips against the dresser. Above the glass as he raised it to his lips his eyes glittered at her, hard and bright. 'Camille had more *savoir-faire* than you ever had or ever will have. She knows what to do to get what she wants. You've never known what it is you want and you've no idea how to get it.'

'Oh.' Kirsty put the glass of whisky which she had hardly tasted down beside the glass of water and with her hands on the arms of the chair she pushed herself upright to stand up, the bare toes of her injured foot resting only lightly on the floor. 'If you're going to be rude I'm leaving,' she retorted furiously.

'You'll have to put your boot on first,' Neil said practically, setting down his glass and coming back to her. 'And to do that you'll have to sit down again.' She didn't move but glared at him defiantly. Standing close to her with his hands on his hips he leaned towards her. 'Sit down, Kirsty. You're not going anywhere. You're staying here.'

'No, I'm not—I'm going home. Oh, what are you doing? Neil Dysart, bring that boot and sock back here at once!' she demanded.

He had picked up her footwear and had gone over to the door. He opened the door and threw the boot and the sock outside. Then he shut the door, turned the key in the lock and pushed the two bolts home. He took the key out of the lock and put it in a blue and white jug on the top shelf of the dresser, then turned to her, his eyes dancing with devilry.

'We're behind a locked door again, Kirsty,' he drawled mockingly.

'You're drunk,' she accused, giving him a scornful glance.

'On two whiskies? Hardly. A little less inhibited than usual, perhaps, but not drunk.' He came back to her and putting a hand against her shoulder he pushed. Kirsty lost her balance and sat down. Immediately Neil sat on the stool, shifting it closer. Resting his arms across her knees, he leaned forward and looked into her eyes. 'When you're angry they change colour,' he whispered. 'They become a deep, almost purple blue, the colour of the loch on a fine day, and looking into them I feel I could drown willingly in them.'

'Stop it, stop it,' she whispered. She put her hands against her cheeks and shook her head. 'Oh, I don't know how you can do it!'

'Do what?' he queried, leaning closer, his breath feathering her lips.

'Try to make love to me when you've been with her.'

'With whom?'

'With Camille.'

'I haven't been with Camille.'

'Yes, you have.' She sat back in the chair as far away as possible. 'You said yourself she went away with you. And in the note she left for Hussein she said she'd gone with you.'

'Did she?' His eyebrows tilted derisively. 'And how did his Excellency react to that?'

'He was very upset. You see, he'd invited her here with her parents so he could propose marriage to her.'

'I know. Camille told me.'

'You knew? Then why did you take her away with you?' she exclaimed. 'Oh, you're even more despicable than I'd believed!'

'Am I?' His eyes glinted dangerously. 'What makes you say that?'

'You must have known, too, that Hussein couldn't ask her to marry him once she'd been with another man.'

'Now, hold on,' he rebuked her sharply. 'Just what do you mean by her having been with another man?'

'She went away with you somewhere yesterday and . . . and . . . well, you and she stayed the night together,' she said uncertainly.

'That's what I thought you meant,' he said, his lips thinning.

'And before she went away with you you did all you could to entice her away. You took her to a dance in the village. You met her in secret and then you eloped with her.'

'I admit to taking her to the village dance,' he retorted. 'I was sorry for her that evening at dinner.' She'd told me she was fed up with staying at the Lodge. She also told me she was sick and tired of waiting for Hussein to propose and seeing him making eyes at you and hanging on every word you said to him.' His upper lip lifted in a sneer and his glance raked her. 'I felt a bit sick myself watching him make up to you and seeing you lap up the attention he gave you. Everyone noticed how besotted he was with you and how you were encouraging him.'

'I did not encourage Hussein!' she flared.

'No?' Neil laughed jeeringly. 'Yet you told me yourself you might marry him . . . for his money.'

'But that was before I knew he was thinking of marrying Camille,' she retorted. 'Once I knew that he was thinking of marrying her I put the idea right out of my head. And I could never do what you did. I could never stoop to do what you did, knowing what you did. Oh, Neil, why did you elope with her? And where is she now? What have you done with her?'

He drew his breath in with a sharp hissing noise as if he had reached the end of his patience.

'More than any other woman I know you have the ability to enrage me,' he said between taut lips. 'Firstly I did not *elope* with Camille. All I did was drive her to Glasgow.'

'Why?'

'When she knew I was going there yesterday she asked me if she could go with me because she wanted to fly to London from there. She said she couldn't stand staying at Balmore any longer and would I help her get away. I agreed because, as I've said, I was sorry for her. I dropped her off in the city where I knew she could get a bus to the airport. I haven't seen her since.'

'Then you didn't stay the night with her,' she mumbled.

'I didn't stay the night with her,' he repeated slowly and with mocking emphasis on every word. 'I've never been particularly attracted to blondes and I found her juvenile chatter about the great time she's going to have once she's the wife of Sheikh al Dukar extremely irritating. She's determined to marry Hussein, you know.'

'No, I don't know. If she's so keen to marry him she shouldn't have gone away with you.'

'She was hoping to draw his attention away from you and back to her, can't you see that? And she told me she intended to phone her parents as soon as she got to London to let them know where she was. Did she?'

'Someone phoned them,' she replied. While he had been explaining he had drawn back from her and she used the opportunity to rise to her feet again. At once he sprang to his feet.

'Where are you going?' he demanded.

'Back to Balmore ... if you would kindly unlock the door and let me have my sock and boot,' she said tartly.

'Is the Sheikh still there?'

'No. He left this morning to go and look for Camille. He's not coming back,' she replied woodenly.

'Are you sure he isn't?'

'Quite sure. Thanks to Camille and to you I've lost a good tenant and a potential buyer for Balmore.'

'Good. I'm glad. It was worth behaving despicably with Camille, as you call it, to get rid of him.'

'You mean you. . . .' Kirsty broke off to stare at him. Mischief and mockery sparkled in his eyes. 'Oh, you've done nothing else but cause trouble since you came back!' she seethed. 'First you rescued the poachers, then you encouraged Camille to run away, to say nothing of how you made me appear to Hussein's uncle by keeping me with you behind a locked door in the turret for an hour.'

'You can blame Ahmed for that,' he replied. 'He did the tale-telling to his boss.'

'But you did ask me to go up to the turret room with you.'

'Only because I wanted to make love to you,' he said softly, coming closer to her and putting his hands on her shoulders. 'As I do now.'

'No, I don't want you to. I. . . .'

His lips covered hers, smothering the rest of what she had been going to say. His arms went around her to prevent her from escaping. She tried not to respond, but the movement of his lips against hers was both seductive and forceful. Her lips parted and her body went slack against his.

Briefly he lifted his lips from hers so he could whisper tauntingly.

'Do you still dare to say you don't want to make

love with me? Your lips and your body are telling me a different story.

Thick lashes shadowed his eyes and his lips curved into the tender loving smile she had come to know so well in this same room four years ago. Her heart leapt in response and as he loosened her hair from its topknot so that it swirled down about her shoulders he kissed her again, a demanding, bruising kiss that made her head whirl. All her misgivings were swept away by the passion which flooded through her in response to that kiss. Her arms went around him, her fingers caressed his neck and tangled in his hair. It was as if they had never been parted; as if the past four years had never been.

'Kirsty, stay here tonight. Sleep with me.'

His voice was deep and a little shaken as his lips moved among the silky fragrance of her hair where it lay against her temple and his arms still held her closely. Through his clothing and hers she could feel the thrust and throb of his desire.

But his words shocked her back to the reality of the situation. Four years ago when he had made the same suggestion she had agreed willingly. Now everything was different. The abrupt manner of his leaving, his silence for four years had changed her from an impulsive girl, willing to give herself in love, into a cautious woman determined to protect herself from hurt.

She tried to pull free of him, but his hands slid down to her waist and tightened. They seemed to her to be unbelievably strong. So did he. He was a strong, ruthless man who was determined to take what he wanted.

'I can't,' she whispered. 'I can't stay the night with you, nor sleep with you.'

'Why not?' Laughter lilted in his voice and he tried to draw her towards him, but she remained stiff and unyielding. 'I know you want to stay as much as I want you to stay,' he continued softly and coaxingly. 'We've been apart for so long, let other people come between us, but now we're together again all the old hungers have awakened.' He managed to pull her closer, his arms sliding around her in a warm embrace, and pressed his cheek against her head. 'I ache for you, Kirsty,' he whispered. 'Deep inside I hurt for you, ever since we met over a week ago on the cliff above the big pool. God knows when I came back to Balmore I didn't expect this to happen to me ... to us ... but it has, and I'm going to ask you again. Please stay here, tonight.'

'No, no, I can't!' Fear of her own responses gave her the strength to resist. She twisted free of his embrace and limped towards the door.

'I could easily make you stay,' he threatened, moving after her.

'I doubt it would give you much pleasure if you did, if you made me stay and sleep with you against my will,' she retorted coolly, her head up, her eyes returning his challenging gaze steadily. She knew only too well how easy he would find persuading her to stay once he touched her again. 'Please, Neil, don't shame yourself or me by doing something we'll both regret later,' she continued. 'Please accept my refusal. I can't stay with you. I ... I don't trust you.'

He was jolted, she could see. His head jerked back as if she had hit him again. For a moment empathy with his pain tempted her to relent, to take back what she had said, to fling her arms about him and offer herself and her love to him unconditionally, regardless of consequences. But she kept thinking of his wife, and she knew that if she gave into her own passionate desires to stay the night with him she would never be able to live with herself comfortably again.

'I'd like to go home now,' she said, turning away and going towards the door. The need to be alone with her misery was becoming overwhelming. She had to get away from him before she broke down and wept for the love they had once known and might have known again if she could have changed her values.

'All right.' He spoke coldly and a little wearily. Behind her Kirsty heard him move to the dresser, take down the jug where he had put the key. Soon he was unbolting and unlocking the door. He stepped outside and returned with her boot and sock. While she put them on he went out again to start his car.

They sat side by side in the front of the Jaguar. Sitting bolt upright and staring straight ahead, Kirsty watched the pale moonlit trunks of trees flit by as the car went along the lochside road. The silence was heavy with unspoken thoughts and feelings. It was so different from the time Neil had driven her back to the Lodge the night they had first met; when he had kept stopping the car at the roadside to turn to her and take her in his arms; when a ten-minute drive had taken over an hour.

Outside the factor's house he said politely without looking at her.

'Would you like me to help you into the house?'

'No, thank you. I can manage.' She opened the door and stepped out, careful not to put weight on her right foot. She glanced inside the car before she closed the door. 'Thank you for bringing me home,' she said.

She slammed the door closed and limped towards the house as fast as she could. Behind her the car reversed and left the courtyard swiftly, with a squeal of tyres. High up in the dark blue, star-pricked sky the full moon seemed to grin mockingly.

CHAPTER SEVEN

PEARL grey mist was peeling back from the waters of Loch Linnhe, the long sea-loch which delves almost into the middle of the Highlands, when Kirsty drove into Fort William next morning.

For her the night had been long and tormented by the demons of churned-up emotions and physical yearnings, and she had been glad when daybreak had come so that she could get ready to visit Dawson, Pettigrew and Tanner. She had dressed in a suit made from fine burgundy-coloured wool and with it she wore a white silk blouse frilled at the neckline, its soft femininity contrasting with the severe tailoring of the suit.

In Fort William she parked the car near the pier and walked back to the main street to the tall white buildings where the lawyer's offices were located.

'Thank you for coming here today, Lady Whyte,' said Douglas Pettigrew, after she had been shown into his room by a secretary. He was a fresh-faced, red-haired man of about thirty-five or six and he looked as if he would have been much more at home on the farm driving a tractor than sitting behind a desk. 'Please sit down.' He brought a chair forward, then went round to the other side of the desk to wait until Kirsty had sat down before taking his seat in a black leather swivel chair.

He leaned forward, placed his arms on the desk and clasped his hands together. His grey eyes stared at her intently.

'To tell the truth I'm not sure where to begin,' he admitted. 'The whole business is so complicated.'

'I really don't understand why you have to discuss my late husband's will with me,' said Kirsty coolly. 'It's before probate at the moment and seemed to be taking a long time to be approved.'

'Probate does take a long time,' he replied. 'Especially if there is some doubt about the will's legality.' He looked down at the desk, frowned, then looked at her again. 'Lady Whyte, you're not going to like what I have to tell you, but I can think of no other way than to put it bluntly.'

'Then please be blunt,' she replied with a slight impish grin. 'I'm really quite tough, you know.'

'Well, here goes. Sir Alec Whyte had no right to leave Balmore to you, because he was never the owner of the estate,' he said.

'But . . . but his father, Sir Ian Whyte, left it to Alec in his will,' exclaimed Kirsty, here eyes opening wide.

'No, he didn't. Sir Ian only left the estate to Sir Alec *in trust*. That means that Alec was allowed to live there and look after the estate while he was alive. Once Sir Alec died the property was to pass to Sir Ian's younger son, Mr Neil Dysart-Whyte, who would also assume the title.'

Kirsty didn't move, but it seemed to her that all sorts of strange sounds twanged and sizzled in her head.

'Go on, please,' she said rather weakly.

'You've heard of Mr Dysart-Whyte, perhaps?' he queried.

'I know a Neil Dysart. He's a surgeon and he's the tenant of a croft on the estate. I know, also, that he is Sir Ian Whyte's illegitimate son,' she said stiffly.

'Er, yes. Just so. Well now.' Douglas Pettigrew rubbed his jaw, and the bristles of his beard rustled. He shuffled some papers on his desk, found the one he wanted and leaning back in his chair studied it.

'It is true that Mr Dysart-Whyte was born out of wedlock,' he announced. 'However, just before he died Sir Ian married Morag Dysart and had the birth of their son legitimatised.'

'Oh. Can that be done?' exclaimed Kirsty.

'It can be done and was done. My father, who was legal adviser to Sir Ian, arranged it, and here is the proof.' He leaned across the desk to hand her the paper. She took it.

'Then why doesn't Neil Dysart use the name Whyte?' she asked.

'You would have to ask him that yourself,' he replied. 'I would suspect that by the time he could use it legally he was already established in his profession as a surgeon and preferred to continue to use the name he was known by. He told me the other day when he was here that he didn't know he was Sir Ian's son until four years ago. His mother told him just before she died.'

'Neil was here, the other day?' Kirsty gasped.

'Yes. You see. . . .' Douglas Pettigrew broke off

and sighed. 'But I'm jumping ahead of myself. To go back to Sir Ian. After he had legitimatised his second son's birth he made his will.' He picked up another document. 'This is it.' He handed it over to her. 'If you read it you will see very clearly that he left the estate of Balmore *in trust* only to his *adopted* son Alec William Whyte for as long as he lived. On Alec's death the title and the property would be passed on, as usual in the Whyte family, to his own eldest son, Neil Allan Dysart-Whyte, to whom he would have willed everything directly if Sir Alec had not existed.'

Kirsty stared down at the printed words in front of her, searching for the word *adopted*. It wasn't hard to find because it had been underlined.

'I didn't know Sir Alec had been adopted. He didn't tell me,' she murmured, putting the document down on the desk.

'Apparently Sir Alec's first wife, Constance, tried several times to have a child but miscarried. So a baby was adopted,' explained the lawyer. 'We have the adoption papers here. Again my father was the lawyer involved.' Documents rustled as he handed them to her.

Kirsty studied them, her brain seeming to burst with bewilderment.

'But if your father was Sir Ian's legal adviser why did he let my husband, Sir Alec, make a will leaving the estate to me?' she asked at last.

'He was not consulted by Sir Alec on the matter of a will or on anything else legal,' said Douglas Pettigrew dryly. 'After Sir Ian's death

Sir Alec broke all connection with this firm, turned all his business over to a firm of lawyers in Glasgow.' His lips turned a downward curve. 'It seems that Sir Alec did not like anyone to remind him that he had been adopted or that Balmore was not legally his, and he knew that my father would never agree to draw up a will leaving the property to you because my father knew about the other will.'

'Then why haven't you told me before now?' demanded Kirsty. 'Why have you taken so long, nearly five months, to inform me?'

'We wanted to find Mr Neil Dysart-Whyte first.' Douglas Pettigrew had the grace to look embarrassed. 'We had to make sure he was alive. It took a while for our letter to reach him. You see, he had moved away from New York and hadn't told Sir Alec of his whereabouts. When he didn't reply immediately we were thinking of writing to him again, but fortunately he arrived here three weeks ago. He had come in answer to our letter, he said, and he was very surprised by what we had to tell him. He had no idea that his father had named him to be heir to the estate after the death of Sir Alec.'

'So what should I do now?' Kirsty was aware of a lightness, as if a burden had been lifted suddenly from her shoulders. She was no longer responsible for Balmore. She didn't have to worry any more about letting it to a tenant or selling it. It wasn't hers to worry about. It was Neil's.

'Now, that is exactly why I asked you to come and see me,' said Mr Pettigrew. 'As the executor of of Sir Ian's will my father has the right to contest the validity of Sir Alec's will before the probate court. Naturally we have consulted with Mr Dysart-Whyte and asked him if he wished to contest Sir Alec's will. He said he would think about it and let us know. In the meantime we thought we should get in touch with you and ask you if you want to go ahead and try to have Sir Alec's will proved.'

'Do I have to give you an answer straight away?' asked Kirsty.

'No, of course not. I realise this must be something of a shock to you and that you must have time to consider the situation. I believe you've let the estate for six months to a tenant.'

'Oh, he's left and he won't be coming back.' Kirsty chewed at her lower lip. 'If . . . if I decide to withdraw Sir Alec's will and Mr Dysart inherits the estate does he become responsible for the mortgage?'

'He does. It isn't a personal debt. You are responsible as Sir Alec's wife only for his personal debts. Perhaps I should also warn you that if you don't withdraw Sir Alec's will you could become involved in an expensive and lengthy lawsuit.' Douglas Pettigrew rose to his feet and Kirsty stood up too, realising that the interview was at an end because he had other clients to see.

'Thank you for your advice,' she said. 'I . . . I'll let you know soon, probably tomorrow, what I'm going to do.'

'Don't be too hasty now,' he said pleasantly, opening the door for her. 'Good morning, Lady Whyte.'

Kirsty walked back to the pier. Sunlight dazzled the water of the loch. Seagulls and terns soared and glided above the few fishing boats which had tied up. Two touring buses had arrived and their passengers, mostly elderly men and women, exchanged jokes and remarks as they gathered together in friendly groups before setting off to explore the old town.

A longing to take off on holiday, to drive away, far away from Balmore and its problems, surged through Kirsty as she unlocked the door of the car. She could do that now. Instead of going north she could drive south, go to Edinburgh to see Duncan and his family, go to Glasgow to see her parents. She could go and never come back, start a new life for herself. She was free, a liberated woman, bound to no one but herself.

But she was also bound to her own emotions and her own sense of values, she thought with a sigh, as she slid behind the steering wheel. She couldn't leave Balmore yet. She couldn't leave until she had decided to relinquish her claim to the estate by withdrawing Alec's will from probate. She couldn't leave until she had seen Neil again and had asked him why he hadn't told her he knew about his father's will.

She started the car and drove back to the main street, automatically turning left and taking the road north. Now that she knew about Sir Ian's will she could make sense of Neil's behaviour the day they had met on the bluff above the big pool. She could understand now why he hadn't liked the idea of Balmore being sold to Hussein.

Then why hadn't he told her he knew Balmore was his? And why hadn't Alec told her Balmore wasn't his? All the way back to the Lodge she tussled with the conundrum, and was no closer to having solved it when she reached the parting of the ways where the road turned to curve round the head of the loch or sloped up the hill to the big house. Stopping the car, she looked over at Cairn Rua. Purple and brown, splashed with patches of bright green, its rocky red summit glowing in the sunlight, it looked inviting, a good place to spend a summer's afternoon, walking and perhaps lazing in the depths of the heather.

On impulse Kirsty drove beside the loch. She would go and see Neil again and have it out with him, once and for all. The small car had trouble getting up the steep hill to the cottage, but eventually she was there, and she stopped it on the level sward of grass.

The cottage door was closed. No one sat in front of it on an old deckchair and the Jaguar wasn't parked beside the house. Neil wasn't there.

At the Lodge she went straight to the big kitchen where she knew Hamish would be having his midday meal with Mary.

'Any dinner for me, Mary?' she asked when she walked in.

'Aye, if you like mince and tatties, there is,' replied the housekeeper, getting to her feet and going over to the cooker. 'Sit yourself down.'

'I was over at the croft on Cairn Rua, looking for Neil Dysart,' Kirsty said to Hamish. 'Have you seen him lately?'

'Aye—this morning. He's away to Skye for a few days, to do some rock climbing in the Cuillins. He says he'll be back on Friday,' replied Hamish in his slow way.

'Oh, I see. Thank you.' Kirsty forced herself to smile as Mary set a plate of vegetables in front of her.

She ate in silence, thinking about Neil. He hadn't hesitated to go away for a change of scene. He hadn't let his emotions or his sense of values come between him and doing what he wanted to do. But then he never had. What he wanted had always come first with him. And if he couldn't get what he wanted, as he hadn't been able to last night when he had wanted her, he just turned his back and went away.

'I'll be in Sir Alec's bedroom this afternoon, if you need me for anything,' she announced as she finished eating and laid her knife and fork down on the plate. 'There's a box of his papers in there that I've been intending to go through before I go away.'

Both Mary and Hamish looked up sharply— the first time either of them had ever reacted quickly to anything she had ever said, she thought sardonically.

'Did you say you're going away?' said Mary.

'Yes. I've decided to have a wee holiday.'

'Och, now I'm thinking that's a good idea, so it is,' said Mary, nodding. 'How long will you be gone?'

'I'm not sure. I'll write to you and tell you when to expect me back. I'll be leaving early in the morning. I'll arrange for all the mail to be delivered to a lawyer's office in Fort William while I'm away. A Mr Douglas Pettigrew will look after all the business to do with the estate.' Kirsty noticed Hamish and Mary exchange knowing glances and knew they had recognised the name Pettigrew. 'All right?' she said enquiringly.

'Aye, that's fine, just fine,' murmured Hamish, and got on with the process of lighting his pipe.

Alec's bedroom was on the ground floor next to the study. It wasn't very big and Kirsty knew that at one time it had been a room where breakfast had been served. Since it faced east it received none of the afternoon sunshine and with its plain dark furniture and curtains it seemed drab and dull that day.

The box where he had stored his personal letters was in the bottom of the wardrobe. It was about four feet long, two feet wide and about a foot deep. It was made from teak and had an intricate design carved on its lid. It was heavy and Kirsty had a struggle to lift it out. The key was on a ring on which Alec had also kept the keys to his desk and filing cabinets and which he had kept on his person at all times. Now that ring was in one of the drawers of the desk, so she went into the study to get it.

The box opened easily and her eyes widened with surprise when she saw it was full of books, all of them bound in black and all of them the same size. Picking up one of them, she found the date of a year printed on it in gold letters and underneath the date the words, Daily Journal. She opened the book and flicked over pages. Most of them were filled with Alec's rather crabbed writing. The books were his diaries which he had kept, judging by the dates on them, for nearly forty years, from the year in which he had turned nineteen until a year before his death when the creeping paralysis had taken away the strength from his hands and had made it impossible for him to write.

Kirsty took all the books out of the box, hoping to find letters stored underneath them. But there were only a few letters, and not one of them was the one she was looking for. She put them back and began to place the diaries on top of them one by one, glancing through each briefly, discovering as she did Alec's bitterness and unhappiness when Morag Dysart had showed her preference for his father; his obsessive love for Balmore and his bitter hatred of Neil.

Skipping over several years, she looked for and found the diary for the year she had first come to work for Alec and read about his reaction to her. She flicked over pages to the day Neil had left Balmore.

'Neil Dysart had the nerve to come and see me again today. He wanted to see Christina to tell her he has to go to New York. It seems he has a chance to work with a great American orthopaedic surgeon. I saw an opportunity to be rid of him. I encouraged him to go. He insisted stubbornly on seeing Christina. He said he wanted to ask her to marry him, and I lied to him. I told him how fickle she is. He was upset but still steadfast. I

told him she is going to marry me, but he didn't
believe me. He asked if he could leave a letter for
her, and I agreed. After he had gone I opened the
letter. There was a proposal of marriage in it. I
burned it.'

Kirsty turned the page and read his account of
his discussion with her about Neil.

'I had to lie to Christina too. I told her Neil is
like his father, lacking in morals where women
are concerned. She took it well. I admire her.
She's clever too—she could help me restore
Balmore. When she's got over Neil I'll ask her to
marry me. If only I could raise some money. The
annuity Father left me is not enough to do what I
want to do. If only he hadn't been so damned
extravagant.'

Kirsty closed the diary and sat for a while on
the edge of the bed thinking about Alec and how
with a few words he had been able to destroy her
trust in Neil and Neil's trust in her. She put the
diary in the box and picked up the one for the
year Alec had made his will. Soon she was reading
about that.

'I cannot bear to think of my beloved Balmore
being inherited by the son of that womaniser who
calls himself my father. Today I have made a will
leaving everything to my dear Kirsty. God knows
she deserves the place, she has worked so hard to
improve it. I've engaged another lawyer to help
me draw up the will. Now I hope and pray it will
not be contested by that old fool Pettigrew.'

Kirsty returned all the diaries to the box and
locked it up. She carried it back to the wardrobe

and left the bedroom. Now she knew what to do. She went back to the factor's house and began to make preparations for her departure the next day.

She wrote to Robert Rankin, Alec's lawyer, and asked him to withdraw Alec's will from probate because she had realised, after reading his diaries, that the balance of her late husband's mind had been disturbed when he had made the will, and she told him to contact Douglas Pettigrew for further information. Then she wrote to Douglas Pettigrew telling him what she had done. Then she wrote to Neil, telling him why she had left Balmore. The first two letters she intended to post; the letter to Neil she left on the desk in the factor's office.

She slept well that night and was up early the next day. After breakfast she carried her suitcases out to the car. It was another misty morning with promise of a warm sunny day. As she drove out of the yard she kept her glance on the road, determined not to look at the view of the loch in case she was tempted to stay. She refused to be held back by sentiment any more. The road before her led into the future, her future, and she had chosen to go forward alone.

In Balvaig she stopped at Jessie's house. Her friend was having her breakfast.

'I've decided to take your advice. I'm going away for a holiday,' said Kirsty. 'The trouble is I don't know where to go. I'd thought of visiting Duncan or my parents, but I've deciced I want to be on my own for a while in a place where nobody knows me.'

'My cousin and her husband run a small private hotel in Galloway, near a little fishing village.' Jessie's glance was bright and shrewd. 'I don't suppose you're too flush with funds and their terms are fairly moderate. If you like I could telephone them for you, tell them you're on the way and you're a friend of mine.'

'I'd be glad if you would. How long do you think it will take me to get there?'

'You should be there in time for dinner this evening. I'll get you a map book and show you exactly where it is.'

Later that afternoon Kirsty stopped her car outside the front door of an imposing house built of blocks of grey granite which stood on a hillside above the small village of Kirkford. Getting out of the car, she stretched and looked about her.

Over the slate roofs and chimneypots of the houses below the hill, she could see the estuary of the river. The tide was in and the blue water was ruffled by a breeze. Several small sailing boats all going the same way, the white triangles of their sails taut and shining, heeled over. They were presumably taking part in a race and were aiming for a buoy which she could just see bobbing on the waves where the estuary flowed into the sea.

She looked back at the house. It looked sedate yet well cared for, a quiet place where she could rest and collect her thoughts together. She went up the few steps, opened the vestibule door and stepped into the hallway. On the small reception desk there was a bell. She pressed it and in a few moments a woman a little older than Jessie appeared.

'I'm Kirsty Whyte. My friend Jessie phoned you and reserved a room for me,' said Kirsty.

'I'm pleased to meet you. I'm Maude Fimlay,' said the other woman, with a cheerful smile. 'And the room is all ready. It's a good thing Jessie phoned, because it was the last vacant room and we've had lots of enquiries this afternoon. The fine weather has brought people on holiday. Now if you would just be signing the register, I'll take you up to your room. Have you ever been to Galloway before?'

CHAPTER EIGHT

FOUR days later, dressed in her tartan pants and wearing a Fair Isle sweater patterned in green and white, Kirsty strode along the firm white sand of a broad beach. Although the day was sunny the wind was strong and grey clouds scurried before it across a sky of pale blue.

Enjoying the sting of salt spray on her cheeks and the roar and hiss of the waves as they advanced and retreated, she walked right to the end of the beach. It was the last day of her stay in Kirkford. Tomorrow she would have to leave because she couldn't afford to stay any longer. Yet she was still undecided about what to do. Should she return to Balmore? Or should she go to her parents' home in Glasgow and start looking for a job?

When she had walked far enough she returned to the hotel and went up to her room. After washing she changed into the blue dress she had worn so often for social occasions at Balmore, brushed her hair and coiled it neatly, then went downstairs to the dining room for dinner, taking her seat at a small table near the window.

She was studying the menu when a voice she recognised only too well said,

'I'd like to sit here, if the lady doesn't object.'

Kirsty looked up slowly. Above the edge of the menu she saw a jacket made from fine greenish

174

tweed. She looked higher and saw a crisp cream shirt and a dark green tie. Even higher she met the cool glance of amber-brown eyes set between short thick lashes. Above them a lock of reddish-brown hair slid forward across a high forehead.

'Do you mind if I sit here?' Neil asked suavely. 'The waitress would like to know.'

Kirsty glanced at the waitress, who was staring at her curiously.

'No, not at all.' She made an effort to appear as suave and cool as he was. 'Please sit down.'

He sat opposite to her, the waitress offered him a menu and departed.

'I found out where you were staying from your friend Jessie,' he said in a pleasant conversational tone. 'Mary Taggart suggested she might know where you'd gone for your holiday.' He looked up from the menu and his eyes were coldly critical. 'Why the hell did you run away, Kirsty?' he rapped.

'I didn't run away, I just left. I decided I needed a change like you did. You went to Skye. I came here,' she retorted, and looked down at her menu again.

'But you don't intend to go back to Balmore,' he accused softly. 'Mary says you took everything you own with you. You left nothing behind.'

She was saved from having to reply by the return of the waitress, who had brought knives and forks to set in front of Neil. When his place was set the waitress took their orders and went away again taking the menus with her.

'I did leave something behind,' said Kirsty. 'I

left a letter for you. Did you get it?'

'I did. That's why I'm here.'

'You should have told me why you'd come back to Scotland, or you should have let Mr Pettigrew tell me,' she said. 'You should have told me about your father's will. Why didn't you?'

Neil picked up a fork and began to make patterns on the tablecloth with the prongs, his eyes hidden by their lashes, his mouth twisting slightly.

'I hoped you and I could work something out, a way of sharing the place between us. I didn't want to take it from you, or fight with you over it,' he told her. 'I was stalling for time by not telling you, time in which I could get to know you again.' His mouth tightened and he flicked a glance across the table at her. 'I gave Pettigrew hell for telling you about my father's will. I was going to tell you myself when we'd sorted out this other more personal matter.'

'What other more personal matter?' she whispered.

'You know what I mean,' he retorted. 'We've fallen in love again with each other.'

'No, we haven't. We're not in love.' She got to her feet. 'Please tell the waitress I've changed my mind and I don't want anything to eat,' she muttered, and hurried away quickly, leaving the room before Neil had risen to his feet.

She sped up the stairs to her room. Taking out the suitcase she had brought up to the room when she had moved in, she began to pack it, throwing the clothes into it anyhow. The case was half full when the doorknob turned, and she looked round, wishing she had thought to lock the door. The door opened and Neil stepped into the room. He closed the door and leaned against it.

'That wasn't a very clever move on your part,' he remarked dryly.

'Oh, please go away and leave me alone,' Kirsty replied shakily, and continued to stuff clothes into the case.

'No. I'm not leaving you alone until you agree to marry me.' he replied.

'Marry you?' she gasped, staring at him. 'How can I marry you when you're married already.'

'I'm not married,' he retorted.

'Yes, you are. Alec told me you married Barbara Gow, the heiress, three years ago.'

'I used to be married to Barbara. But I'm not married to her now and haven't been married to her for over a year. She and I split after twelve months of marriage. She found she didn't like being married to a surgeon who was dedicated to his work and who didn't have time to dance attendance on her all the time.' His voice rasped with bitterness. 'So she left me, and I wasn't a bit sorry when she did.'

'Oh!' Kirsty's legs felt suddenly shaky and she slumped down on the edge of the bed. 'I didn't know. I . . . I'm sorry.'

'About what?'

Neil lunged away from the door and came over to the bed. Lifting the half-full suitcase off the bed, he put it on the floor and sat down beside her. Every nerve quivering in response to his nearness Kirsty kept her glance on the case on the floor.

'I'm sorry your marriage broke up,' she muttered.

'You don't have to be sorry. Barbara and I married for all the wrong reasons. She wanted a man who would be her escort, who would be content to walk in her shadow. And I . . . .' He broke off, and Kirsty looked at him. He was also staring at her case, his face set in grim lines.

'And you?' she prompted, and he twisted on the bed to face her.

'I married her on the rebound from being in love with you,' he said harshly. 'When I didn't get an answer to the letter I left for you I came to the conclusion that you were everything Alec had said you were.' He laughed shortly when she looked away, shaking her head. 'You still don't believe me, do you? You don't believe I was so deeply in love with you my world turned upside down when you didn't answer my letter. To your way of thinking men aren't supposed to have feelings that can be hurt.'

There was a short silence. Evening sunlight poured into the bedroom through the window, gilding everything. Outside a thrush warbled its last song of the day.

'Barbara had hurt her leg in a skiing accident, and Weingarten let me operate on it,' Neil said more quietly. 'The operation was successful. Her gratitude was overwhelming.' He laughed again, shortly, in self-derision. 'She made love to me, proposed marriage to me. She was wealthy, an heiress, well known, and I knew it would further my career if I married a New York socialite. The attendant publicity would help me make it to the top in my profession.' He drew in his breath. 'We deserved to break up. There was nothing deep in our relationship. We didn't really care about each other; we were just dazzled by each other's outward show. She was attracted by the glamour surrounding a young surgeon who had saved her leg. I was . . . well, I've told you I was in a hell of a mess emotionally speaking and had decided to put fame and fortune before anything else.' There was another silence then he added softly, 'You are going to marry me, aren't you now that you know I'm free to marry you?'

'I don't know. I'm not sure that I can,' she muttered.

'So you're still not trusting me. You still believe what Alec told you about me,' he said, his voice low and bitter. 'Yet I've never asked any other woman to marry me, Kirsty. I've never wanted to share my life with any woman the way I'd like to share it with you. I asked you to marry me four years ago in a letter. If you'd received it and had accepted my proposal we'd be married now. We might have had a child. Oh God, Kirsty, when I think of the time we could have been together and haven't been together, all because Alec didn't give you my letter, I feel murderous towards him!'

His voice grated and his hands clenched on his knees. She reached out and laid a hand over one of his, her fingers stroking the tanned skin soothingly.

'Please don't feel like that about Alec. We must both forgive him for what he did,' she whispered. 'I think he must have been mentally unbalanced and very jealous of you. He burned your letter.'

His hand turned under hers and opened to grasp her fingers tightly before she could withdraw them.

'How do you know?' he demanded hoarsely.

'I found his diaries and read parts of them. They're in a box in his bedroom at the Lodge. If I'd only opened the box when he died and had read them then I'd have known he was never the owner of Balmore and so he couldn't leave it to me in his will. And I'd have known you were telling the truth about your letter,' she explained.

'He wrote it all down?' Neil exclaimed. 'Why?'

'I think he was always a very lonely person, not given to confiding in other people, so he confided in a diary. Writing down what he had done was like making a confession and perhaps eased the guilt he felt about wanting to be revenged on your father and mother for making him suffer. Your mother was right. He did hate you, because you were the product of your mother's love for your father. He lied to you about me because he wanted to hurt you and he lied to me about you, not because he wanted to hurt me but because he wanted to hurt you again through me.'

'And he did. He did,' he sighed.

'He also hated you because you were the real son of Sir Ian and would one day possess Balmore.' Kirsty's voice faltered slightly. 'That's why he made a will leaving it to me. He loved

Balmore more than any person. It was his obsession.'

'I had no idea that he'd been in love with my mother,' Neil said. 'No idea at all. It explains a lot.'

'I didn't know until Mary told me. He met your mother when he was a student in Edinburgh, and took her home. She met your father and never looked at Alec again. He was terribly hurt, and soon afterwards the disease began to show itself. In his diary he admitted that he contemplated suicide at that time. I think it was then he transferred his affection from people to plants and animals, to the estate.'

'You seem to have understood him. Did you love him?'

'I did, but not in the way you mean. I admired him and I enjoyed working with him. But I never felt comfortable with him, I never wanted to put my arms around him or to rest my head against his shoulder. I never wanted to sleep with him,' she added, looking down at their clasped hands.

'Poor Alec,' Neil said softly. 'You're right—we must forgive him, even though he hurt both of us.' His glance was slightly mocking as it met hers. 'But maybe I'm presuming too much. Maybe you weren't hurt.'

'Oh, I was. I was! I was miserable for weeks, for months after you'd gone away. And it's been hard to forgive you, to start trusting you again. Knowing you were married didn't help.'

'But I wasn't married, and I'm not married now. I started to tell you in the turret room that you were on the wrong track, but you wouldn't stop to listen.'

'You didn't try to tell me the other night at the cottage,' she reminded him tartly, trying to pull her hand free and failing. The strong surgeon's fingers gripped hers masterfully.

'I'd forgotten that you didn't know,' he replied. 'Do you mean to say you refused to stay the night with me because you believed I was still married to Barbara?' he said tautly. 'Was that why you said you didn't trust me?'

Sensing that he was angry, she tried to free her hand again and shifted away from him along the bed as she nodded.

'Then why the hell didn't you say so?' he thundered, coming after her.

'I don't know, I don't know,' she babbled. 'Oh, Neil, don't be angry with me. I've been so confused since you came back, wanting to love you, wanting to be with you yet not daring to in case it led to disaster.'

'If you'd asked me I could have told you I wasn't married, couldn't I?' he said, his eyes glinting dangerously. 'You know, I could punish you for not asking me. I spent one of the most miserable nights of my life because you refused to stay with me.'

'You don't have to punish me. I've been punished already. I went through hell that night too,' Kirsty said. He had released her hand and had moved away from her, and his sudden withdrawal bothered her. 'How would you punish me?' she asked curiously.

'By walking out of here and driving away,' said Neil, flicking a narrowed glance at her. 'Why should I bother to stay with a woman who doesn't know what she wants and doesn't know how to love? In fact, I'm beginning to wonder why I came after you. Hell!' He raked fingers through his hair and leaned forward to rest his elbows on his knees and his head between his hands, 'I must be going crazy, behaving as if I were in my early twenties instead of in my mid-thirties, running after a woman who's rejected me twice within the space of two weeks and who's probably going to reject me again if I try to kiss her.' He pushed back his sleeve to look at his watch. 'Seven-thirty. Any idea what time they finish serving dinner here?'

'No.'

Kirsty edged along the bed closer to him. Putting out a hand she touched his shoulder. Her fingers spread along the smooth fine tweed of his jacket to the nape of his neck and twined in the thickness of his hair.

'I'm glad you followed me,' she said softly.

Neil turned his head slowly to look at her. She watched his glance slant down to her mouth. Then she was watching his mouth too, seeing the lips part as they came nearer. Longing to feel their pressure against hers and to know again the touch of his hands, she lifted her mouth enticingly, parting her lips, and from under her drooping lashes watched his lips come closer, feeling long dormant nerves quiver alive in anticipation of being excited by his touch.

'I'm glad you're here, glad you've come,' she whispered. 'Please don't go away from me again.'

Following the urgings of passion at last, she loosened the knot of his tie and began to flick undone the buttons of his shirt. Her eager hands pushed open the shirt and her fingers slid greedily over the hairy warmth of his chest, pressing and pinching until she heard his sharp intake of breath. With a sigh she rested her head against him. Under her ear his heart changed beat.

'How strongly your heart beats, strong man,' she whispered. 'And your skin is like velvet. Oh, Neil, I've wanted to do this for a long, long time!'

'At last you admit it.' He spoke thickly, his arms going around her, tilting her sideways, taking her with him as he lay back on the bed. His hand twined in her hair. He dragged her head back from his shoulder and his mouth possessed hers with rough hunger, his teeth bruising the tender skin of her lips.

His savagery tasted sweet to Kirsty and awakened a desire in her to rouse him further. No longer shy, she caressed him, her hands touching him wherever they could, her mouth feasting on his.

'I love you, Kirsty,' he murmured against her throat. 'I love you and I want you. Are you going to marry me? Dare I ask you again?'

'Yes, I'm going to marry you,' she replied. 'Because I love and want you. I know now I want to be a real wife and mother after all. I'm tired of being subservient to an obsession.'

His lips sought hers again and again, and as the

weight of his hard sinewy thighs pressed against
hers she knew she could no longer refuse the
demands of his desire. Nor did she want to refuse.
Her arms slid around him to hold him down
against her, while her body twisted and lifted
against his inviting invasion. .

For a few moments she swung among stars
and flew in outer space, then crying and sighing
came slowly back to earth to the soft crushed
firmness of the bed, to the silken hardness of his
shoulder beneath her cheek and the warm velvet
slackness of his limbs entwined with hers.

In the afterglow of fulfilment they slept a little,
waking only when their limbs grew chilly. Neil
pulled the quilt over them and within its shelter
his lips worshipped her again. After a while she
said,

'Shall we live at Balmore?'

'You can live there if you wish, but I won't be
there all the time,' he answered, rubbing his nose
against the soft curve of her cheek.

'Why?'

'My work as a surgeon still comes first and it
always will. The reason I came back was not really
because I wanted Balmore but was to take up a
position at a teaching hospital in Edinburgh. I
start there at the beginning of September.' His
fingers played in her hair. 'Perhaps I should have
told you this before I asked you to marry me, but
do you think you can stand being left alone many
times? Can you put up with a husband who's often
late home? Or who has to leave suddenly in the
middle of a dinner party to which you've invited

important guests?' Bitterness rasped in his voice again and she guessed he was thinking of the way Barbara had behaved when he had been late or had left in the middle of dinner or even in the middle of the night.

'I'll be able to put up with having a surgeon for a husband because I love you,' she replied, tracing the line of his lips with the tip of her finger. 'I'll also have my own life to lead, you know, looking after our home and our children. And perhaps I'll have a job too, when the children are older, so you won't have to dance attendance on me all the time. We'll have a house near the hospital so you won't have far to go to work or to come home.'

'Sensible Kirsty,' he said. 'No wonder I love you.'

His lips claimed hers again and for a while there were no more words.

'But what about Balmore?' said Kirsty when, breathless from being overtaken by a new wave of passion, they lay relaxed in delicious lethargy.

'I've decided to give it to the National Trust, once I've inherited it,' he replied.

'All of it?'

'No. I've discussed the matter with Hamish and some of the other people who work on the estate. Archie Thornton and Will Andrews would both like to buy their farms, so I think we should give them the chance to buy at a low price in view of their long tenancies.' Neil rolled on to his back and stretched lazily. 'As for the rest, there's really too much of it to keep to ourselves, and I've never wanted to be an absentee landlord like my father was. I'd like to make it possible for more people to enjoy its beauty, so I've asked Doug Pettigrew to approach the Trust about offering it to them as a park. After the mortgage is paid off, of course.' He turned back to her and leaned up on an elbow. 'What do you think, Lady Whyte?' he asked.

'I think it's a wonderful idea. Will you give the house to the trust too?'

'No. We'll keep it with a few acres of land, for a place to retreat to and so that you can keep your hand in planting trees and gardening. I wouldn't like you to hanker too much after your job as factor,' he teased.

'Thank you,' she whispered, winding her arms about him and drawing him down. 'I think Alec would have approved.'

They kissed again, slowly and gently, enjoying their new freedom to caress each other without striving for culmination until both of them became aware of strange noises.

'It's me,' said Neil. 'I'm damned hungry —I haven't eaten since breakfast. Once I'd found out you were here I kept on coming.' He lifted his head and scowled down at her. 'You prevented me from having any dinner, so what are you going to do about it? Do you think they'll feed us here if we go and ask them nicely? Or should we drive into the nearest town and look for a fish and chip place?'

'They might feed us here. But where are you going to stay for the night? I know that every room has been booked in the hotel for the past few days.'

'I'm staying the night here,' he said, sliding off the bed and beginning to pull on his clothes. 'In the room next to this one. When I explained to the owner of the hotel that I'm a close ... very close friend of yours, she was most understanding and said she could let me have her daughter's room because the girl is away for the night. Not that I'll be needing a separate room, the way things have turned out,' he added, giving her a wicked glance over his shoulder. 'That bed is big enough for the two of us, as we've just proved.'

'Neil Dysart-Whyte, you are the most arrogant, conceited mischievous man I know!' Kirsty retorted, pausing in the middle of dressing herself to pick up a pillow and hurl it at him.

Laughing, Neil caught the pillow and hurled it back at her. She ducked, and the pillow hit the bedside lamp. The lamp slid to the edge of the bedside table wobbled, then fell to the floor with a crash. The light bulb shattered and the parchment shade became separated from its frame and crumpled.

'Oh, now look what you've done!' gasped Kirsty.

'You started it,' he replied, coming across to her and sliding his hands up her bare arms as if fascinated by their smooth silkiness. 'You started it four years ago when you came to the cottage on Cairn Rua. You're a dangerous lady,' he whispered, bending his head and tormenting the lobe of her ear.

'No, I'm not, I'm not! Please don't say that,' she protested, but she didn't pull away from him.

Her arms went round his neck and they stood close to each other. Her arms went round his neck and they stood close to each other, their bodies not quite touching, his hands at her waist. 'And I don't want to be dangerous,' she whispered. 'I just want to be loved.'

'And you shall be loved, my beloved temptress. You're tempting me to love you as you stand close to me with your shoulders gleaming white under the mantle of your black hair, your blue eyes dark and mysterious. A siren, that's what you are, tempting me to my downfall . . . and to go without my dinner.'

'But what are they going to think when we tell them about the broken lamp and when we don't go down again this evening to ask them for dinner?' asked Kirsty.

'*They* can think what they like, whoever *they* are. You and I are going to be much too busy making up for lost time, renewing our love for each other.' Neil's hands swept over her back as he pressed her against him. 'I told you it wasn't over, in the turret,' he whispered. 'I told you there were still some embers of love left just waiting to be fanned into a flame. Do you believe me now? Do you trust me now?' He pushed her away a little so that he could look into her eyes, the expression in his own one of doubt.

'Oh, yes, I trust you now,' she said sincerely, putting her arms around his neck again and lifting her face to his. 'You've rekindled the flame. I love you, I always have, but I wasn't sure about your feelings for me until today.'

The expression of doubt passed from his eyes like a cloud drifts away from the sun. Topaz-bright, his eyes glowed with passion before his lips possessed hers and she felt she was being kissed again by the young man she had met in the violet-tinted dusk of another summer evening. Her lost lover had come back to her at last, and as the flame of love burned steadily, fusing their hearts together, it was as if they had never been parted.